THE MASTER OF BLACKTOWER

I was not afraid of Mr Gavin Hamilton, despite his looks, his manners, and—I was sure of this now—his deliberate attempts to frighten me. But I could imagine how the rest of the world would react to him, and his method of hiring a secretary. The idea charmed me so that I burst out laughing, but once out in the street I sobered. The situation had its humorous side; but, all the same, there was something a little sinister about my new employer.

I had offered him my hand upon leaving, and he had deliberately put his own hands behind his back and given me a formal bow. Perhaps he wore gloves because his hands, like his face, were disfigured. That was natural enough. But if a gentleman refuses to take a lady's hand, the least he owes her is an explanation.

The sun was shining brightly on the dusty street, but a cloud gathered over my spirits. Blacktower House . . . it had an ominous sound.

THE MASTER OF BLACKTOWER

Barbara Michaels

A TANDEM BOOK

published by
WYNDHAM PUBLICATIONS

A Tandem Book
published in 1976 by
Wyndham Publications Ltd
A Howard & Wyndham Company
123 King Street, London W6 9JG

First published in Great Britain by
Herbert Jenkins Ltd, 1967
Published by Universal-Tandem
Publishing Co. Ltd, 1969
Reprinted 1971
Reprinted January 1972
Reprinted by Tandem Publishing Ltd
October 1976

Made and printed in Great Britain by
Hazell Watson & Viney Ltd, Aylesbury, Bucks

ISBN 0 426 17785 1

CHAPTER 1

THE Black Tower of Dunnoch.

I saw it first at twilight. The Highland mountains were purple in the fading light, the western sky a brilliant tapestry of gold and crimson. Against the fiery northern sunset the ruined tower rose in jagged silhouette, still standing guard over Blacktower House, which sprawled along the slope of the hill below.

The coach jolted and swayed as the tired horses swung into the last steep rise. I hardly felt the jolting, or the bite of the wind that pushed insistent fingers through the velvet upholstery. A different sort of cold chilled me; I shivered and drew the folds of my mantle closer.

I was tired and an easy prey to nervous fancies. It had been a long journey from London to this lonely glen buried in the heart of Scotland's highest mountains, long not only in miles but in experience. I had never been to Scotland. It was like another world.

The month was April, the year, 1853. Spring had not yet dared to venture into the Highlands. The gorse and heather were brown and shriveled, and the bare white trunks of the birch trees looked cold. All that day, the only colour had been the sombre black-green of the pine trees, and the harsh purple of the mountains. One would never think that in London the soft pale flowers were pushing through the earth—lavender crocuses, and daffodils and butter-yellow primroses. The new grass there was a tender April-green—like the grass in the churchyard of St. Clothilde's, on a day two weeks earlier.

The memory was as sharp as a knife. When I closed my eyes I could see it again : the sweep of delicate green broken by white marble crosses and weeping angels, softened by a grey veil of rain—and the austere rectangle

5

of the newly dug grave at my feet. Not only my father was being laid to rest in the quiet churchyard outside London, but my whole world.

Rain dripped off the budding trees on to the brim of my black mourning bonnet and trickled down my cheeks. The ebony plumes on the horses' heads were sodden with water; the black umbrellas of the mourners shone as if they had been varnished. There were not many mourners —only the servants and a few elderly colleagues of father's, who had braved the wet to pay their last respects to an honoured scholar and antiquarian. "I am the Resurrection and the Life; and whosoever believeth in me . . ." The minister's voice was blurred by haste. He wanted to be done with it, and go back to his fireside and glass of port.

At my side, Mr. Downey shifted his feet and contorted his face to restrain a sneeze. No doubt, he too was thinking of his own fireside, and so were the others. Only Father would not be going back to his fire. He would stay here, in the rain, under the quiet grass.

Mr. Downey was father's lawyer, and he was at my side because there was no one else to take that place. He had been kind, in his dry, legal way, but as soon as the service was over he led me firmly towards the waiting carriage. We had business to discuss, he and I—unpleasant business—and I was as anxious to be done with it as he was.

A fire was burning in the library when we reached the house. The room was cosy and warm; the ruddy light shone on Father's big desk, with his cracked leather chair behind it, and on the book-lined walls. At the sight of the familiar room and the empty chair behind the unnaturally tidy desk, my eyes filled with tears. I offered the lawyer a glass of wine as an excuse to turn my back. Taking a glass myself, I drank it down. The sherry ran warmly through my body and into my cold hands and feet. I poured another glass, ignoring the lawyer's disapproving stare, and sipped it slowly, gazing out of the window at the grey pencil lines of rain. Then I was ready. I took off my bonnet and flung it on to a chair, and turned to face Mr. Downey.

I had caught him staring. He quickly averted his eyes, but I had seen the direction of his gaze. I pressed my hands against my hair, flattening the springing curls.

"I wish I could cut it off! Or dye it black, to match my dress—"

"That would be very foolish," said Mr. Downey, deploring female hysterics. "A lady's hair is her crowning glory, and yours is a becoming shade of—er—auburn."

"Father called it red-gold," I said softly. "He quoted Homer... I beg your pardon, Mr. Downey. You've been so kind to me. I'll not trespass on your time any longer. What is it you want to say?"

Mr. Downey's thin sallow face remained impassive, frozen by years of legal caution; but I think my outburst worried him. He didn't want a weeping woman on his hands.

"Perhaps this is not a good time. Your father told me you were accustomed to assist him in his affairs; but you are very young..." He studied me thoughtfully, stroking his long bony nose, and then he said, surprisingly, "It has been a strange life for a young girl—your mother dead since your infancy, no companions of your own sex and station—"

"I needed none," I said coldly, resenting the implied criticism of my father. "Papa was all I needed—friend, teacher, parent.... Please, Mr. Downey, don't... remind me. Tell me the truth, and let's be done with it. I'm destitute, am I not?"

"Two hundred a year is not destitution."

"But neither is it independence."

"A young lady of eighteen has no need of independence." Mr. Downey made it sound like a nasty word. "Your aunt will certainly offer you a home."

"My aunt dislikes me intensely, and has ever since I informed her, at the age of five, that she looked like her own pug dog."

Mr. Downey gave an exasperated sniff.

"I would suspect you of being flippant, Miss Gordon, on any other day but this. What about your aunt's son—your cousin?"

"Cousin Randall? Yes . . . I know everyone expects that Randall and I will marry. That, Mr. Downey, is why I was hoping for independence."

"But—but—my dear Miss Gordon, your cousin is an eminently respectable young man! And don't forget he inherits your father's property! Mr. Randall Gordon is a young gentleman of modern, liberal opinions. He feels . . . not an injustice . . . let us say, a misfortune, in the law which prevents a daughter from enjoying her father's estates."

All at once I thought how much Father, who delighted in absurdities, would have enjoyed this ridiculous speech. I said demurely, "Am I to understand, Mr. Downey, that Randall wants to marry me as a practical demonstration of his modern, liberal opinions?"

I had underestimated Mr. Downey. He had to tighten his lips to keep from smiling.

"Miss Gordon, you have looked into a mirror often enough to know why a young man might want to marry you—whatever his opinions. As a matter of fact," he continued, more soberly, "I received a letter from Mr. Randall Gordon only this morning. He expressed his regret that owing to his mother's poor health, he was unable to return from Baden in time for the funeral."

I was unable to hold back a sniff. Mr. Downey frowned at me.

"Your aunt has been ailing for years; you know that. And your father's illness and death were very sudden. As I was saying, Mr. Randall particularly expressed his interest in *you*."

"Dear Mr. Downey." I leaned forward and touched his hand. "I can't marry Randall. Not even to oblige you."

"What is your alternative?" Mr. Downey sighed, but he sounded less annoyed than he had every right to be.

"Why," I said airily, "I shall seek employment."

"In what capacity, pray? As a companion or governess?"

"You needn't be sarcastic, Mr. Downey. Oh, yes, I know those are the only respectable occupations open to a woman. But it's so unfair! For years I've been Father's secretary and assistant. He trained me; he told me no man could have served him better. Why can't I use those skills?"

Mr. Downey's wooden jaw dropped. I had really shocked him; only his belief that I was mentally unsettled by grief spared me a severe lecture.

"My child, we can't change the world, even if we want to. I'm sure you're as clever as any girl in England. But you could never obtain a position as a private secretary."

"Why not?"

"Why—why—because, Miss Gordon, a governess is employed by the lady of a house; a secretary is employed by the *gentleman*. A secretary spends hours alone—alone! —with his employer. Behind closed doors, Miss Gordon! Need I say more?"

I was tempted to widen my eyes and beg for further explanations. But I really didn't have the heart to vex him any more.

"No," I sighed, "you needn't. But I think you are insulting the gentlemen of England."

"I do not say that you would be—necessarily—in danger of—er—insult. Not from all gentlemen, certainly. . . ." Mr. Downey did not sound at all certain. He abandoned that position. "I do say that no one would employ you. Custom is too strong."

"At least I might advertise. There would be no harm in trying."

"There most certainly would! Such an advertisement would be open to the most unpleasant misconstruction. I insist that you do nothing of the kind."

Mr. Downey's voice had overawed many an angry client. There was no point in arguing with him, so I bowed my head and closed my lips. He mistook silence for

9

submission and allowed himself a bleak, three-second smile.

"Mr. Randall Gordon expressed the wish," he said, "that you remain here until he and your aunt return, which will be within a fortnight. By then, I feel sure your good sense will have told you what your course of action must be."

I smiled meekly, and said not a word; and I went on smiling while I saw him to the door. Then I went back to the study and sat down in Father's big chair. It was an antique ruin of a chair; I had been threatening for months to throw it away. I was glad now that I hadn't. For a little while I sat upright, moving my hands along the cracked leather. Then I drew a sheet of paper to me, dipped Father's pen into the onyx inkwell he had brought home from Greece, and began to write.

It took a week for the answers to my letters to come in. All were to colleagues of my father's, who had known him, and knew me. All of them informed me—so politely —that they did not require a secretary. I should have owned defeat then. But Father was a stubborn man, in his quiet way, and I am his daughter. I advertised.

That was a mistake. Mr. Downey had been right and I had been horribly wrong. The advertisement *was* open to misconstruction. I had two replies. I came home from the second interview with my fingers still stinging from the slap I had bestowed on the "gentleman" who was looking for a "trained antiquarian secretary". Antiquarian, indeed!

Dusk had fallen before I reached the house. Too worn and beaten even to ring for tea and a fire, I went at once to the library and sank into Father's chair. Desperately I tried to summon up Father's courage and sense of fun. But at that point I could see nothing amusing in the interview I had just gone through.

Twilight deepened into night as I huddled against the worn leather of the chair. Outside the window the lights of London cast a pale reflection on the sky. In less than a week Randall would be home. With the casual arrogance of his sex, which at that moment I thoroughly detested, he would expect me to marry him.

A good indication of my mental exhaustion was that I seriously wondered whether I shouldn't do just that. It would be easy to give in, and stop trying. Surely the alternatives were worse than Randall.

I thought of Miss Mills, my aunt's companion—a withered dry stick of a woman, always dressed in shabby brown. She blinked continuously, and there was a nervous tic in one of her cheeks. "Where is my shawl, Miss Mills?" "Mills, fetch my wool at once!" "The dog must be washed, Mills; what have you been doing all morning, you lazy creature?" I could almost hear my aunt's shrill voice. I had always despised Miss Mills, even while I sympathised with her. Now I realised that her disgusting humility wasn't weakness, but a grim necessity for survival.

Then there was the girl—Miss Allen?—who had been governess in Lord A———'s family. One of our maids had told me about her; the stories were all over London. She had eloped with the youngest son, and Lord A——— had cut the boy off without a penny. Then the gallant youth had denied the marriage and abandoned her. No one knew what had become of her. "The river?" suggested my housemaid, with a roll of her eyes.

Miss Mills or Miss Allen—slavery or disgrace. On the whole, I thought I preferred disgrace. But neither fate was attractive.

Miss Mills or Miss Allen—or Randall. I hadn't seen him for months; it was hard to remember what he looked like. I knew he was tallish, with brown hair thinning on top and a bushy moustache of which he was inordinately vain, but I couldn't seem to summon up his features. His face was round, and always somewhat flushed; he dressed elegantly. A little too elegantly, perhaps? His gloves were too tight. Or perhaps his hands were too plump—plump and puffy, and unpleasantly cold to the touch.

I was shivering; the room was chilly without a fire. If I marry Randall, I thought, he will have the right to touch me whenever he pleases with those cold hands.

I was pacing up and down, wringing my own hands in distraction, when Ellen brought in a note a messenger had just delivered. I was in no great hurry to read it. I anticipated an invitation from Mr. Downey, who had already suggested that I come to stay with him and his wife. Worst of all, the message might be an announcement of Randall's arrival. I told Ellen to light the fire and bring my tea, and I drank two cups before I looked at the note. Then I realised it was written in a hand I did not know.

The handwriting was a man's, undoubtedly—heavy, black, sprawling recklessly across the page:

"If D.G. who advertised herself as a trained antiquarian secretary, will call tomorrow at the Travellers' Hotel, at 10 A.M., she may present her credentials for a position. Ask for Mr. Gavin Hamilton."

My first impulse was to toss the note into the fire. I had already had two interviews with gentlemen who wanted to offer me a position. But when I looked up, it seemed to me that three phantom shapes stood grimacing at me from the shadows—withered Miss Mills, ruined Miss Allen—and Randall. I knew then that I would be at the Travellers' Hotel at 10 o'clock.

The Travellers' Hotel was a quiet, respectable establishment in Bloomsbury, near the new Museum. I asked for Mr. Hamilton, and the clerk directed me to an upper floor. My hands were damp inside my gloves when I knocked. After an interval a deep man's voice told me to come in.

Sunlight flooded the room from the windows opposite the door and blinded me so that I saw only the outline of the man who had spoken. He was tall and held himself like a gentleman, but I could see little more than that.

He stood without moving or speaking for a long time. The silence grew awkward. I was nerving myself to speak when, with a curious squaring of his shoulder, he moved forward, out of the glare, and I saw him clearly for the first time: Mr. Gavin Hamilton, Master of Blacktower.

I was struck speechless by the sight of his face. Ugliness I was accustomed to; none of my father's friends were noted for manly beauty. But the countenance that confronted me was worse than ugly. It was deformed. Across one side of his face, from brow to chin, ran a livid scar that puckered his flesh and distorted the shape of his mouth.

The rest of his face was regular, although the features were too strongly marked to be called handsome. He had a long, lean face, with high cheekbones and a straight, prominent nose. His eyes were dark and wide-set under heavy brows. He wore no moustache, and his thick black hair was cut shorter than was the fashion. Some men, with such a scar, would have tried to cover it with as much hair as possible. Not Mr. Gavin Hamilton.

He gave me ample time to assimilate his appearance before he spoke.

"Sit down," he said, in a harsh voice. "You, I take it, are D.G. What do the initials stand for?"

"Damaris Gordon." I sat down—mercifully there was a chair near at hand, for I don't think I could have walked to one. "My father is—was—Dr. Andrew Gordon."

"I thought as much. I heard of your father's death. In fact, we are distantly related. Did he ever mention his connection with the Hamiltons of Dunnoch?"

"No—I don't think so."

"Check the genealogies, if you doubt me. I will be candid, Miss Gordon. If I had not identified 'D.G.' with your father's daughter, I wouldn't have answered your advertisement."

"I see." Even after the first shock had subsided, I still found it difficult to look at his face. I dropped my eyes to his hands, and got a second shock. Although he was dressed for indoors, in a dark-grey morning suit and white shirt, he wore gloves—not proper kid gloves, but black silk ones that clung to his hands as if they had been painted on.

He observed my reluctance to look at him, and he sat

down in a chair where the sunlight fell pitilessly across his scarred cheek.

"You seem ill at ease, Miss Gordon. Do you see the open door on your right? Within the next room is a lady in my employ, who is chaperoning me. Mrs. Cannon!"

Within the doorway he had indicated a lady appeared. Her wrinkled face and white hair were those of an elderly woman, but her frock of peacock blue trimmed with bows of crimson velvet would have been more suitable on a girl. The white hair was a mass of braids and coquettish curls, and the reticule she carried in fat, mittened hands was trimmed with pearls and silk. I was to learn that a harmless love of fine dress was one of Mrs. Cannon's weaknesses. On this occasion I was startled by her appearance, but reassured. The wide blue eyes were as candid as a baby's, and almost as vague; the puckered rosy mouth widened in a smile which I couldn't help returning. Then, at a gesture from her peculiar employer, she retired.

"Do you feel that the proprieties have been observed?" Mr. Hamilton asked sardonically. His voice was deep and harsh, with a hint of a burr. "Then we will proceed. I had thought of offering you a position. But I had not expected to find you so young and so . . ."

He didn't finish the sentence, which left me to wonder, uneasily, what he had omitted to say. My cheeks burned and I was tongue-tied—an unusual situation for me!

"I must say," remarked Mr. Hamilton, without removing his keen black eyes from my face, "that your advertisement astounded me. What is your family thinking of, to allow you to do such a thing? Surely your aunt has a home for you?"

He did know my family, then. I was so relieved at discovering this that I answered him honestly. "If I must be dependent on charity, I prefer a stranger's to that of my aunt."

"I see your point. I have met the lady. But what about your Cousin Randall?"

"What about him?" I demanded, stiffening.

"Why, it is generally understood that he is your betrothed. Have you quarrelled? I warn you, Miss Gordon, that my need of secretarial assistance has limits. I won't help you tease Cousin Randall."

I forget precisely what I said in answer to this outrageous statement. By the time I finished my back hair had escaped its net and was coiling furiously about my neck; and Mr. Hamilton was in a convulsion of mirth.

"That's enough—that's enough! I have the picture."

I took my gloves from my lap, and rose. "I bid you good morning, Mr. Hamilton!"

He sprang to his feet and intercepted me as I swept towards the door. "Wait. My laughter was in poor taste, but you invited it. Sit down, and listen to me."

I was still very angry—but not so angry as to forget why I had come. I sat down.

Mr. Hamilton, back in his own chair, studied me across the table for some moments without speaking. Finally he said, in a businesslike voice, "Your duties would consist of cataloguing and arranging my library. You would also take dictation. I am prepared to pay a salary of fifty pounds per annum. Does the arrangement suit you?"

"Yes . . ."

"Those are the advantages of the position. Because I am, for all my sins, honest, I will tell you the disadvantages. My present home is in northern Scotland, far from the comforts of civilisation. The only ladies of your own class are Mrs. Cannon, whom you have just seen, and—a young lady."

He stopped and frowned at his hands, encased in those extraordinary gloves. Then he said, without looking at me, "The young lady is my daughter. She is an invalid, unable to walk. Because of her handicap she has been badly spoiled. She seems even younger than her sixteen years."

"What a tragedy," I said, thinking I understood what he wanted to say. "I'd be happy to do anything possible for Miss Hamilton. No doubt she's had governesses, but when one is bedridden further study helps to pass the time. I might tutor her in Greek, or—"

His shout of laughter stopped me in mid-sentence.

"Annabelle, and Greek lessons! You have no idea how comical that is, Miss Gordon. The girl hasn't the brains of a gnat, and her character is no more pleasing. I was only trying to warn you what you can expect from the little idiot. Personally, I advise you to avoid her. I do."

I was aghast at his brutal speech, and I suppose my face showed it, for he said irritably, "Sit down and stop scowling. I know you don't like me to laugh at you, but I really can't stop to apologise every time you say something absurd. Well—what do you think? Do you want the position?"

The question was like a dash of cold water. I forgot my indignation in a surging tide of simple, ugly fear. Here it was, the chance I had stopped hoping for—and without the unpleasant conditions of the first two interviews. I had an illogical, but certain, impression that Mr. Hamilton would not offend me in that way. Nor was I daunted by his rudeness or his brusque manners. Then why, why did I hesitate?

He was watching me intently, a half-smile pulling his twisted mouth still further awry. The long black fingers of his right hand drummed impatiently on the desk.

"You hesitate?" he said, in the same harsh voice I had first heard. "I don't wonder."

I raised my bowed head and looked him squarely in the face.

"I accept the position."

I don't know why I said it. It was as if someone, or something, else spoke through my lips. But, oddly, once the words were out I was no longer afraid.

Mr. Hamilton's smile vanished, and his brows drew together in a formidable scowl. "I withdraw the offer!"

"No, you don't. I have a witness."

"I doubt that. Mrs. Cannon is probably asleep. She usually is. One last chance, Miss Gordon. Haven't you a friend—a solicitor, at least—whom you might consult before putting your head into the lion's paws?"

I pictured Mr. Downey, listening to an account of this mad interview. It was a terrifying thought.

"No indeed! I accept, and that's that. When do we leave for—for—"

"Blacktower House." Mr. Hamilton rose when I did, and came towards me. When he stopped I had all I could do not to retreat. He was so tall that the top of my head barely reached his chin, and he seemed to loom over me like a mountain.

"Blacktower House," he said again. "We leave two days hence, at ten in the morning."

All the way down the stairs I went over the details of the strange interview just concluded. No, I was not afraid of Mr. Gavin Hamilton, despite his looks, his manners, and—I was sure of this now—his deliberate attempts to frighten me. But I could imagine how the rest of the world would react to him, and his method of hiring a secretary. Mr. Downey—oh, dear, how he would scold! The idea charmed me so that I burst out laughing in the middle of the lobby, and the sedate clerk behind his respectable desk gave me a scandalised look. Once out in the street I sobered. The situation had its humorous side; but, all the same, there was something a little sinister about my new employer. I had offered him my hand upon leaving, and he had deliberately put his own hands behind his back and given me a formal bow. Perhaps he wore gloves because his hands, like his face, were disfigured. That was natural enough. But if a gentleman refuses to take a lady's hand, the least he owes her is an explanation.

The sun was shining brightly on the dusty street and on the massive Ionic façade of the Museum, but a cloud gathered over my spirits as I walked towards the corner to wait for an omnibus. Blacktower House ... it had an ominous sound.

CHAPTER 2

FOUR days later, as Mrs. Cannon and I emerged from the Royal Arms at Dunkeld, the wet drops that fell on our faces were more snow than rain. We had reached Dunkeld late the previous night, after an exhausting journey by railroad; and I, for one, stifled yawns behind my hand as I shivered on the steps of the inn and watched the pale light of morning touch the east with grey.

Dunkeld was then the terminus of the railroad. Mr. Hamilton's coach was waiting to carry us over the remaining distance; but Mr. Hamilton was not with it. The ostler told us he had already departed, on horseback.

I had scarcely seen him since our first interview. When I arrived at the railroad station in London with my worldly goods strapped on top of a hired carriage, he had shut me and Mrs. Cannon into a coach reserved for ladies, and disappeared. At Dunkeld he reappeared long enough to escort us to the inn, and then he vanished again.

As soon as the carriage left Dunkeld, Mrs. Cannon fell asleep. I was tired, too, but the strange new scenery fascinated me. After we left the village the road climbed steadily, and we passed a few stately houses surrounded by ample grounds. Overhanging rocks and trees, still bare of foliage, lined the way. In summer, of course, the scenery would be magnificent. The barren elms and beeches would be green, the heather would make a purple carpet over the moors, and the distant mountains might not look so grim against a blue sky in the sunshine. But now the prospect was dismal, and the wildness of the terrain increased as the morning wore on. The ascent grew steeper, and enclosing rocks drew in. A white waterfall slid down the dark rock wall, breaking in clouds of spray. And always the hills loomed higher—bare brown peaks with snow crowning their tops.

I felt extremely small under those frowning slopes—small and foolish. Independence was very well, but perhaps I ought to have been independent at less distance from my only relatives. What did I know of Mr. Gavin Hamilton, after all? That he had a scarred face and an uncouth manner, and employed an elderly housekeeper who was never more than half awake. Hardly enough information to justify placing myself so completely in his power.

I looked at Mrs. Cannon, and my dismal mood lightened a bit. Swathed in a wonderful mantle of purple taffeta lined with fur, Mrs. Cannon slept as placidly as a baby in its cradle. Her mouth was slightly ajar, displaying a set of china teeth too perfect to be natural. On her head was the latest style in bonnets—a broad-brimmed straw with ribbons three inches wide. They were tied in a huge bow under her chin, and she looked for all the world like an enormous lavender pussycat.

We stopped for dinner at Castleton, a straggling collection of huts on a small space of broken ground. And this, I thought in discouragement, was the nearest town to Blacktower House!

Dinner consisted of mutton, a thick soup of lentils, and boiled pudding. Mrs. Cannon ate enormously and fell asleep again as soon as we went on. I sat with Black's *Picturesque Guide to Scotland* open in my lap, but the carriage bumped so badly that I couldn't read. I knew, already, what the *Guide* had to say about my new home: "The wildest, most desolate part of the Highlands." It was not overstating the case. The rugged slopes of the Cairngorm Mountains were all around us now. The road was hardly more than a cart track strewn with stones. A stream, sullen and grey, ran along beside the road.

As the red ball of the sun dropped below the mountain horizon, we came into a region which, even after the wilderness we had passed through, brought a gasp to my lips. The road plunged into a canyon, barely wider than the carriage. The dim light that might have penetrated from above was cut off entirely by pines that ringed the canyon mouth and clung precariously to the steep walls. I was thrown back against the seat as the carriage began to climb. A sudden shower of water struck the window, and I saw a wavering white curtain, ghostlike in the gloom, on my right—a waterfall that thundered down the cliff to break just beside the road.

"The Gorbals," said a drowsy voice. "This is the entrance to the glen, my dear. We'll be home soon..." A muffled snore followed.

The homely sound restored my equilibrium; but I didn't care for the Gorbals. I had never seen anything less like earthly landscape. I was glad when the panting horses reached the top of the incline and we shot down an equally steep slope into the glen.

There were no stately homes here, only rock and brown, dead heather, and once a flock of dirty black-nosed sheep. The light drew in behind the enclosing hills, and all the land grew dark except for the glowing tapestry of scarlet in the west. At last we passed through a tiny village—low thatched huts that huddled flat on the stony ground. Then we were on the last slope, and the vision of the Black Tower rose before my startled eyes.

At the top of the slope we came out on to a wide sweep of gravel and passed through heavy walls into a courtyard lit by red flaring torches. Mrs. Cannon awoke, rolled out of the coach, and hurried towards a door.

It led into a stone-floored passage that was even colder than the out-of-doors had been. Somewhere near at hand I smelled cooking and assumed we were in the back part of the house, near the kitchens. Mrs. Cannon trotted briskly on ahead of me, through corridor after corridor, and finally we passed through a door into an entrance hallway. Wooden floors had been laid down over the original stone, and there were carpets, very grateful to my cold ankles. In one wall was a heavy oak door, probably leading to the main carriage entrance. A handsome sweep of stairs went up to the first floor.

"We use only the West Wing," Mrs. Cannon explained, puffing as she mounted the stairs. "The rest of the house is ruinous and far too large."

The West Wing alone seemed immense to me. The corridors here were also carpeted, and lit by candles in wall brackets. At last Mrs. Cannon stopped before a door and threw it open.

"This is my room. Now do sit down, my dear, while I see what arrangements have been made for you."

She tugged at a bellpull, and before long a maidservant answered the summons. She was young and sturdy-looking, with flaxen braids wound around her head, and wore brown homespun with a white apron and cap. Her plump rosy face would have been pretty if it had not been so sullen.

"Come in and close the door," said Mrs. Cannon sharply. "Miss Gordon, this young person's name is Betty. She will answer your bell as well as mine. Speak up, you foolish girl," she added, and for a startled moment I thought she was speaking to me. "What room have you prepared for Miss Gordon?"

"The Red Room, ma'am."

"Quite suitable. Well, Betty, don't stand there gaping; show Miss Gordon to the Red Room."

The old lady had already settled herself before the fire, with both plump feet on the fender. I rose, not surprised at her cavalier dismissal; I had already found her to be kind, but chiefly concerned with her own comfort.

As I went towards the door she said drowsily, "I dine here, Miss Gordon. Will you join me? Betty will fetch you . . ."

I thanked her; but I think she was asleep before the door closed behind me.

The Red Room, three doors down the hall from Mrs. Cannon's room, was as cheerful as its name. A fire leaped in the hearth, casting a warm glow upon crimson draperies and bed curtains. The floor was covered by a bright-figured Turkish carpet.

Betty had scarcely closed the door behind us when it burst open again. Without even a knock, a sour-looking manservant entered, threw my boxes unceremoniously on the floor, and departed.

I looked helplessly from my poor maltreated boxes to the empty doorway, and then at Betty. Her face was expressionless, but I thought I detected a gleam of sympathy in her eyes.

"Well," I said, smiling, "the boxes are here, at any rate. Will you please unpack for me, Betty?"

After the girl had gone, I pulled a chair up to the fire and sank into it with a sigh of relief. I was almost drowsing there in the warmth when Betty returned.

"If you please, miss, I am to ask if you wish help in dressing."

"I am dressed, thank you. If Mrs. Cannon dines formally, she will have to excuse me."

"The Master has sent to say that you will dine with him."

The Master, indeed, thought I. My first reaction was negative. I opened my mouth to say that I was too tired to dine in state that evening. But then I realised that I was being naïve. I was not Mr. Hamilton's guest, but his servant. The invitation was a command.

Some perverse impulse made me dress in my best frock, although its low neckline and short sleeves left my shoulders coldly exposed. The black moiré was becoming to my hair, at any rate, and the skirts rustled when I walked. Four stiff petticoats underneath made them flare— and the extra layers of clothing kept out some of the chill. I had no jewels, even if I wanted to wear them; the mourning brooch of jet with a strand of Father's hair was my only ornament. I twisted my hair up from my face and let it fall from a high crown in back, binding it with a black ribbon.

When I turned from the dim image in the mirror, Betty was gaping at me.

"Will I do?" I asked, with a smile.

"You look beautiful, miss!" I had been right; she was a pretty girl.

Feeling much more cheerful, I followed her down to the drawing room. It was nice to know that I could win a response from someone in the house, even a servant. The drawing room surprised me, though. Traditionally it is a woman's apartment, but there were no dainty Dresden figures or flowered draperies in this room. The furniture was massive, old-fashioned stuff, heavily carved and black with age. The walls were hung with hunting prints, and bristled with the antlers of poor dead deer. Oddly enough, that was the first time I thought of Mrs. Gavin Hamilton. Mr. Hamilton had a daughter, so presumably he had once possessed a wife. Evidently he was a widower. But I wondered why his wife had never redecorated this room.

Mrs. Cannon was like a butterfly in a blacksmith's shop against the dark, masculine furniture. For once, she was wide awake, and it seemed to me that she was also slightly pop-eyed with surprise. Certainly she had given me the impression that she didn't dine with the Master. She had dressed herself, to suit the great occasion, in a blue-and-silver brocade with a lace bertha and puffings of silk. I estimated that she must be wearing at least eight petticoats; her stoutly corseted little body rose up out of the mass of skirts like a bust from a haystack. There was a strong suggestion of lavender water from her general vicinity.

I turned from the fascinating spectacle of Mrs. Cannon in formal dress to make my curtsy to my employer. He had not changed; he was still wearing the same travel-stained tweed suit and heavy boots he had been wearing the night before. He asked me how I had survived the journey; and I replied, superfluously, that I had survived it well enough. Then the conversation languished. Mr. Hamilton applied himself to a decanter of port. Mrs. Cannon watched him like a faithful dog who doesn't quite know what is expected of it, and I warmed my toes at the fire.

Dinner was announced by a singularly nasty-looking old man in a dirty kilt and jacket. The tartan interested me, since I assumed it was that of the Hamiltons, but I couldn't make out the pattern because of its incrustation of filth. Mr. Hamilton offered Mrs. Cannon his arm; she blinked at him in a startled fashion, and took it. I was left to follow behind.

The old servant led the way, carrying a heavy silver candelabra, as we left the West Wing for an older part of the house. The corridor was like a long cave, stone-walled and stone-floored. An icy draught blew down it, setting the candle flames to flickering wildly. I felt as if I were walking ankle-deep in snow. Then the old man set his shoulder against a massive panelled door, and we entered the dining room.

It must have been the Great Hall of the original house. There were candles on the table, which was long enough to seat thirty guests at once, but they made only a small pool of light in the midst of the great gloomy cavern of a room. The beams of the ceiling were lost in a sea of shadows; hanging from them were shapes that looked like giant cobwebs.

The food was cold by the time it reached us, having been carried down those wintry corridors all the way from the kitchens in the West Wing. Mr. Hamilton appeared not to notice. He talked animatedly about the antiquities in the Hall and what I had taken to be cobwebs were the tattered flags and banners of ancient Hamiltons. He pointed out portraits on the walls, too. I supposed they were there, but I couldn't see them. My feet felt like blocks of ice. As soon as I decently could I looked at Mrs. Cannon and made signals of distress, hoping she would give the signal for us to withdraw and leave Mr. Hamilton to his wine. But she was sitting with closed eyes, and a vague smile. I started to rise.

24

Mr. Hamilton's hand closed upon my wrist. "Wait. I want you to hear something."

His fingers were as cold and stiff as those of a corpse, and the black silk felt slippery against my skin. I sat down at once. I was already shaking with cold, and if an extra shudder went through me, I flattered myself that he hadn't noticed it. As soon as I was seated he took his hand away. Then into the frigid air came a sound of unearthly music—soft clear notes, falling like drops of water on to a frozen pool.

"There are advantages to living in a barbaric country," said Mr. Hamilton blandly. "I suppose few English gentlemen possess a resident minstrel in this day and age. Up there, Miss Gordon—behind you."

I turned, my gaze following the direction of his outstretched hand. Now that he pointed it out I could see the outlines of a balcony or gallery high up on the northern wall.

"Very interesting," I said, trying to keep my teeth from chattering. "But couldn't we hear him in the drawing room?"

"The music is more effective here," said Mr. Hamilton shortly. The cold seemed to invigorate him; there was a flush of colour on his high cheekbones, and his eyes sparkled.

"Davey," he shouted, lifting his head. "We have a visitor tonight. Give her one of your best."

There was a break in the music and a tentative ripple of notes, as if the musician were seeking inspiration. Then the strings found a pattern; and the voice began to sing.

The voice was that of an old man, but it was clear and true despite its tremulousness. I knew the ballad; it was the story of the unhappy maid of honour of Mary, Queen of Scots, who found herself with child by the queen's husband Darnley. Driven by desperation, the girl tried to conceal her guilt by an abominable act. She took the newborn babe and

"... put him in a tiny boat,
And cast him out to sea,
That he might sink, or he might swim,
But he'd never return to me.

Old Davey was a master; I could almost hear the miserable girl's voice. I turned to my host with a smile of delight; and my smile froze as I saw his face.

He rose, his black hands clenched on the table top, and shouted something in a voice thick with fury. The words were Gaelic; I recognised the language, but not the meaning. The music stopped as if a knife had slashed the strings.

"But—what's wrong?" I stammered. "He sings beautifully."

"He knows better. He knows he is never to sing that song in this house...." Mr. Hamilton drew a deep breath; the dark blood began to recede from his face. "You were right," he said quietly. "It is too cold here."

Before I could move or speak he had snatched up the candelabra and left the room, at a walk so rapid that it looked like flight.

CHAPTER 3

THEY say one never sleeps well the first night in a strange bed. Certainly I didn't, that first night at Blacktower House. The wind whispered at the windowpanes, and the dying fire made patterns of shifting light and shadow on the crimson red curtains. Still, I think I would have slept soundly, being physically exhausted, if my mind had been at ease. I had never seen a man's face look the way Mr. Hamilton's had looked when he lifted himself out of his chair and shouted at the singer.

Deserted, Mrs. Cannon and I had made our way back to the drawing room after the Master's abrupt departure, and a painful trip it was, because the old lady's distress turned her into a dead weight on my arm. But during the windy walk I remembered something. The name of the tragic lady of the ballad was Mary Hamilton.

Still, thought I, rolling and tossing in the big bed, that didn't solve the problem of Mr. Hamilton's inexplicable rage. The song was not history; it was only a song. And even if the story were true, why should a man like Mr. Hamilton go into fits of sensibility over the reputation of a remote ancestress?

I wanted to know, not only out of idle curiosity, but because Mr. Hamilton and I lived in the same house. If he was subject to such rages as that. . . . I told myself I was being foolish, but I couldn't forget his face—black with fury, the mouth misshapen even beyond the distortion of his scar.

I expected to dream of that face, or of poor Mary Hamilton—but I didn't. When I awoke, rested and refreshed. I was thinking of something altogether different. A good night's sleep had put the events of the previous evening into proper perspective; I could dismiss them as strange, but unimportant. There was someone else in the house about whom I had been curious from the first; and in this case I could satisfy my curiosity without delay.

It was a grey, misty morning; fog obscured the windows of my room. When Betty brought my breakfast I asked her which was Miss Hamilton's room. She told me it was the fourth door down the hall, next to Mrs. Cannon's, but her eyes opened wide and she was obviously surprised that I should ask. It was a small thing, but it confirmed my already formed notion that the young lady was neglected, and made me all the more eager to become her friend. So great was my crusading zeal that I went straight to her room after breakfast. I knocked and went in without waiting for an answer.

I don't know what I expected—a barren attic furnished with cast-off chairs and cots, I suppose. Instead, I found myself on the threshold of a princess's boudoir, out of a child's fairy tale. It was the most overdecorated room I had ever seen—pink Chinese wallpaper with designs of peacocks and fruit and flowers, rose damask hangings at the windows and at the gilded bedstead. The carpets were blue, with fat cabbage roses all over them. Knots of ribbon and silk rosebuds hung from the most unlikely places and festooned the window hangings, and a huge golden baroque mirror hung where it would reflect the bed. There was a great deal of furniture, all inlaid or lacquered or carved—an ebony cabinet with tortoise-shell marquetry and gilt bronze mountings, a writing table with Sèvres porcelain placques and spindly gilded legs. It was like stepping into the heart of a giant rose, all pink and gold. Then a whiff of stale, heavily perfumed air struck me, and I wrinkled my nose. A rose, perhaps; but one that was past its bloom.

In the centre of the big bed, propped by lace-trimmed pillows, sat a young girl. She wore a bedgown of the same eternal pink, trimmed with white fur. Golden ringlets, elaborately curled, fell on her shoulders. A book was open on her lap, and even from the door I could see that it was not a novel, but one of the new books of fashion, with pictures of doll-faced ladies wearing the latest, most exaggerated modes.

Then I looked from the fur and the satin and the golden curls to the girl's face—and the fairy tale ended. The eyes that met mine, in a cold, unwinking stare, were pale-blue framed by lashes so fair they were almost invisible. The mouth was a thin ungenerous line that drooped at the corners. The cheeks were a sickly dead white. In short—the young lady was plain.

"Who are you?" she demanded in a thin, querulous voice. "What do you mean by bursting in here?"

"I do beg your pardon, Miss Hamilton," I said. "I was so very anxious to meet you! I am Damaris Gordon, your father's secretary."

I came towards her, extending my hand. It took resolution to keep it extended while she frowned at it, and then at my face. At last she gave me a feeble handclasp.

"How very red your hair is," she remarked. "I have never seen hair of that colour before."

"Fair hair is prettier," I agreed.

Sarcasm was wasted on Miss Hamilton. "Is my father going to marry you?" she asked coolly.

"Why—why, no—certainly not! Whatever gave you such an idea?"

"Janet—my maid—said he might. She said you were young and not ill-favoured, in spite of your ugly hair." Her blue eyes inspected me and then dropped, obviously for purposes of comparison, to the simpering ladies on the page of the fashion book. "You aren't beautiful," she decided, "but perhaps a man might find you pleasing."

"My dear Miss Hamilton—you shouldn't say such things! What do you know of men, a little thing like yourself?"

"I have read many novels, and the men in them are often infatuated with women of the servant classes."

This was going a bit too far, even for an invalid. But before I could say so she went on.

"If you aren't in love with my father, why did you come here? Why did you leave London for this wretched place?"

"London isn't so fine as you may think. It's only a great grimy city."

"Oh, no! The balls, the shops, the fine houses, the court —have you seen the Queen? What is she like?"

Of all the inhabitants of London I was the least equipped to discourse on balls and the graces of the nobility, but I had a good imagination and no scruples about using it. The girl listened open-mouthed to my colourful tales, and her manner grew, if not more respectful, at least more cordial. I played Scheherazade until one of the maids—the Janet of whom she had spoken, I assumed—came to take away the breakfast tray.

"Your father will be expecting me to begin my duties," I said. "I must go now."

"Very well," said the princess royally. "But come back this afternoon."

"I will if I can," I said, seeing the lonely child under her imperious air. "If your father doesn't need me."

"Tell him I want you. He gives me whatever I want."

I would have dearly loved to have explored that statement, and the contradictions in the relations between father and child—the opulent furnishings of her room and the cold hostile way he spoke of her. But the maid, Janet, was still in the room. She was a big rawboned woman with a sly, obsequious face. I would never have chosen her to look after a delicate but spoiled young girl. My own maid, Betty, had a far more honest face.

Well, I thought, as I ran down the stairs, Miss Annabelle Hamilton is not my problem. Or—I stopped outside the door of the drawing room as a thought struck me—or is she? Perhaps her father had been hinting that I teach her manners, instead of Greek! She certainly could use some instruction, but perhaps I wasn't the best of tutors myself. Smiling, I opened the door and found the Master waiting.

This morning he wore the Highland costume in which the menservants were dressed. The plaid was dark, mostly greens and blacks, with a narrow red thread running through it. With the plaid kilt and grey knee stockings he wore a coat of matching grey and a white shirt, open at the throat. The odd costume suited his tall figure; he was the very picture of one of the Highland chiefs who raised the clans for Bonnie Prince Charlie.

Except for his black-gloved hands. I was growing used to his scar, but his gloves still shook me.

"So," he greeted me, "my spies tell me you spent the morning with my daughter. What do you think of her?"

"She is rather pitiful. And—charming, of course."

"Oh, come now! Didn't she favour you with her frank opinions as to your appearance, character, and behaviour?"

"No one could take offence at the words of a child."

"She is sixteen. But if that's the worst you can say of her, she must have restrained herself. No doubt she has taken a fancy to you."

"I did my best to make her do so," I said, smiling as I remembered my fictitious description of Her Majesty and Prince Albert at a court ball.

"How noble we are this morning! I hope your Christian intentions last, although I doubt it. But enough of that. Your duties are not to cater to Annabelle's whims. Come along."

The library was opposite the drawing room, on the main corridor of the West Wing. Windows filled one wall and the remaining three were lined with bookshelves. An iron gallery, reached by a flight of narrow stairs, had still more shelves. Under the windows stood a big desk covered with books and papers. In its design the room was a handsome one, with moulded cornices and a fine Adam fireplace. But the litter was incredible. Books were everywhere except in their proper place—piled on the floor, tumbling from chairs and tables and ledges. Dust covered everything in the room except the desk, and as Mr.

Hamilton closed the door I heard a scrabble of claws behind the shelves.

With an exclamation of horror I bent to pick up the nearest book.

"These volumes are being ruined! And this is the rare third edition of Maxwell's *Antiquities*. Mr. Hamilton, indeed—!"

"I see I chose my librarian well," said that gentleman with a smile. "You nurse that filthy book as a cat does a kitten."

"Speaking of cats, I must have one."

"Ah, yes. I forgot that proper young ladies are afraid of mice."

"Well, I'm not afraid of them! But I don't want them dining off your leather bindings."

"A suitable cat will be supplied. Do you want to begin today?"

I looked dismally at my dirty hands. "Yes, after I change. My oldest frock will be best."

"I did not employ you as a housemaid," said Mr. Hamilton. "One of the servants will do the actual cleaning."

He opened the door and shouted. Before long there was a shuffle of feet in the passage, and the old man who had announced dinner the previous evening appeared. He was still wearing the same filthy kilt and jacket, or an exact copy of them, and he planted himself before his master with legs apart and arms akimbo, without deigning to glance at me.

"This is Angus," said Mr. Hamilton, "my devoted valet, majordomo, butler, or what you will. Angus, Miss Gordon is about to restore the library. Send cleaning materials and one of the scullery maids."

The old man's eyes were sunken between his bony cheeks and tattered grey brows, but I saw them roll in my direction. He muttered something in Gaelic. Mr. Hamilton shot back a retort in the same tongue. It was a biting reproof; I could tell that from the tone, without understanding a syllable. Angus was unimpressed. The look he gave his master was ugly in its open malignancy.

"He is a filthy, disagreeable old man," said Mr. Hamilton calmly. "You will ignore most of his unpleasant remarks as beneath your notice. But if they ever exceed the bounds of common decency, or if he is lax in obeying an order, report the matter to me."

He and Angus began to argue—there was no other word for it—about the servant to be assigned to me, and the details of the work. I stood watching them. At a casual glance they were totally unlike—one young and straight, the other old, bent and ugly. And yet . . . They would have been the same height if it had not been for Angus's stoop, and the bones of their face were oddly similar. I knew then why the plaid suited Mr. Hamilton so well. Like Angus, he was a typical Scot.

Well, I had known that; Hamilton is an old Scottish name. I shook myself out of my reverie as Angus turned to go. He looked at me directly for the first time. I returned his glare with one of equal intensity. Angus and I, it was obvious, were not going to get along.

I named the "suitable cat" Toby, after a childhood pet. Toby the second didn't resemble his predecessor, who had been a plump grey tabby with bland yellow eyes. The new kitten, a product of the stable, was a lean black beast, and his eyes were a brilliant green. He was prepared to work for his keep, and he did. At first I started nervously whenever a mouse squeak came from behind the shelves where Toby's long furry tail waved vigorously as the only visible sign of the combat going on. Later I became hardened to the sounds, and they diminished in frequency as Toby's reputation spread among the rodent population. He was a dignified animal; his only bad habit was that he insisted on bringing the dead mice out to be admired. I could hardly scold him, since that was what he was here to do; so I admired his prey without ever looking at it directly, and, after bumping his head against my ankles, Toby took it away.

33

I had suspected, in London, that Mr. Hamilton was hiring me out of charity. The library reassured me; it really did need care. But, charity or not, I meant to earn my salary. I worked like a slave in the dust and grime, and April passed into May without my noticing it.

One morning as I was settling down to work the door opened. I had been expecting the scullery maid and didn't look up until a large shadow came between me and the sunlight.

"Have you ever wondered," enquired Mr. Hamilton, "why ladies are not admitted to the professions? Look at yourself! Your hair is covered with dust; your face is pale, and you are beginning to stoop like Angus."

"My appearance, sir, is my own affair."

"Quite true. But your health is my affair. As your employer, I order you to exercise daily. Do you ride?"

"No," I said quickly, without adding that I was afraid of horses.

"Then you ought to learn. Go up and change your dress."

"I—I have no riding costume."

"A lady's riding costume is only another set of skirts. Wear something warm—and clean. I don't care to be seen with a person who looks like a scrubwoman."

Naturally, this taunt provoked me into putting on my best day dress—a redingote skirt of green poplin with a jacket bodice that flared out below the waist. It had a narrow white collar and the new pagoda sleeves, piped in darker green velvet. It was a perfectly absurd costume for riding, of course. But when I came into the courtyard Mr. Hamilton's black eyes raked me from head to toe, and he said nothing. So I concluded that I had passed inspection.

He was already astride his horse, a tall grey with a wicked, rolling eye. I was glad to see that he had chosen a milder-appearing animal for me. It had its eyes closed, and it looked as if it wanted to lie down.

I was determined not to let Mr. Hamilton see that I was afraid, so I fed the animal some sugar, expecting at any moment to feel the great teeth snap on my hand. But the questing mouth was as soft as velvet. Somewhat reassured, I accepted the help of a groom and scrambled ungracefully into the saddle. Mr. Hamilton watched my thrashing skirts with discourteous amusement.

"Hook your knee over the saddle," he ordered. "You must learn not to kick a horse in that hysterical fashion. Any animal but Flame would have run away with you before this."

"Flame?" I looked incredulously at the horse's nodding head.

"She was a lively infant, and bright red-brown in colour." Even as I watched, the laughter left his face. He said slowly, "Yet the destiny of the animal cannot be altered. We are what we are; no training can wipe out faults that are bred in the blood and bone."

He turned his horses's head towards the gate, leaving the forbidding words adrift in the air, like fog.

I caught him up outside the court, and said earnestly, "You can't mean what you said just now. That's fatalism —it leaves no hope of redemption, for body or soul . . ."

He had been sitting his horse in brooding silence, his head bent. At my words he looked up.

"I do not believe in the soul," he said curtly. "I referred to the physical animal."

He gathered up his reins and leaned over to give Flame a smart slap. She stumbled forward with a groan of protest.

"I'll have a whip for you next time you ride," said Mr. Hamilton, eyeing my gallant steed critically. Then he said, with a quick sidelong glance, "Aren't you going to comment on my heretical statement about the soul?"

I knew he was baiting me, so I said primly, "Your beliefs are no concern of mine. But I don't agree with any of your conclusions."

"Of course you don't. For all your intelligence, you are a very unworldly young woman. Do you always believe the best of everyone, and everything?"

"Why, no," I said, taken aback by the bitterness of his

tone.

"You know that there is evil in the world, that not everyone is to be trusted, or believed? I doubt that you do. Where, after all, could you have learned such unpleasant truths? Not from your father, surely."

His hands relaxed on the reins. His horse stopped. We sat facing one another, and under the intensity of his gaze my eyes fell.

"There was the butcher," I said, hoping to strike a lighter note. "I soon learned that he was not to be trusted. Mutton for lamb, beef for veal—"

"And did it never occur to you to apply the lesson learned from the butcher to men who offer you positions in remote country houses? What, in heaven's name, possessed you to come here with me?"

He leaned forward, hands clasped on the pommel, his face dark and angry. I couldn't move away from him without moving Flame, who was not easily stirred. I felt my heart pounding heavily.

"There is—there is such a thing as judgment," I began hesitantly. To my relief his grim expression lightened. He took up his reins.

"That will do. In a moment you will mention your feminine instincts, and I can't endure that sort of argument."

We rode on in silence, following a twisting path that climbed the hill behind the house. I was intent on keeping my seat, and meditating on the conversation that he had concluded so abruptly. It was with a start of surprise that I saw the rough walls of the Black Tower looming just ahead.

Mr. Hamilton drew rein upon the narrow level space around the foundations. The stones were rough and incredibly massive; weather and time had darkened them to their present hue, from which the Tower derived its name. I urged Flame up to the walls, and put my hand on the stone, which was cold and harsh.

"It was a strong fortress," I said musingly. "How did

36

such a place ever fall?"

"Oh, there is some tale or other about it," said Mr. Hamilton indifferently. "The treachery of the ladylove of an ancient chief of Dunnoch. His enemies cut his throat at her feet—and then cut hers, as a reward for her betrayal. You picked a poor place for a retreat, Miss Gordon. The Highlands have never been civilised, and the Highlander is still only a savage in a kilt."

I smiled at him, refusing to be baited, and after a moment he rode on around the Tower's southern corner.

The level space atop the ridge was large enough only for the Tower itself, with a narrow ledge around it. Almost at the horses' feet, the ledge fell away into a steep rocky slope that ended, far below, in a narrow glen. The hills to the west were lower than those behind us, and I could see beyond them to the moors, covered now by a faint veil of the palest green. Upon this colour the darker surface of the road looped in and out of sight and finally disappeared in a sweeping curve towards the south—to Edinburgh, to London.

With an effort I dragged my eyes from the road and the thoughts it evoked, and looked at the slope below. Our ride wouldn't take us that way, certainly. Nothing less sure-footed than a goat or mountain sheep could have travelled on that rocky slant. I said as much to Mr. Hamilton.

"You forget that other sure-footed animal, man," he replied.

"Surely not!"

"Oh, yes. Do you see the smoke down below? The cottage there belongs to one of my crofters. When he has business with me he comes over the hill just here. Look; you can make out the path."

There was a path, of sorts; it wound between the rocks and the contorted pines that clung tenaciously to the bitter ground. Yes, it could be climbed. But if the climber slipped he would roll, amid an avalanche of stone, all the way back down to the valley floor.

"I wouldn't care to walk that path," I admitted.

"It's not difficult; I have done it. But now look behind you."

To the east the glen lay spread out before me like a map, looking clean and peaceful from that height, with the grey stone houses huddling low to the green-washed ground, and with the bare beautiful hills beyond. Then I looked to my left. Blacktower House lay below.

I had not realised its size and extent. The original central portion must have been nearly as old as the Tower. It was built of the same rough, time-darkened stone, with twin towers flanking the old entrance. The wings to right and left were of lighter stone; they had wider windows and thinner walls than the central section. On one side a wall was joined to the stables and offices to form a court-yard. Even in the spring sunlight the house was not an attractive dwelling. As it crouched upon the slope it had an air of neglect and indifference that could not be reduced to any specific detail.

I turned my back on it and looked in the opposite direction, along the length of the glen. A flash of brightness, as of sunlight striking some polished surface, caught my eye.

"What is that?" I asked, pointing.

"That must be the windows of Glengarrie. Strange how the light strikes them."

"Another house? Or a town?"

"Glengarrie is the nearest big house. It used to belong to the Dunbars, but it has been empty for years."

He stood up in his stirrups, straining his eyes towards the far-off sparkle. When he settled again into his saddle I couldn't tell from his expression whether he had seen anything or not. It hardly seemed possible; the distance was too great.

"Well," he said, with an air of decision, "what do you think of the world into which you have come? I warned you that it would be isolated—confined. . . ."

I raised my eyes from the peace of the glen to the hills

beyond. They were rocky and forbidding, like a series of enclosing walls; but they had a savage beauty of their own.

"No, I don't feel confined," I said. "'I could be bounded in a nutshell and count myself a king of infinite space—'"

"Spare me your literary allusions," the Master broke in. "And what of myself? Has Mr. Shakespeare a comforting quotation to suit me?"

I thought of one at once—it was from *Macbeth*—but it wasn't very flattering, so I decided to keep it to myself.

As I pondered, the Master said sharply, "Look at me."

He was leaning towards me, his face only inches from mine. His black eyes were cold, without their usual spark of mockery.

"Are you afraid of me?" he asked.

"No!" I said, promptly and defiantly. And then, in wonder, as I realised I was only speaking the truth, I added, "No, I'm not."

For a long moment his eyes held mine, searching. Then, without another word, he jerked the horse's head about, and led the way back down the hill.

CHAPTER 4

AFTER that we rode out several times each week, and spring ventured cautiously into summer. Even that luxuriant season was sparse and "near" in the Highlands; yet it had its own austere beauty. Birch and rowan put on fresh green leaves, and the heather bloomed purple. When the weather was fine one could see for miles in the clear air. Mr. Hamilton pointed out the separate peaks and told me their odd-sounding Gaelic names—Ben Macdhui, Ben Avon, Ben-na-Bhourd. One bright morning he showed me a tiny pyramid on the far western horizon which he said was Ben Nevis, more than thirty miles away.

I went to Miss Hamilton's room that morning, after we returned to the house. I had taken to calling her Annabelle now, and she called me Damaris; but we were still far from intimate. That day the perfumed staleness of the room seemed worse than usual after the winy air of the hills. I went to one of the windows and threw it wide open.

Annabelle gave a shriek. "Close it at once! I can't endure cold air!"

"It's not cold enough to hurt you. Only see the sunshine!"

I came back to the bed and stood beside it, to be sure there was no draught. She was well sheltered by the bed curtains, where she crouched like a small sultana in her silken tent.

"This stale air is bad for you day after day," I said. "Don't you ever leave your room?"

"You forget." The blue eyes shot me an angry look. "I am a cripple."

"I don't know anything about your condition. How did you lose the use of your limbs?"

"I fell into the water when I was a small child. The

40

burn is very wide and deep at the mouth of the glen, before it goes over the falls. . . ." Her voice trailed off, and her eyes looked inward. Then she gave a little jerk and said quite calmly, "I was in the icy water for hours. It paralysed my legs."

"Do you remember that?"

"Oh, no. . . . No, Mrs. Cannon told me."

"If you were in the water so long, why didn't you drown?"

"The current threw me against a rock," said Annabelle glibly. "My head was out of the water, but my legs hung down in the burn."

"Perhaps you were cut or bruised by the rocks."

"No. It was the cold water."

I sat down on the bed beside her. "That's nonsense," I said bluntly.

"Why—why—you don't know anything about it! How dare you say such a thing?"

"I dare because you aren't Cleopatra or Semiramis, and can't order my head cut off if I displease you." I smiled into her sullen face. "I studied some anatomy with my father. Will you let me look at your legs?"

"Oh, go ahead." Annabelle threw herself back against the pillow and glowered at me. "But don't pretend you know about medicine. You're just inquisitive like the rest of the servants."

I ignored the last remark, having found this the best way of coping with her insults, and drew the covers back. Her poor white limbs were as thin as those of a child. But there were no scars, and the structure of the bones seemed to be faultless.

Finally I drew the coverlet up and rearranged it.

"It's strange," I said, half to myself. "I can see nothing wrong."

The moment the words were out of my mouth I regretted them. Annabelle's head turned sharply. We stared at one another for a moment, I in consternation, and she—well, there was the dawn of an idea in her

41

glittering eyes, an idea which I knew I must put down at once, before it could flower into hope. I had no business suggesting such a thing to her. The fact that it hadn't occurred to me until I spoke didn't excuse my carelessness.

"But of course I'm not a physician," I said quickly. "A doctor would have known—and you must have had the best—at the time of the accident."

"I don't remember any doctors," said Annabelle.

This was the sort of statement she was fond of making —negative, hostile, implying persecution and neglect. I knew her better than to take her seriously.

In an effort to get her away from the subject, I said at random, "How was it that a small child was allowed to wander near such a dangerous spot?"

Annabelle was slow in answering. Finally she muttered, "The nurse was careless, I suppose. After my mother died, everything went to pieces here."

It was the first time that I had ever heard anyone mention the former Mrs. Hamilton. I forgot all else in an upsurge of curiosity.

"When did she die?" I asked.

"When I was born. I killed her. That," she added calmly, "is why my father hates me."

"Annabelle! Where did you get such a wild notion?"

"It's not a wild notion. It's true!"

"Well, you certainly don't remember *that*. And I know Mrs. Cannon never told you such a thing."

"No one had to tell me! It's like that novel, *Lord Ellsworth's Secret*. My mother was very beautiful, and my father loved her madly. He hates me because I killed her."

"Your father doesn't hate you."

"Oh, yes, he does. Look—I'll show you something, if you promise to keep it a secret. I've never shown it to anyone else."

"I promise."

Annabelle stretched out her arm towards the table beside the bed. Then she gave me an oblique, sly look.

"Hide your eyes."

I covered them with my palms. There was a great rustling and rattling from the head of the bed, and finally Annabelle said, "Now you can open them."

She was sitting up against the pillows, holding a flat oval shape of wood about five inches in length. She handed it to me.

"That was my mother. Wasn't she beautiful?"

I looked dubiously at the portrait—a miniature on ivory, yellow with age. The gilded frame was worn. The face was like those of the simpering dolls in the fashion book, round-cheeked, with rosebud mouth and languishing dark eyes. The black hair hung in ringlets over the plump white shoulders.

I looked at the face for a long time, and the painted black eyes seemed to return my stare with bland indifference. Something about the picture roused a dim disquiet; but although I stared and thought, and thought and stared, the impression would not solidify. Finally I gave up and handed the portrait back to Annabelle.

"She is beautiful," I said mendaciously. "Thank you for showing it to me."

She made me cover my eyes again while she restored her treasure to its hiding place, and then I rose to go. Still the odd impression—that there was something not quite right about the portrait—haunted me. I was almost at the door before I remembered what I had meant to say earlier.

"Why don't you come downstairs for a bit after dinner? One of the men can carry you."

"Oh, no." Annabelle shrank back into her pillows.

"I'm sure it wouldn't hurt you. Come now, I want you to see what I've done in the libarary. And you must meet Toby."

"Who is Toby? A servant?"

"No, not a servant. I won't tell you who he is. You must come and see for yourself."

"Well . . . all right." She returned my smile with a twinkle that made her look almost pretty. But, being

43

Annabelle, she had to have the last word. "If I hurt myself, it will be your fault."

I was willing to risk it. It seemed to me that the danger to her body was less than the danger to her mind if she remained isolated and brooding in her own room. Already she was losing the ability to distinguish between fact and fancy. That wild tale about her mother, for instance...

I stopped in the middle of the hall, struck by a new idea. The tale was wild; but could I be sure it was untrue? I didn't know anything about the history of the family. If I wanted to help Annabelle I would have to learn something about it.

I knew this was just an excuse to justify my shameless curiosity. But it gave me the courage to keep on being curious. I decided to talk to Mrs. Cannon.

Talking to Mrs. Cannon wasn't as easy as one might think. Only three topics interested her : food, dress, and the misbehaviour of the servants. Whenever I tried to introduce another subject she always smiled faintly, and began to snore. Still, I had never met an elderly lady who didn't like to gossip, and I went to her room for dinner that day with a fixed determination to find out what I wanted to know.

As soon as we had finished the main part of the meal, during which time the good lady's attention was fully absorbed, I asked casually, "How long ago did Mrs. Hamilton pass away?"

"Mrs. Hamilton?" The old lady blinked, and added two more spoonfuls of sugar to her tea. Finally she said, "Fifteen years. Or was it sixteen? Annabelle is sixteen. It must have been fourteen years ago."

I sighed inaudibly. Well, I had known it wouldn't be easy.

"How did she die? Was it in childbed?"

"Childbed?" Mrs. Cannon pondered, spoon poised over her cup. "Why, no. No, not in childbed. Annabelle was two years old when her mother passed away. She is the only child. There never was—"

44

"But how did the lady pass away?"

"How? Let me see. Consumption—or pleurisy? Pleurisy, I believe. I had an aunt who perished with that complaint. She made a beautiful end; it was most edifying for all beholders."

"I'm sure it was," I said hastily; for Mrs. Cannon seemed about to launch into a detailed description. "You weren't here, then, when Mrs. Hamilton—er—perished?"

"No. No, I was not." Mrs. Cannon put down her spoon and took a sip of the treacly tea. "I was called to my position after Mrs. Hamilton's death—being a distant connection of the family, like yourself, my dear. And a pretty state of affairs I found when I arrived, I can tell you!"

"Really?"

"Only fancy—the Master had dismissed every servant in the house! I presume he blamed them for carelessness—the child's accident, you know. She was still very ill when I came, and he himself, poor man, shouldn't have left his bed."

I opened my lips to pursue this ambiguous remark; but Mrs. Cannon, launched on one of her favourite topics, swept on.

"Yes, I was told to bring a complete new staff with me from London. And that was no simple task, I assure you. The servant classes today are not what they were in *my* time. All they care about nowadays is copying their mistress's wardrobe in cheap materials, or flirting with the butcher's boy. Oh, that reminds me. I caught that hussy Betty in a most compromising position with Ian, the Master's groom, yesterday. And I know she has her eye on my blue satin bonnet with the ostrich plume—"

I thought that Betty would look much better in this particular bonnet than Mrs. Cannon did, but of course I didn't say so.

"I suppose English servants wouldn't want to come so far," I said, trying to get her back on the subject. "But isn't that a curious thing, to discharge all the servants?

The nurse, perhaps, might be held to blame. But all of them—with an ailing child in the house . . ."

It was too late. Mrs. Cannon's head had fallen on one side. A beatific smile curved her mouth, and her eyes were fast shut. Quietly, I tiptoed out.

I smiled at myself in the mirror as I brushed my hair and straightened my cuffs. So Betty was compromising herself with the Master's groom! I had come to like the girl. Her glum looks were only a mask. She responded, quickly and touchingly, to kindness.

I found Mr. Hamilton in the courtyard, mounted to ride out. Ian was holding his stirrup, and I looked at the groom with new interest. I had always preferred him to the other servants; he was quiet, but not sullen, and he had always been courteous to me. He certainly was a well set-up young man—tall, with the high cheekbones and thin, swarthy face of most of the Scots I had seen. Betty could look further and do worse, I thought.

"I want to bring Annabelle downstairs today," I said to her father. "Will it injure her to be moved?"

Mr. Hamilton's hands slackened on the reins; his spirited grey, mistaking the movement, pranced impatiently. Mr. Hamilton swore at Ian for not holding the animal—an unfair criticism, since Ian's start of surprise had been no more reprehensible than his own.

"It won't hurt her," he said. "But are you out of your mind?"

I could hardly explain my reasons there, under Ian's interested eye, and with half a dozen other servants loitering around. So I simply stared calmly back at Mr. Hamilton, and after a moment his lips parted in a reluctant smile.

"No, you never deign to explain yourself, do you? Very well. Ian, go up with Miss Gordon and carry Miss Annabelle—where? The library? Miss Gordon, are you trying to annoy me? Well, so be it. The library. But have her out by four o'clock. I will be using the room after that."

Ian, staring fixedly off into space, looked as deaf as a

46

sound man could look; but I was hot with anger as I led him into the house and up the stairs. It was brutal of Mr. Hamilton to speak of his daughter so, and in front of the servants.

We found Annabelle dressed in an elaborate gown of blue silk, which fastened down the front with dozens of little buttons. She made the trip downstairs easily in Ian's strong arms, and when he had gone I arranged an afghan carefully over her knees, and stood back to observe the effect.

A little excitement seemed to do her good. I realised, with some surprise, that she would be a handsome girl if her cheeks had the bloom of health and her face a happier expression. She glanced around the room, at the neat shelves and the rows of books.

"It looks very nice," she said graciously. "Now where is this Toby person?"

I brought him out from his favourite lair, behind the twelve thick volumes of Mr. Hume's *History*. Toby was no longer the wild rangy kitten from the stable; he had grown fat and sleek with his diet of mice. His black fur gleamed, and his whiskers were immaculate. Being a tolerant animal, he was always willing to form a new acquaintance. He settled down in Annabelle's lap and began to purr.

The girl's pleasure was pitiable. She had never had a pet; and she touched the warm, vibrating ball of black fur with a respectful admiration I had never seen her display towards a human being. I was determined to make this a festive affair, so we had an elaborate tea, with scones and jam and cakes. Toby condescended to partake of a dish of cream, and, in his usual spirit of experimentation, sampled a cake as well. He was at his best, like a host exerting himself to be entertaining.

I had told Ian to come back at four. When he appeared, Annabelle's face crumpled like a baby's.

"Oh, must I go? I'm not tired—truly, I'm not."

I certainly wasn't going to tell her the real reason we

had to vacate the library at four o'clock. So I merely said that she ought not to tire herself the first time. She gave in, much more gracefully than I had expected, and Ian bore her off.

That was the first of our little parties, which occurred several times a week. By tacit permission the room was ours for two hours, and no one disturbed us. But eventually the inevitable happened. Ian was late in coming, and Mr. Hamilton was early.

Annabelle had been teasing Toby with a feather as he lay, feet up, in her lap, more like a kitten than a grown cat with a living to earn. When the door opened she looked up; and her face froze. The alteration in her features struck me so forcibly that I turned on my employer with a look that was by no means respectful.

"You are too early," I said.

"Would you like me to go away?" he inquired, in a tone of deadly humility.

"No, I suppose you may come in. I'm sorry we can't offer you tea. We ate it all up."

"Thank you." He advanced, looking formidably tall. "Good afternoon, Annabelle. Good afternoon, Toby."

"Do you know Toby?" asked Annabelle, forgetting herself in her surprise.

"Very well. He sits on my desk when I write letters, and criticises me."

Mr. Hamilton bent over and touched the cat's head. From the corner of his eye he looked at his daughter. There were curiosity and mild surprise in his look—nothing kinder than that.

I heard a clatter of feet in the corridor and Ian entered, looking unnaturally red and flustered.

"Beg pardon, miss—sir. I was delayed—"

"It doesn't matter, Ian," I said. Mr. Hamilton said nothing.

I went upstairs with Annabelle, who was once more her old sulky self. She didn't need me to settle her into her bed—her maid, Janet, was waiting for her—but I needed

48

time to compose myself. Several times in the past I had tried to work up courage enough to speak to the Master about his daughter; and each time my nerve had failed. Now I meant to speak. But I wanted to be sure I was in complete command of myself before I went back to the library. Anyone who wanted to argue with Gavin Hamilton needed all his wits about him.

He was seated behind the desk when I burst into the library. Glancing up, he waved me to a chair. I sat down. And then, before I could open my mouth, he did something that took my breath away by its studied rudeness. Reaching into a drawer of the desk, he took out a handful of one-pound notes and gave them to me.

"Your first quarter's wages," he said.

I had taken the money without thinking, as one automatically receives anything that is offered. Now my fingers clenched, crumpling the crisp paper.

"Do you want to speak to me?" the Master asked blandly.

I looked up from the crumpled notes in my fist.

"That was prettily done."

"Oh, I have few scruples; you ought to know that. But I see you aren't intimidated. Come, speak up; let's get it over with."

"I want to speak to you about Annabelle," I said, glaring.

"Really? What a surprise!"

"Be as sarcastic as you like," I said angrily. "It will only prolong a discussion which you seem anxious to cut short."

"I beg your pardon." His face smoothed out into a courteously attentive mask; but I knew very well he was laughing silently behind it.

"First about her physical health," I said. "What is wrong with her? Why can't she walk?"

"I have no idea," said the Master indifferently.

"There is no mark or scar—" I stumbled over that word, but Mr. Hamilton only cocked a mocking black eye at me and smiled. I finished. "There's no mark on her body—no visible reason why she shouldn't walk."

"I know that. The doctors told me years ago that they couldn't account for her condition. Neither can I."

"You—you did have doctors, then?"

He had been leaning back in his chair, teetering idly on two legs of it. Now the front legs came down with a crash, and he leaned forward across the desk, scowling at me.

"What sort of brute do you take me for, Damaris?"

"Nothing. I mean—no sort. Forgive me."

"Granted." He tipped his chair back again, but the eyes that watched me were still furious. "Go on."

"As to—as to her mental conditon. I wanted to bring her downstairs, to give her a new interest, because I am concerned about her fantasies. She has told herself romantic tales, and now she believes them."

"What sort of tales?"

"About her mother." The chair legs came down again, but I went doggedly on. "She told me her mother had died in giving birth to her."

"That's not true."

"I know."

"How the hell *do* you know?"

"Mrs. Cannon—"

"That doddering old biddy!" I realised, with an odd foreboding, that he had relaxed again. "She knows nothing about it. Annabelle's mother died of typhoid. In London. Now. What else?"

I shook my head dumbly. Typhoid. Mrs. Cannon had said pleurisy. But she hadn't even known Mrs. Hamilton. She was old and vague. There was no reason not to accept Mr. Hamilton's statement. And yet—why had he been so alarmed at the idea that I knew something about the lady's death—and so relieved when he found that my source was Mrs. Cannon?

"What else?" he repeated.

"Nothing else."

"I frightened you," he said, more gently. "I'm sorry,

Miss Gordon."

He had called me "Damaris" before. I didn't answer him. I was too confused to think of anything to say. And I could hardly deny that he had frightened me, when he had —just a little.

When he spoke again, I knew he had dismissed the subject, now and forever. "I must go to Edinburgh tomorrow. I'll be away for some time. Is there anything you want? Any message to send?"

"No. Thank you."

He made a gesture of dismissal, at once lordly and casual. I crept, like a mouse, from the room.

He left before daylight the next morning. After breakfast I went out myself, on a mission I would never have dared to begin while he was in the house. I was looking for Annabelle's mother.

There was no church of any denomination in the glen. A travelling minister came once a month to hold services in the blacksmith's house—the biggest in the village—and to marry or read burial services over any of the villagers who required such attentions. Anyone in need of religious consolation in the meantime had to walk or ride over the pass into Castleton. But, although there was no church, there was a small graveyard on a ridge not far from Blacktower House, and I rode Flame over there.

Pines, melancholy even in the sunlight, leaned over the low stone wall that surrounded the cemetery. The ground was weed-grown and rough, the markers half buried in gorse. The majority of the low slabs were of mountain granite, with laboriously carved inscriptions, usually just the name and dates of birth and death.

I let Flame's reins dangle; there was never any need to tie her, since she never moved if she could help it. Then I went to have a closer look at the graves.

In the northeast corner, separated from the humbler graves by a tottering iron railing, was the burial place of the Hamiltons. Most of the graves were old, the stones worn almost smooth by weather; on one I made out a date that might have been 1578. A great majority of the Hamilton graves that did have legible markers dated to the 1600's and early 1700's, but there were a few later monuments.

I crawled over the ground on hands and knees, searching the crumbling stones. My hands got dirty and my skirt grass-stained, but when I rose to my feet I was satisfied of one thing: Annabelle's mother was not buried here.

I mounted Flame, who sighed reproachfully when I pulled her head away from the weeds she was cropping, and started back towards the house. The trip had been a waste of time; and I had known from the start that it would be. Mr. Hamilton had said that his wife died in London. She must have been buried there. Even Mrs. Cannon hadn't said explicitly that the lady had been living at Blacktower House when she died.

Storm clouds were gathering over the cruel high slopes of Ben Macdhui. A sudden wind flattened the heather, baring the smooth grey stems. It was going to rain.

Rain did fall, most miserably, and it continued for a week. Mr. Hamilton did not return; and I went on with my ridiculous search for a woman who had been dead for fourteen years. No one bothered me. When the Master was away Mrs. Cannon slept all the time instead of only half the time, and the servants abandoned all pretense of working. I wandered, unseen and undisturbed, through the house.

And as I walked, my candle held high, through room after deserted room, a kind of horror grew upon me—horror of the abandoned chambers with their mouldering draperies and rotting furniture, and horror of the direction my thoughts were taking. For nowhere in the house was there any trace of the woman who had been its mistress—no dress she might have worn, no bed she might have slept in, no trinket she might have touched.

I saw the old nursery, where Annabelle had lived as a child. Nothing had been moved; the toys were crumbling

52

to dust on the grimy shelves. I touched a stuffed doll, and the painted china head went rolling off the shelf and came to rest at my feet, where it grinned imbecilically up at me. I even invaded Mr. Hamilton's bedchamber, an austere cell on a cross corridor of the West Wing, far from Mrs. Cannon's room and mine. No woman had ever shared that room with him.

I should have stopped after I explored the West Wing. The rest of the house obviously hadn't been inhabited for years. But by then I was obsessed. Somewhere, surely, there must be some sign that Annabelle's mother had existed. Not even a husband's grief could explain the deliberate, systematic removal of every object that had once belonged to her. It was as if someone were trying to deny that she had ever lived.

On Thursday I decided to explore the Great Hall and the rooms near it. I took Toby with me. Like all cats he enjoyed exploring, and I had come to feel the need for companionship in the darkened passages.

Outside the rain fell with dreary persistence, and fog obscured the windows as I passed through the door under the main stairs and into the stone-floored corridor that led towards the Hall. The candle flickered in the draught. Even Toby seemed subdued. He trotted close at my heels, like a little black dog, and didn't mew once.

By daylight the Hall was not as grim as it had been by night, but it was still melancholy in its vast decay. The fitted flagstones of the floor glistened with damp. High up on the eastern wall was a row of windows filled with crude yellow and red stained glass that changed the clouded daylight to the lurid hue of a smoky fire. Directly across from the main door, where I was standing, was the minstrel's gallery. I could see only the high carved balustrade of blackened wood. On the fourth wall, opposite the windows, was a mammoth stone fireplace. On the chimney hung a collection of rusting weapons—claymores and spears, a long dirk or dagger with its blade discoloured by a substance that may or may not have been rust, and a pair of matched fencing foils.

In the centre of the chamber stood the long table, with twenty chairs about it—I counted them, half-unconsciously, in an effort to steady my nerves. Each had a high back and seat and arms covered with velvet. There was very little additional furniture, only a carved oak chest on either side of the fireplace, and a row of wardrobes, or presses, bound in iron bands, below the windows. I couldn't see what, if anything, occupied the wall under the gallery; the whole area was lost in shadows.

I tried to open one of the presses. At first I thought it was locked, but then the stiff hinges gave way with an uncanny squeal, and I almost fell over backward. The shelves inside were filled with dishes and glassware. The china was thick, coarse stuff, with a crest, which I took to be that of the Hamiltons, but everything was covered with a layer of dust as thick as grey velvet.

I wiped my fingers on my skirt and looked about. The antique weapons and old furniture would have been interesting to an antiquarian. But I was not an antiquarian today; I was only a busybody, and there was nothing for me here.

I crossed the room, and found, under the minstrel's gallery, a door of massive oak studded with nails. Somewhat to my surprise, it opened easily. The hinges had been freshly oiled. Standing on the threshold I lifted my feeble candle high, and saw another stone-floored passage. It was pitch black. No other light showed, and the passage ended in darkness.

Suddenly Toby, crouched at my feet, began to growl.

The sound, in that place, was enough to start me shaking. Then I saw what the animal's keener senses had already caught. Something was moving towards us from the far end of the corridor.

I stood rooted to the spot, unable to retreat even to the doubtful safety of the Hall. As the form drew nearer I heard a shuffling sound and hoarse, asthmatic breathing. At that I took courage. Whatever approached, it was something that breathed—something alive.

Then a face thrust itself forward into the yellow circle of candlelight. I didn't recognise it at first, so grotesquely did the candle shadow its features. The mouth opened, displaying a row of brown, broken teeth.

"Aye, I thocht as much," muttered a croaking voice. "Peekin' an' pryin' aboot the house, as if ye were already mistress."

It was hard to understand Angus even when he condescended to speak his vile brand of English, but I caught his meaning at once. No longer moved by superstitious fears, I frowned at his ugly face.

"How dare you say that!"

"Och, I ken weel it's Hamilton yer after—ye fule of a lassie! Better wed wi' the Black De'il himself!"

"I don't want either, thank you."

"Yer lying," said Angus pleasantly. "But ye'll not have him—not Hamilton. Aboot the ither, I canna say." He emitted a series of croaking grunts which were evidently meant to be laughter.

Decidedly, Angus in a temper was more endurable than Angus amused. I stepped back involuntarily to escape the horrid parody of mirth. Angus's head followed me, like that of an old turtle. His wrinkled yellow claw shot out and caught my hand.

"Ye'll not have him," he repeated. "Not Hamilton. He's had enough o' women, wi' the ither one."

I couldn't have moved if I had wanted to. The bony fingers were clamped like a vice.

"What other one?" I hardly recognised my own voice. "You mean Mrs. Hamilton, don't you? Angus—you were here then. I know you were. What happened to Mrs. Hamilton? How did—how did she die?"

Angus's knotted fingers relaxed He blinked at me, as if startled.

"Ask th' Master," he growled.

"What do you mean?"

"He's the ainly one who kens." His voice dropped to a

55

hoarse whisper. "She rode awa' one day, fourteen years ago—out towards the falls. An' he rode after her. An' she niver came back. No mon alive saw her again—but Hamilton." He dropped my wrist and bent over in a paroxysm of gasping laughter. "Aye, ask Hamilton how she died! Why dinna ye ask him?"

I fled then, with Toby spitting and snarling behind me —back through the Hall and the cold stone corridors. The candle flame flickered and went out as I ran. And all the way down the length of the Hall and into the corridor beyond, the sound of Angus's goblin laughter followed me.

CHAPTER 5

HUDDLED on my bed, with Toby in my arms for comfort and every candle in the room alight, I still couldn't rid my ears of the echo of Angus's laughter. I had locked and bolted my door—the first time I had done such a thing since coming to Blacktower House. Why, I wondered, as my fingers soothed Toby into a rumbling purr, why did the Master keep a demon like Angus about? There was no love lost between them; often I had seen Angus's eyes blaze with hatred as he looked at the man he was sworn to serve. And Mr. Hamilton despised Angus. Yet, when Annabelle was hurt, he had dismissed the other servants and kept Angus.

Mrs. Cannon had exaggerated, of course, when she said all the servants had been away. Some of them had to stay, to tend the sick child, and it should have been obvious to me from the first that Angus had always been here. Angus, and . . .

And Davey? The old minstrel who had sung for me the night I came?

Davey was Scottish, certainly. He was an old man, from his voice. My fingers tightened on Toby's fur, bringing a warning growl from his throat. Once again I was sitting in the frigid hall, where the torn banners hung like cobwebs overhead, hearing the Master's furious voice saying, "He knows he is never to sing that song in this house!"

What a fool I had been, to forget the minstrel! Surely he would talk to me; he wouldn't be cruel and frightening like Angus. I coaxed Toby into purring again. Yes, tomorrow I would talk to Davey.

That night the rain stopped. When I went out into the stableyard after breakfast, the world glittered as if newly washed. I was looking for Ian. He was the only one of the

57

servants who was neither rude nor stupid; he would tell me where to find Davey. I hadn't seen the old man, or heard him, since that night so many weeks before. Perhaps, I thought, he lives in the village. But when I found Ian, stitching harness in the leather shop near the stable, and asked him my question, he scratched his head.

"Auld Davey? I'm feared ye canna speak wi' Davey, miss."

"Why not?"

"Why, ye ken, auld Davey's deid."

"Dead?" I repeated numbly. "How—when did he die?"

"He was an auld mon, miss, verra auld. He deied in his sleep. It was a month ago—twa months, even."

He was very old. He died in his sleep. Two months ago . . . not long after he had sung a forbidden song, and been bitterly reprimanded by his master. An old man who had been at the house from the first, dead now, before I could speak to him—question him.

I came out of a grey fog of suspicions to find myself standing in front of the house, between the two tall pines that flanked the carriage drive before it swept around into the courtyard. Under one of the trees was a big rock shaped like a rough seat. I sat down on it, and in the cool shade my head finally stopped spinning.

From this place I could look out over the glen towards the Cairngorms. The soft blue slopes seemed very near; I could see the silver line of a waterfall on Ben Macdhui. A group of black dots detached themselves from the tree line and wandered out across a stretch of mountain pasture —red deer, perhaps, those beautiful, graceful trophies of Highland hunting. A bird soared high over the glen, the musical trill of its song sinking like drops of water.

I realised that I was not watching the bird, or seeing the mountain slopes. My eyes were fixed on the road that wound through the glen and disappeared. It was the road to Edinburgh on which, at any time, Mr. Hamilton would come riding home.

I wanted him to come. I had a fancy that, if I saw him,

the black, ugly suspicions that had planted themselves in my mind must appear in their true light—as unpleasant imaginings, nothing more. I had been making mysteries out of a man's natural reticence about his private emotions, and an evil old servant's attempt to frighten me. I had too little to occupy my mind. Since Mr. Hamilton was gone, I had missed our rides. I had missed him . . .

And why not? I asked myself defiantly. He was the only intelligent, stimulating person in the whole glen. But —but it would not be wise to grow dependent on him, or any other person. I'd be wiser to find some healthy occupation—something dainty and ladylike, something that required concentration.

The wild beauty of the scenery gave me the answer. The next day I brought my sketching pad and pencils to the bench under the pine. I can't say my efforts were ever successful; the bold grandeur of the terrain was too much for an amateur's skill. But it pleased me to go on, to see if I could improve; and it did occupy the time. Mr. Hamilton still did not come home.

One afternoon I sat in my usual place, drawing. The day was so clear that I could see the purple shadows in the canyons and corries that laced the slopes of Ben Macdhui, and the air was so warm that I had unbuttoned the first two buttons of my black crepe basque. The drawing was not right—not quite—and yet it seemed to me that I had finally caught the stern yet graceful slope of the peak. Now if I could trace the line of trees just below. . . . I glanced up from my sketch to look at it. Then I leaped to my feet, letting sketch and pencils fall to the ground. Just behind me sat a gentleman on horse back.

He was a young man and a handsome one. Waving yellow hair crowned his head and a neat moustache of the same straw-blond drooped over a well-shaped mouth. His chin was small and pointed, his nose as narrow as a woman's. He was elegantly dressed in a brown riding suit and high polished boots. A golden stickpin glittered in his cravat. His hands held a black hat, which he had removed on seeing me; they were covered with fine kid gloves, of a pale primrose shade.

This apparition was off his horse as soon as I moved. He made me sit down again, restored my drawing materials, and begged my pardon, in one impulsive breath.

"Not at all, sir," I said, recovering myself. "It's not your fault that I was absorbed in my work."

"I can see that you were." The young gentleman peered at my crumpled drawing. "Exquisite work! Admirable taste! One can see that you have had the best drawing masters."

"Oh, no. My father—"

"Yes, of course. I know him by reputation."

"Indeed?" I studied the gentleman. He didn't look like the sort of man who would admire my father's abstruse scholarship, and on closer examination I found he had one feature that was not so pleasing—his eyes. They never met my gaze squarely, but darted from my black dress to my hands and—I thought—lingered too long at the open neck of my basque.

I put my pencil down and buttoned up my bodice. "Were you looking for someone?" I asked. "You are a stranger here, I believe."

"Forgive me!" The gentleman bowed gracefully. "I am Sir Andrew Elliott. My sister and I have taken Glengarrie for the summer."

"Really? I'm surprised I hadn't heard of it."

"This is a rude, isolated spot, where news travels slowly." Sir Andrew sat himself down on the ground at my feet, and sighed pathetically "I vow, a horrid spot! How does a lady like yourself endure it?"

"If you feel that way, I wonder that you came here."

"Oh, but—I was thinking of a continuous, year-round existence. For one summer it is well enough. My sister, Lady Mary, is not well. The air of the Highlands was recommended to us."

"I am sorry to hear that your sister is unwell. Is she receiving visitors?"

Sir Andrew's blue eyes shifted. "As to that—her health varies so, from day to day—"

I didn't press the subject. Certainly I had no desire to sally forth in bonnet, parasol and gloves, to pay formal calls. Even if a secretary was supposed to pay such calls! I rather thought she was not.

Sir Andrew broke into my idle thoughts. "Your social activities, I observe, are also curtailed. I trust that his lordship—that is to say, it is not for Lord Dunnoch, I hope, that you wear mourning?"

"Lord Dunnoch?" I repeated in astonishment. "I know his name, of course; he is said to be the wealthiest peer in Scotland. But I would hardly put on mourning for him, even if I knew him to be dead. Which I don't."

My words astonished Sir Andrew as much as his question had surprised me. His mouth dropped open, and he was on the verge of speaking when we were diverted by the sound of a horse approaching at full gallop. Sir Andrew rose to his knees, his hands filled with the wild daisies he had been idly plucking, and turned to look towards the road.

I knew the rider, although he and his horse were still miniature figures at the foot of the hill. Somewhere on the road he had changed into his favourite Highland garb; the dark-green tartan stood out strongly against the silver-grey of his horse's flank. They seemed to fly, they came so quickly; before long the animal came to halt, in a cloud of dust, and Mr. Hamilton was staring down upon Sir Andrew.

"Who is this?" he demanded curtly.

Sir Andrew was at a disadvantage, squatting at my feet and still clutching his handful of daisies. He rose without his former grace.

"My name is Elliott. Sir Andrew Elliott..."

"Sir Andrew and his sister have taken Glengarrie for the summer," I explained, when the young man's tongue failed him.

Mr. Hamilton transferred his attention to me.

"Good afternoon, Miss Gordon."

"Good afternoon, sir."

Poor Sir Andrew was at a loss. He tried not to look at the Master's face; but his gaze would go creeping back. I knew it was a startling sight for someone who had never seen it before. But when Mr. Hamilton addressed me the young man started.

"Miss—Miss Gordon?" he stammered.

Really, I thought, the man is impossibly gauche. Must I make all the explanations?

"Sir Andrew had only just arrived," I said. "I hadn't yet introduced myself. I am Damaris Gordon, Sir Andrew, and this is Mr. Hamilton, who owns Blacktower House."

"I see," said Sir Andrew.

"Do you?" The Master's face hardened. "Miss Gordon is a young relative of mine, Sir Andrew, who has obliged me by consenting to act as my secretary—and as my daughter's friend."

I had no idea why they were staring at one another so oddly, nor did I care. All at once I was seized by one of those moods of lighthearted gaiety, when everything seems amusing. The behaviour of the two men struck me as particularly comical; Mr. Hamilton invited Sir Andrew to come into the house, although he obviously wanted him to go away; Sir Andrew politely declined, but his desire to come in was equally obvious. Sir Andrew explained about his sister's delicate health and Mr. Hamilton expressed his regret, without, it was clear; feeling the faintest interest in the lady or her health. Sir Andrew made his bows; Mr. Hamilton bowed; I bowed. Sir Andrew mounted, and rode off—still bowing.

Mr. Hamilton stared after his retreating figure.

"There goes a pretty specimen," he said, half to himself. "I wonder what he's after."

"Why should he be after anything?"

"Everyone is—man, woman and child," said Mr. Hamilton, with a grimace. "It only remains to discover what it is they want."

He rose and went off towards the courtyard. Being used to his abrupt ways, I prepared to follow at my leisure. I tried to smooth out my poor drawing, but it was spoiled. One of the horses had set a hoof in the centre of it.

On the whole, I thought, as I strolled towards the house, I was glad Sir Andrew had come to the glen. At least he would give us something new to look at. And what a handsome fellow he was! Certainly his pink-and-white complexion was easier to look at than Mr. Hamilton's swarthy, scarred face.

Sir Andrew called, and called again. He seemed to find our society fascinating—heaven knows why! Although Mr. Hamilton made it a point to be present at each meeting, he was gruff and, at times, barely civil. The conventional social inquiries became, in his hands, a form of inquisition.

"There are Elliotts in Inverness and in Glen Airlie. Which branch are you connected with, Sir Andrew?"

"You say, Sir Andrew, that you attended school in England. What school was that?"

And so on. Not only did Sir Andrew have to face the Master's questions, but he had to run the gauntlet of the servants as well. I suppose they found life so dull that any new face was interesting. Every time Sir Andrew called, one or another of them discovered an errand in the front part of the house, or "happened" to be outside taking a breath of air. Even Angus condescended to some "peekin' and pryin'" of his own; and once I found Sir Andrew in conversation with Janet, Annabelle's rawboned maid. She scuttled away as soon as she saw me, and Sir Andrew greeted me with relief written plain on his face.

"Gad, what uncouth gabble these local peasants speak! I vow, I couldn't make out a word the woman was saying."

I dismissed the matter without a second thought, which was utter folly on my part. I ought to have known at least part of what was happening, but I was too concerned with private feelings of my own, which left me confused and unsettled. I soon found out what Janet had been doing with Sir Andrew when I received a royal summons from Annabelle.

I went to her, feeling a bit guilty. I had neglected her of late, being busy with my inquisitiveness. Annabelle made it clear that she felt neglected.

"I wish to go downstairs this afternoon," she announced.

"Your father has asked me to write some letters. Tomorrow, perhaps."

Annabelle took a deep breath, stiffened her back, and went into a violent fit of hysterics.

I was frightened out of my wits. I thought she was dying. Her face turned blue and the whites of her eyes showed all around the pupils. The veins in her throat stood out like ropes with the violence of her screams.

I caught at her flailing hands. "Annabelle, Annabelle— what's wrong? What hurts you?"

The screams became intelligible. "You don't want me to see *him*! You're trying to keep him for yourself! Acting as if you were the mistress here—and you're nothing but a cheap, vulgar—"

Luckily, her vocabulary was inadequate to express her feelings. She took a deep breath and screamed again. I put my hands over my ears. Then it occurred to me that they might be better employed; I slapped her.

Annabelle stopped screaming and began to cry.

"It isn't fair," she sobbed. "I'm the lady of the house— not you! Why can't I see him?"

"You may see him, and welcome," I said coldly; and, as Annabelle raised a radiant face, I added, "But not today. If you behave like a child, you must be treated like a child. Tomorrow, if you can show me that you know how to act like a young lady, you may come down."

Annabelle started to protest, but she caught sight of her face in the mirror, and thought better of it. Her face was bloated, and her elegant coiffure was in shreds, the strands of hair hanging like weeds over her puffy cheeks.

"All right. But if you forget—"

"I won't forget."

Out in the corridor I met Janet. She bobbed a curtsy and tried to slide past me. I put out my hand.

"It was you, Janet, who told Miss Hamilton of Sir Andrew's visits."

"Oh no, miss!"

"Come, I know it was. Don't you realise that such information should come from Mrs. Cannon or from me?"

She rolled her eyes and let her mouth hang open.

"All right, Janet," I said helplessly. "In future, control your tongue."

It was a stupid thing to say, like telling the wind not to blow. Janet gave me one look before she went past me, into Annabelle's room; and I knew that I had made an enemy—without deriving any benefit from it.

After dinner I went to the library, ready to take dictation, but Mr. Hamilton wasn't there. I hadn't been waiting long when the maid announced Sir Andrew.

He wore a new costume, undoubtedly the lastest fashion —a brown shooting jacket with innumerable pockets, pale-fawn trousers very tight in the calves, and a tweed cap.

"All alone, Miss Gordon?"

"I am waiting for Mr. Hamilton. He wished to dictate some letters."

"The perfect secretary." Sir Andrew's smile widened. "I wish I could afford such a luxury."

I moved away from him and sat down in Mr. Hamilton's chair. The desk was now between us.

"Perhaps you would like to ride out and meet Mr. Hamilton," I suggested.

"An excellent idea—if you'll accompany me."

"No, I think not."

"I'm afraid Mr. Hamilton has forgotten you. I saw a horseman riding away from the house as I came up."

"That's curious. He definitely told me—"

"It does seem strange that he could neglect such a—er —secretary. But perhaps he had another appointment."

Sir Andrew's smile was becoming tiresome, and so was Sir Andrew. He came around the desk and put one hand on the back of my chair.

"Very well," I said rising. "Let's go after him. The air here seems oppressive to me.'

There was no one in sight by the time we came out of the courtyard, so we rode off along the path on which, Sir Andrew solemnly assured me, he had seen the horseman go. The weather was hot and sticky. The leaves hung still. A thunderstorm was brewing. I was tempted to turn back, but Sir Andrew on horseback was less of a problem than Sir Andrew on foot, and the path led in a direction I had never explored—towards the entrance to the glen.

I could understand why Mr. Hamilton never rode this way. The path ran along the hillside, high above the glen, where the pines grew in thick clusters and coarse underbrush slowed the horses to a walk. Through occasional gaps in the trees one could see the road far below, and the white water of the burn tumbling along beside it. The burn was wider here than it was near the village; it ran fast and deep.

Finally the trees thinned, and we emerged into a kind of sloping meadow. The path had led downhill for the last mile, and we were only ten yards above the burn, which formed a wide pool before plunging over the hill beyond in a fierce cascade. The banks of the pool were high and steep; in its centre was a group of large rocks, like an island.

I drew rein, and Sir Andrew came up beside me. I scarcely noticed him. It had come to me, with a prickling of the spine, that this was the scene of Annabelle's childhood disaster.

The sun had gone in by now, under gathering clouds. In the strange light of the imminent storm the sparse grass was grey; the shapes of the twisted trees and the scattered stones were black. The water of the pool lay still and dark, reflecting the shadowed sky. But out towards the centre there was a slow, ominous swirl, as if hidden

66

currents sucked below the surface.

Beside me Sir Andrew was very still. He looked out across the grim pool with a sober expression. I hadn't expected him to be so sensitive to atmosphere, for if ever a place spoke of nature's hostility to man, this was that place.

Finally he drew a long sigh and turned to face me with a forced smile.

"What a ghastly spot," he exclaimed.

"Yes—it is. Let's go back."

"No, we must stay and outface it. Otherwise it will master us."

I rather liked his spirit, so when he dismounted I did the same. I sat down on one of the rocks and he flung himself down at my feet.

"What is there about this place?" I murmured, watching the subtle, secret swirl of the grey water.

"I can't say. But just now—as I looked—a shiver ran through me, as if someone had walked on my grave. An old superstition, Miss Gordon—and a particularly silly one, I fancy."

I made no response. Sir Andrew was silent for a time. Then, without warning, he rose to his knees and put his arms around me.

I was too stunned to move or protest. Sir Andrew, with perfect coolness, proceeded to kiss me. His moustache tickled, and in the first moment I felt like laughing at the whole ridiculous performance. But my amusement died a quick death. He was very strong. When I tried to free myself, his arms tightened till they bruised my ribs. Struggle as I might, I couldn't break away from him until, at last, he let me go of his own accord. I stumbled to my feet and ran to where Flame stood placidly cropping the grass.

When I turned he was just behind me. I put out my hands.

"Don't—don't, or I'll take my whip to you! How dare you behave so?"

"It's your fault," he said, stepping back a pace and regarding me from under his lashes. "You're uncommonly lovely, Damaris. You drive a poor devil out of his wits. By God, I don't blame Hamilton for hiding you here. But why do you stay? You don't love him, do you?"

"Love him?" I repeated stupidly.

"No, of course not. A less lovable man I've never met." He took advantage of my numbed surprise to embrace me again. "I'm offering you escape, Damaris," he grumbled against my hair. "I'll show you London, Paris, the great glittering world. I'll never desert you. How the rest of them will envy me!"

The meaning of his words finally penetrated. I raised my whip and struck at his face.

He caught the blow on his arm; but the gesture, and my expression, must have convinced him.

"The answer is No, I take it," he said coolly.

I turned my back on him and mounted. As I began to ride off he caught the reins away from me.

"Wait. I'm sorry if I offended you. Believe me, there are many women who wouldn't have been offended."

"Let me make one thing clear, Sir Andrew," I said, still shaking with rage. "You have made a mistake—a natural one, for a man of your type. I am not Mr. Hamilton's—" Strangely, I couldn't say the word—I, who prided myself on speaking plainly! "I am his secretary, nothing more. Give me those reins."

I snatched them away and turned Flame back towards the house. I meant to gallop away in a fine passion, but Flame would have nothing to do with such nonsense; Sir Andrew caught me up easily. We went on in smouldering silence for a time. Finally Sir Andrew said, "I told you I was sorry. Don't be a prude, Damaris—oh, hell, Miss Gordon, then! Why must you be so confoundedly serious about a small error in judgment?"

I said nothing, not trusting my voice. We were almost in sight of the house before he spoke again.

"You won't tell Hamilton—will you?"

I would rather have died than mention the subject to anyone—least of all to the Master! But I was in no mood to relieve Sir Andrew's anxiety by telling him so. We parted in silence; I left him at the door and marched into the house without looking at him.

I had forgotten about the appointment I had with Mr. Hamilton, and I would have avoided him if possible. But I had to pass the library on my way upstairs, and he heard me. The familiar harsh voice called my name, and, when I hesitated, called it again, more insistently.

He was at his desk. There were papers spread out before him, and the room was dark, almost as dark as evening.

"I'm sorry I forgot the letters," I said, staying near the door. "Do you want to dictate them now?"

He looked up sharply. I suppose my voice sounded strange.

"No. Where have you been?"

"Riding. I—forgot about the letters."

"So you said. Did you ride alone? Come here—why are you hovering by the door?"

I obeyed, knowing that my hands were unsteady and my hair still disarranged by Sir Andrew's embraces. Still, the room was dusky; perhaps he couldn't see me clearly.

"What's wrong?" he demanded. "Your hands are shaking. Has something frightened you?"

"No."

The wind was rising. It rustled among the bushes by the open windows like a live thing. The heavy drapes bellied out in a sudden gust.

Mr. Hamilton rose to his feet and stood over me.

"With whom did you ride? The young lout from Glengarrie? Oh, come, Damaris, don't lie. I always know when you lie to me. Something has upset you. What is it?"

I could hardly tell him the truth: that Sir Andrew's insulting assumptions had struck home in a way he never intended. Now I saw myself and Mr. Hamilton as the rest of the world must see us—and I saw something else that was even harder to bear. I stood twisting my hands together to keep them steady.

"The weather upsets me," I muttered. "It's so close. If only the storm would break!"

A great stroke of lightning, sharp as a sword, split the clouds and struck close at hand. The crash of the thunder rolled and echoed between the hills.

It was too much for me, after an afternoon of mounting mental shocks. I shrieked and clutched with my hands, like a child snatching at his mother's skirts. When I came to myself a moment later, my hands were twisted in Mr. Hamilton's lapels and my head was buried in his shirt-bosom. I tried to retreat—and discovered that I was caught, by the hair, among the buttons of his coat.

"I am very sorry," I said, into his shirt. "But my hair seems to be caught."

I expected one of his infuriating laughs. It didn't come.

"Stand still," he said harshly, "and stop struggling. I'll untangle you."

I wasn't struggling; but I decided not to say so. I felt his fingers working away, and none too gently; I had to bite my lip now and then at an especially painful tug. But at last the pulling stopped. I waited for him to tell me to remove myself, but he said nothing. Slowly I raised my head, and stood transfixed.

Directly before my eyes I saw his hands, poised and open, the black-gloved fingers standing out in sharp outline against the white of his shirt. Coiled around his wrist, caught by the magnetism of the silk, was a long strand of my hair. The red-gold tendril ringed the black silk like a bracelet.

Suddenly the poised hands moved, twisting fiercely among the masses of my loosened hair, tilting my face up towards his. A second livid bolt of lightning split the dark sky beyond the window. Then I saw blackness, like thick velvet, against my closed eyelids.

It was like the lightning, bright and fierce, and over almost as soon as it began. He stepped back in one quick

70

bound, like a man leaping away from an unexpected chasm. In the gloom I heard the ragged catch of his breathing.

The rain began, beating the waiting earth and flooding in through the open windows. I retreated step by step, stumbling over a chair, bruising my arm on a table, but never turning my back. I found the door with my hands and went up the stairs as if sixteen devils were after me.

CHAPTER 6

THUS I passed another sleepless night at Blacktower House; not the first, and certainly not the last. Morning, which brought blue skies and a beaming sun, brought no relief to me. All morning I hid, like a coward, in my room. I was prepared to plead that weakest of female excuses—a headache—if anyone inquired after me. But no one did.

Of course, he must know how I felt although I had not discovered it for myself until the previous day. No man could hold a woman in his arms and not know. My lips had answered the insistence of his, my arms had held him. I could close my eyes and feel that embrace again, as if it had been burned into my body.

I knelt by the window staring out at the purple hills and seeing nothing. Yes, he knew that I loved him. But he cared nothing for me. That sudden, insane embrace meant no more than a temporary madness. If Gavin Hamilton had wanted me, he would never have let me run away from him.

About noon I saw him in the courtyard. One of the grooms brought his horse, and he mounted and rode out through the gate. I watched his tall, erect figure until it vanished behind the wall.

Then I remembered, like a memory from another world, that I had promised to bring Annabelle downstairs that afternoon. I could keep my promise now without fear of meeting the Master. I would have to face him sometime. But not, I thought desperately, not today!

I was all the more willing to oblige Annabelle because I had a notion that Sir Andrew wouldn't venture to show his face again, but I underestimated his impudence. No sooner had I got Annabelle settled—flushed and excited and dressed in her most elaborate tea gown—than the maid announced callers.

I might have said something, even in front of Annabelle. But Sir Andrew was too clever for me. He had brought his sister with him.

She made me think of fire, and that was odd, for her beauty was all blonde and ivory, with none of the dusky warmth of dark skin and hair. Her skin was flawless, ranging from creamy white on throat and brow to a soft rose in her cheeks, and a darker rose on the small, perfect mouth. Her wide blue eyes were framed by long lashes much darker than her hair. She was an inch or so shorter than I was, and beautifully formed. Her rounded figure was set off by an elegant riding costume of dark blue, cut to fit tightly at bust and waist before it flared out into wide gored skirts.

Annabelle was frankly gaping at her—one of the dolls from her fashion books come to life. I was in little better command of myself. I left it to Sir Andrew to make the introductions, which he did with perfect aplomb. No one would have guessed that he had never met Annabelle before. Leaving her to his sister, he took a chair by my side.

"Aren't they lovely together?" he asked, in tones that must have been audible to both ladies. "Two fair divinities, side by side—a joy to behold."

"My I offer you some refreshments?" I asked through my teeth. "It's early, I know; but you have had a long ride."

Sir Andrew grinned impudently at me, and accepted. After the tea things arrived, we all relaxed. Or perhaps I should say, I relaxed; for no one else seemed in the least self-conscious. Lady Mary chatted brightly about balls and theatre parties to Annabelle. The girl listened, fascinated; but her eyes kept straying to Sir Andrew, who was fingering the rose in his buttonhole and smirking impartially on us all.

"I'm glad to see that Lady Mary's health has improved so suddenly," I remarked, not without malice. "From what you said, I assumed she wouldn't venture out this summer.

The Highland air *is* miraculous.!"

"I said her health varied considerably," Sir Andrew answered imperturbably. "And I, for my part, am delighted to see Miss Hamilton so well. Your description led me to expect a pallid, childish invalid; instead, I find a beautiful young lady."

Annabelle overheard the remark, as she was meant to. She gave me a look of pure loathing. I didn't care what she thought of me, but I hated to let Sir Andrew's lies pass unchallenged. Before I could compose a reply, however, there was an interrupton. Toby came out from behind the books where he had been sleeping, and stretched himself. He saw the teapot and the plate of cakes and came towards Annabelle with his tail twitching eagerly. He bounded into her lap and demanded food.

Lady Mary jumped to her feet, upsetting the heavy carved chair. Her pretty face had gone all awry.

"Andrew! Get it away!"

Annabelle's hand froze on Toby's head. Perhaps it was her shocked surprise that affected the cat, or perhaps it was something else. At any rate, the hair on his back lifted and he began to growl. His green eyes blazed at the lady.

Sir Andrew's easy laugh broke the tension. "Change places with me, Mary. Dear Miss Hamilton, don't be alarmed, I beg. My sister has a sad antipathy towards animals. It's a hardship for me, since it means I cannot keep a pet; and I vow I love the little dogs and cats."

In a moment he was sitting in the chair his sister had vacated so abruptly, leaning over to stroke the cat's neck and smiling into Annabelle's enraptured face. With a little laugh Lady Mary crossed the room and took Sir Andrew's chair next to me.

"Don't scold me, Miss Gordon. Indeed, I can't help myself."

"Not at all," I said meaninglessly. "Let me take Toby away."

"Oh, no—I see that he is Miss Hamilton's pet. He doesn't bother me now, truly."

She bothered Toby, though. He never took his eyes off her. After a while he rose with great dignity and departed through the open window, tail switching and nose high. When he had gone, Lady Mary was more at ease. She kept up a gay conversation, delighting me with her witty observations on manners and society.

Then her comments gradually changed to questions. What sort of man was Mr. Hamilton? Was he young and handsome? Had I lived long in Scotland? Didn't I miss London and its gaieties? What did I do to amuse myself?

She was a skilful questioner. No inquiry seemed impertinent, coming from her smiling mouth. Before I realised it, I had told her a great many things—about my father, his sudden death, and my search for a position. She was such a fine lady that I expected her to cool towards me when she realised my dependent status, but her manner didn't change at all, that I could see.

All the while I was aware that Annabelle and Sir Andrew were enjoying themselves immensely. I couldn't hear what they were saying, thanks to the lady's prattle, but as I watched Annabelle's transparent face, I began to wish I could.

The afternoon light grew golden, and at last Lady Mary rose to leave. Sir Andrew's reluctance to go was expertly feigned; his eyes lingered wistfully on Annabelle. She, less well trained, made a face like a child being torn away from a party. I frowned at her, but she didn't see. She was busy arranging her hand elegantly as if she actually wanted Sir Andrew to kiss it. He took it in both his hands, and then pressed his lips, not against the back of her fingers, but into the palm.

The irritation that had been boiling in me all afternoon came to a peak. "What nice, gentlemanly manners Sir Andrew has," I said, ostensibly to his sister. "I'm sure they suit Paris, but I find them a trifle exaggerated here."

She smiled, but said nothing. Sir Andrew turned to me.

"Miss Gordon, if you must be a chaperone, don't be a spoilsport. There—I shall kiss your hand, too."

I barely succeeded in biting back a cry. His fingers crushed mine painfully but slyly, and it was not his lips but his teeth that I felt on my palm.

Lady Mary appeared not to notice. "Come along, Andrew, and stop teasing Miss Gordon."

They took their leave with smiling grace. I smiled and bowed, too—nursing my bruised hand in my skirt. I wondered if Annabelle had seen her cavalier's gesture. She had not; her eyes were blind with adoration.

After Ian had carried Annabelle upstairs, I sat down and thought about what had happened. It was inevitable that Annabelle should fall in love with Sir Andrew. Perhaps it had already happened. He was handsome enough and polished enough to win the heart of any girl— especially the sort of girl that didn't look beyond blue eyes and a golden moustache. With any normal girl I would have shrugged my shoulders and let nature take its course.

But Annabelle was not a normal girl. She couldn't even move by herself. She was inexperienced and highly nervous. When Sir Andrew rode out of her life, as he certainly would at the end of the summer—twirling his moustache and waving a casual good-bye—well, I didn't like to think of the state Annabelle would be in. It seemed better to nip the flirtation in the bud. Sir Andrew had every intention of encouraging it; he and his sister had pressed me to visit them, and had spoken to Annabelle of meeting soon, and often. So it was up to me to kill young love, and the most effective way of murdering it was to speak to Mr. Hamilton. Although I abhorred the position of talebearer and spy, I didn't know what else to do.

I decided to ask Mrs. Cannon's advice—not because I expected she would have anything useful to contribute, but because I had to talk to someone. She was asleep when I invaded her room, and it took me some time to get her to understand what I was talking about.

"Speak to Mr. Hamilton?" she repeated, blinking. "Oh, my dear, you can't do that now. He has gone to Edinburgh. I don't know when he will be back."

"Gone—to Edinburgh? He said nothing about it—yesterday—"

"It was a sudden decision, I fancy. He is such a hasty man; he takes odd notions and acts upon them, with no consideration for others."

I busied myself in smoothing the pleat of my black skirts. "Did he mention why he was going?"

"Why should he?" Mrs. Cannon opened her eyes very wide.

I shook my head, having no answer. But for a moment the memory of my own personal troubles rushed in upon me. Mr. Hamilton had no more wanted to face me than I had wanted to face him. Either he was running away from an awkward situation—or he had done what any honourable man would have done in his place. He had gone to see whether he could find me another position.

There was no use thinking about it, not then. I forced myself to return to the original problem, but I had to shake Mrs. Cannon awake before I could proceed. Taking my silence for satisfaction, she had begun to snore again.

"I want to talk to you about Sir Andrew Elliott," I said loudly. "If Mr. Hamilton is away, our responsibility is all the greater. Sir Andrew and Annabelle have met. He will be visiting us regularly, and Annabelle is—well, you know how she is. I'm not sure it is wise for them to become attached to one another."

My conversations with Mrs. Cannon always progressed limpingly. She had to sit and think over every statement I made, with much rolling of eyes and muttering, before she answered. After going through this process she said, "Do you think he is growing attached? To be sure, it is a piece of extraordinary luck; no one could have expected it. We must do all we can. A new frock, perhaps. . . the pink satin I brought from London."

"But—but Mrs. Cannon," I gasped, "you misunderstand me completely! Sir Andrew is a man of the world, young, wealthy, handsome. Now he is bored and looking for amusement. But he would never marry Annabelle! She can't even—that is, she isn't—"

I hesitated, thinking to spare her modesty. I forgot that, for all her primness, she had been raised in an age far more frank than ours.

"Are you referring to Annabelle's infirmity? It need not interfere with her duties as a wife."

"Perhaps not. But how can we know that Sir Andrew is sincere? He seems to me a great flirt."

Several times Mrs. Cannon had surprised me by coming out of her fog and displaying a certain shrewdness. She now gave me a glance so keen and so knowing that I felt as if Sir Andrew's kiss were visible on my face.

"I expect he *is* a flirt. Gentlemen often are. However, Miss Gordon, a gentleman may flirt with a woman—but he *marries* an heiress. Annabelle will be one of the greatest matches in Scotland when Lord Dunnoch dies."

I caught my breath. Of course—of course! That accounted for a great many things—including Sir Andrew's erratic conversation the day I first met him. He had taken me for Miss Hamilton. Oh, yes, it was all clear to me now. He was handsome and young; but perhaps he wasn't as wealthy as his fine clothes and air of breeding suggested.

"I had no idea that Mr. Hamilton was related to Lord Dunnoch."

"His lordship is Mr. Hamilton's elder brother. You really didn't know? But Mr. Hamilton's title—he is the Master of Dunnoch, you know. That is the title of the heir in Scotland."

"I never thought about the title. It did strike me as offensively servile—almost feudal. But it suits him . . ."

Mrs. Cannon stared uncomprehendingly.

"I expect that is why Mr. Hamilton left so suddenly today," she offered. "Lord Dunnoch's health is very precarious."

"But has his lordship no sons?"

"He had. Two fine sons." Mrs. Cannon sighed lugubriously. "One died in infancy. The other, alas, was drowned in a boating accident at Oxford last spring. That is why we were in London in April. The news of his son's death sent his lordship into an apoplexy. We thought for a time that Lord Dunnoch would follow his heir into the Realms of Everlasting Bliss."

I looked at her askance, but she was perfectly serious.

"And," I said, "there is no chance that his lordship will have other children?"

"Dear me, no. Her ladyship died several years ago. His lordship is considerably older than Mr. Hamilton, and since his seizure he has been bedridden, and only partially conscious. It is only a matter of weeks, perhaps, before Mr. Hamilton becomes Lord Dunnoch."

I took leave of Mrs. Cannon and went back to my room. I was chagrined at my own stupidity; it almost seemed as if I had not wanted to find out the truth. Why, Mr. Hamilton had mentioned the Hamiltons of Dunnoch the very first time I talked to him. Yes, but there were so many branches of these old families, some of them poor as church mice, and his style of living had never suggested expectations. As for Annabelle . . .

Always Annabelle! I was tired of talking about her, tired of worrying about her. She didn't need my worry. She would be the greatest heiress in Scotland. Sir Andrew suited her perfectly. They were both silly, shallow, and selfish. No doubt they would be very happy together.

My mood was no better the next day. I couldn't seem to settle down to anything. The library was forbidden ground —too many memories—and I didn't feel like sketching. I wandered into Annabell's room and found her and Mrs. Cannon in the throes of dressmaking. Rose-coloured satin covered the floor like a luxurious carpet and Mrs. Cannon crawled over it like a giant beetle, wielding her shears, while Annabelle watched and commented from the bed.

That was no place for me. I retreated, in a glummer mood than before. I knew, of course, that I was wandering about the house in an attempt to put off the one thing I ought to be doing—writing to my cousin Randall. If I had entertained any lingering hopes (and, dear Heaven, I had!) they were shattered by Mr. Hamilton's departure. I knew I ought to make arrangements to go before he sent me away.

Perhaps, if Randall had been a different sort of person, I might have written him, but even then I probably wouldn't have. The truth was, I had lost my self-respect, my pride, and all the other chilly, ornamental virtues. I could no more cut myself off from the Master than I could crawl into my grave and pull the earth in after me. If he wanted me to leave, he would have to send me away.

Once I had admitted this to myself, I felt a little better. There is a certain relief in facing the worst. But I was still restless; the house oppressed me. I went out to the stable and asked Ian to saddle Flame for me.

I don't know why I decided to ride to Glengarrie—perhaps because there was nowhere else to go. I had never been there, but it was impossible to miss my way; all I had to do was to follow the road and the burn. The way led through thickets of dark pines, where sunlight dappled the ground in delicate, shifting patterns, and across open stretches of heather. Finally I saw Glengarrie before me.

It was a newer mansion than Blacktower House, and much smaller. There were no wings, only a three-storied oblong. The façade was graceful, with high, wide, windows, and a terrace in the Italian style. Shrubs in tall urns flanked the steps, and roses twined over the balustrade.

When I rode up to the wide steps, a man shuffled into sight from behind the house. He touched his cap and took my reins, but didn't offer to help me dismount. I was glad of that; compared to him, the servants at Blacktower House were actually prepossessing. He was a huge fellow with hulking shoulders, who looked as if he would be more at home in the prize ring than the servants' quarters of a great house.

I was mounting the steps when Lady Mary appeared in the open window to the right of the door.

"Miss Gordon! What a delightful surprise! Please come

in."

I did so, the window being of the French type, and found myself in a drawing room which had the bare look of most rented houses. The green carpet had once been good, but the nap was worn down in some places. The furniture was heavy and old-fashioned. The only objects that suited the occupant of the room were a crystal bowl, filled with pink roses, and a new piano. However, Lady Mary was sufficient ornament herself. She wore a pale-green embroidered muslin, open at the neck, and trimmed with cream-coloured Valenciennes lace at throat and elbow cuffs. In my old black frock I felt like a dowdy scarecrow beside her.

We talked of the weather, and exchanged compliments on one another's health. Then she picked up a fan that lay on the table—a dainty thing with mother-of-pearl sticks and a painted scene of shepherdesses—and waved it languidly to and fro.

"Do you expect Mr. Hamilton back soon?" she asked.

"I don't know."

"I confess, I am curious to meet him. I understand that he is a widower."

"Yes."

"Of long standing, they say. Strange that he has not married again. Was he so devoted to his wife?"

"That would be the most reasonable explanation, I suppose."

"Not necessarily." Lady Mary's eyes twinkled. "He might dislike women—or like them too well to settle on one."

"I'm sorry not to be able to satisfy your curiosity," I said distantly. "But I know nothing of his personal affairs. Gossip doesn't interest me."

She shot me a quick blue glance over the edge of the fan. It hid her mouth, so I was unable to judge her reaction to my rudeness.

"Alas," she said gently, "I'm not an intellectual like yourself, Miss Gordon; I don't share your admirable indifference to gossip. And really—Andrew has brought home such curious tales from the village alehouse—"

"What tales?" I said sharply, conscious of an odd premonition.

"Fie, Miss Gordon, you are not as impervious as you claim! I ought to tease you by claiming, in my turn, an indifference to gossip. But I won't be so unkind. The tales refer to Mrs. Hamilton—and how she died."

"She died in London. Of typhoid."

"The villagers don't think so."

I rose and blundered over to the window. The air in the room suddenly stifled me.

"It was so long ago—no one would remember—"

"Ah, but they do. Not that she came to the village; she was aloof and contemptuous of those people; and how they resented it!" She lowered her fan; the pretty mouth was curved in a smile. "But they remember her. You see— she was very beautiful."

"What do they say, those ignorant wretches in the village?"

She watched me through narrowed eyes.

"There was bad feeling between husband and wife, you know. The servants often heard them quarrelling. They say he struck her."

"Is that all they say?"

"No." Lady Mary unfurled her fan. I watched, half hypnotised, as her white hand moved it back and forth, back and forth. "They say Mrs. Hamilton fled, from his jealousy and his threats. They say he followed her, and caught her at the pool, near the falls. They say she is still there—deep down in the black water, by the rocks."

For one moment the whole room heaved, like a ship in a storm. Then my eyesight steadied, and I said calmly, "That is a lie."

"Oh, it must be," Lady Mary agreed cheerfully. "But it is a charming tale, is it not?"

"I wonder if he knows what they are saying."

"I take it he does; and doesn't care."

"But he must care! If they suspected this—this horror,

why didn't someone accuse him?"

"Child, you don't understand these peasants. It's only a good story, like the tale of the Black Lady of the Tower. But I agree that the situation is unwholesome."

"Unwholesome! He ought to have them soundly thrashed."

She sighed. "Mr. Hamilton is not so unhappy, if he has advocates as devoted as you ... I didn't believe the story, either. But I thought you ought to be warned."

"What on earth do you mean?"

She rose and came towards me, her skirts swaying gracefully.

"Miss Gordon, you are young, and alone in the world. Perhaps you'd be happier in some other house. I have friends in England, and on the Continent. May I interest them in your situation?"

Now was the time to tell her that I had already decided I must begin thinking of finding another position. She meant what she said; her face, her voice, spoke unmistakably of sincerity and concern.

"No—I thank you. I'll not go. Lady Mary, indeed, you mustn't believe these tales!"

"You mean to stay, then—whatever happens?"

"Whatever happens."

"I'm sorry."

She turned away. I stood clutching at the worn velvet draperies; the floor still felt unsteady under my feet. I was shaken, not so much by the story, but by the fact that she believed it. How else could I explain her anxiety for me—genuine anxiety, I was prepared to swear!

I heard steps on the terrace, and turned to see Sir Andrew strolling up and down outside. He paused to pick a rosebud and fasten it to his lapel; then he looked up and saw me at the window.

"Miss Gordon—a pleasure! May I come in, or am I interrupting some girlish secrets? Confess—you were talking about me!"

"No, you vain creature," said his sister, laughing. "We

were, in fact, discussing Mr. Hamilton."

He came across the room towards her, and she raised her face for his kiss. They were a handsome pair, not only in their blonde good looks; but in their unconcealed devotion to one another. Sir Andrew straightened, one hand still on her shoulder. There was a mischievous gleam in his blue eyes as he looked at me.

"What poor taste you display, ladies. I've already warned Mary that she will find Hamilton's appearance shocking. How did the poor devil get that ghastly scar?"

"If you knew him better," I said hotly, "you wouldn't notice the scar. You would see the fineness of the spirit within."

Sir Andrew laughed heartily. Lady Mary smiled. I felt my cheeks grow hot. Would I never learn to stop betraying myself? The lady saw my chagrin. Her smile faded, and she tapped her brother briskly on the arm with her folded fan.

"Andrew, you are quizzing Miss Gordon. You are rude. Pray, Miss Gordon, don't go. Andrew shall beg your pardon."

"No, I must go. It is late."

"I do beg your pardon, Miss Gordon." Sir Andrew looked penitent—all of him except his eyes. "Alas—still determined to go? I'll fetch your horse, then."

He was pacing up and down in front of the house when we came out. Flame's bridle was over his arm, and he looked uncommonly thoughtful. But when he saw us he looked up with a brilliant smile.

"Would you like me to ride part of the way with you?"

"No. thank you."

"I see I'm still in disgrace. Well, I must endeavour to work my way back into favour another day."

At the turn in the road I looked back. Lady Mary stood on the terrace, framed by the twining roses. The breeze lifted tendrils of pale-gold hair off her white forehead. Her eyes glowed like sapphires.

I carried that picture with me, after she and the house disappeared from view. Sick at heart, I took no notice of my

84

surroundings until a sudden, startled movement of the horse brought me to my senses. And just in time; only a quick clutch at the pommel saved me from being thrown off.

I realised then that Flame, the somnolent, was ill at ease, and had been ever since we left Glengarrie. In any other horse her behaviour would have been called skittish; she had been shying at every daisy beside the road. My unconscious mind had noted it, and my body, better trained than I realised, had adjusted. But the last sudden start had been too abrupt to be ignored.

I pulled Flame to a stop. Even then she kept moving restlessly, lifting her feet in little prancing motions. I stroked her neck.

"What's wrong?" I asked. "Are you afraid of something?"

She turned her head towards me and rolled her eyes piteously. All at once I was afraid, but not of Flame. I remembered the old stories, that animals sense presences that are invisible to human sight. I looked uneasily over my shoulder.

Of course there was nothing—behind me, or anywhere else. We were in the midst of a small copse of fir trees. The soft breeze stirred the pine needles with a dry rustling sound; there was a rush of grass as some bird or small animal passed through the glade. But nothing else. I was absurd to think that anything could be here, lurking and malignant, at such an hour. Ghosts came at night, to draughty passages and crumbling walls. They did not walk through pinewoods on sunny summer mornings.

All very true—but some part of me was not convinced. A mindless panic swept through me. I dug my heels into Flame's sides, and leaned forward in the saddle. And with a wild scream she bolted.

I was spared the shame of being run away with. At her first plunge I fell off, striking the earth with a violence that knocked the breath out of my body.

For a time I lay still, breathing in the scent of the pine needles in which my face was buried, and waiting for the ache in my limbs to subside. Then I thought I heard the pound of a horse's hooves, and I tried to sit up; but when I rested my weight on my left hand it gave way, and I collapsed with a gasp of pain.

The hoofbeats came nearer, and stopped; a man's voice cried out in alarm, "Good heavens, Miss Gordon, what has happened? I had business in the village . . . wanted to spare you my company . . . but how fortunate that I happened to be following! Are you badly hurt?"

"Thank you, Sir Andrew," I said letting him raise me to a sitting position "I'm all right; my wrist is sprained, I think."

"Can you stand? Yes. . . . No pain? Well." He drew a long breath. "One sprained wrist is the total sum. You were lucky, Miss Gordon. You might have struck your head, or caught one foot in the stirrup, and been dragged."

"I can't understand how it happened. Flame is the gentlest of horses."

"She was rough enough this time. I suppose she is still running."

My eyes caught a flicker of russet brown at the far end of the clearing.

"No, there she is, Sir Andrew! Peering through the trees like a naughty child."

I called; and out came Flame, head bowed and reins trailing. She came mincing towards us, still stepping with that odd unease, but plainly anxious to see what had happened to me. When Sir Andrew went to meet her she waited for him and let him take her bridle.

He talked to her for a time, stroking her neck and examining her feet and sides. He adjusted the saddle and came towards me, leading an obedient horse. His face was a mask of puzzlement.

"She is certainly calm now," he admitted. "Did you hear any insect noises before she bolted?"

"Not particularly. There are always bees in the heather—"

His brow cleared. "That is what happened, depend

upon it. She must have been stung."

"I would have thought it takes more than a little bee sting to rouse Flame," I said with a smile.

"Well, Miss Gordon, what do you say? Are you the woman to mount the horse that threw you? I do believe she is quite recovered now."

I looked dubiously at Flame. To be truthful, I would have preferred to walk home. But the mild penitent eye that met mine reassured me. I had a silly notion that I might hurt Flame's feelings if I refused to give her a second chance.

She moved like an angel the rest of the way. Sir Andrew insisted on accompanying me, and I didn't refuse the offer. When we reached the courtyard he told Ian what had happened. The groom was visibly distressed.

"It's nae canny," he exclaimed. "The beast hasna the spirit to bolt."

"I would have thought so, too," I said. "But it appears we underestimated her."

Ian's scowl remained fixed. He eyed the placid animal suspiciously, and I wondered if he too suspected ghosts in the pinewoods. But then he looked at me and said, awkwardly but sincerely, "I hope, mistress, you're no harmed."

"Oh, no. It was a bee, no doubt, as Sir Andrew suggested."

"Maybe it was," said Ian, in a voice heavy with doubt.

He led Flame away and I turned to thank Sir Andrew. He waved my gratitude away with a modesty that was really quite charming, and when he asked permission to call next day, to make sure I had had no further ill effects from my fall, I could hardly refuse him.

As I stiffly mounted the stairs, towards my room and a bowl of steaming water, I thought, with a wry smile, that the adventure had been miscast. How Annabelle would have revelled in being run away with, and rescued by the gallant knight on his chestnut steed! Provided, of course, that she didn't fall too hard.

CHAPTER 7

Mr. Hamilton came back that night. I saw him from my window when he rode into the courtyard. After dismounting, he stood for a time looking up, it seemed to me, directly at my window. I shrank back behind the draperies, although I knew he wasn't really looking for me, and couldn't see me.

I was sick with apprehension next morning when I went to the libarary. But I knew there was no point in postponing the meeting. I hadn't written Randall; I had told myself I would wait till the Master came back, and see what happened. Well, now he was back, and I would see.

He was not in the room when I entered, but someone else was, seated on one of the big chairs with her little feet dangling and her hands folded in her lap.

"What are you doing here?" I demanded, forgetting my manners in my surprise.

"The Master sent for me," Mrs. Cannon said. "I wonder what he wants."

My heart sank, although I had thought there was no lower place for it to go. Did he need a witness for what he had to say to me?

We sat in silence for an interminable time, Mrs. Cannon humming to herself in a wheezy voice, I sitting with my eyes fixed on a book, which I didn't see. At last he came. He was wearing the kilt, its pleated skirt flaring with the length of his stride.

"Good morning," he said. "Mrs. Cannon, how do you do?"

I assumed the first greeting had been directed to me, but since my eyes were lowered, I couldn't be sure. I watched his hands, since I didn't dare look at his face. Black-gloved, long and thin, they sorted a pile of papers that he had brought into the room with him.

Then his hands stopped moving and he said, in a loud, harsh voice, "What has happened? Have you hurt yourself?"

I realised that my sleeve had slipped up, and that the edge of the bandage on my arm was showing.

"It's nothing," I said, quickly trying to adjust my sleeve. "A sprained wrist. Flame threw me."

"Flame?" His voice was incredulous.

"I assure you, it's minor. You know what a clumsy horsewoman I am."

He said nothing. Still I couldn't meet his eyes. Instead I watched his hands, which went back to sorting the papers. He took several envelopes from the pile.

"Mrs. Cannon, here are some letters for you. I found them waiting at Castleton. And—one for you, Miss Gordon."

Mrs. Cannon received her letters with a murmur of thinks, and I sat turning mine over in my hands. I knew whom it was from. The unformed, careless script could only be that of one man.

So I read it, and felt, all the time, that the Master's eyes were watching me. When I had finished, I folded it back into the envelope.

"Cousin Randall?" inquired a sardonic voice.

"Yes."

"What does he say? Let me see it."

I looked up in surprise at this outrageous demand, and withdrew the letter from the imperious grasp that was almost upon it.

"No, indeed," I said, and couldn't help smiling. "You wouldn't care for it."

"I think I can guess at its general tone. May I ask, as a mere—employer—whether his communication affects your plans? Is Cousin Randall coming to snatch you from this den of wickedness, or has he cast you off in virtuous horror?"

It was the old, familiar mocking tone; and without

realising it I found myself answering him as I would have done a week earlier. But when I looked at him I knew it was not the same—that it would never be the same again.

"A little of both," I said. "He admonishes, warns, and scolds. Then he—he offers me a safe asylum, if I ever wish to seek it."

"I see." Mr. Hamilton's brilliant black eyes clouded. "And what will you do?"

"I—don't know."

Dimly I was aware of Mrs. Cannon staring from one to the other of us in complete bafflement, as if we had suddenly started speaking Chinese. I felt a tide of warmth creep up from under my collar over my cheeks and brow. The Master gave me no help; he sat regarding me with the stony solemnity of an idol.

"What do you advise me to do?" I asked.

"I would be grateful if you would stay here for the rest of the summer, at least. That would suit my plans best. But, of course, if you wish to go at once . . ." He shrugged, indifferently.

And I said—humbly, cravenly, "I'll stay."

"Thank you."

"I trust," said Mrs. Cannon tentatively, "that you had good reports of Lord Dunnoch?"

"No. His health is worse, if anything."

Mrs. Cannon clucked sympathetically, but I thought there was a gleam in her eye. No doubt it would suit her vanity to be housekeeper to a peer. And, of course, the Realms of Everlasting Bliss were waiting for the present incumbent.

"Thank you for my letter," I said, rising.

Mr. Hamilton nodded, and reached for an account book. Mrs. Cannon, however, remained seated. She cleared her throat portentously.

The master put down his book and looked at her in surprise. "Yes, Mrs. Cannon?"

"Sir Andrew Elliott called while you were away."

Mr. Hamilton, through years of experience, had learned

how to deal with Mrs. Cannon. He folded his hands and remained silent, waiting with a patience I hadn't expected in him. After a short time Mrs. Cannon produced a second sentence.

"He brought his sister, Lady Mary, to call also."

"I see. And?"

"Annabelle met them both."

Mrs. Cannon heaved a sigh and settled back in her chair. She seemed to think she had explained the situation adequately—as, in fact, she had. Mr. Hamilton's patient smile changed to a look of alert interest.

"And has Annabelle sent you to tell me what she wishes to wear for her wedding?"

Mrs. Cannon's baby mouth trembled at his jeering tone. I interposed.

"Matters have not gone that far yet."

He turned to me with an air of relief at having someone less sensitive to deal with. "Don't tell me Annabelle doesn't fancy herself madly in love!"

"She doesn't confide in me. But I imagine she does. Wasn't it inevitable?"

"Surely. I'm prepared to believe her capable of almost any idiocy. What about the sentiments of the prospective bridegroom?"

"How on earth would I know how he feels?"

"I fancy you might know a great deal." Under his scrutiny my eyes fell, and he continued, still in that mocking voice. "Do you remember what I said about Sir Andrew the first time I met him? 'I wonder what he's after.' Perhaps now you can answer that question."

"Perhaps I can guess. But—"

"Stop hedging. You've seen him with Annabelle. Is he after her?"

"I—think he may be."

"Of course he is. Why else would he have come to this 'damned dreadful hole,' as he calls it? I ought to have known immediately. But I was misled into thinking—"

He broke off abruptly. There was a brief silence. Then

he said, "You see, Miss Gordon, how easily these matters are settled? In five minutes we have agreed that Annabelle wants Sir Andrew, and Sir Andrew wants Annabelle. It only remains to decide whether we shall give them what they want."

"You must decide that," I said.

"No, no. You and Mrs. Cannon are the experts on matters of the heart. How do you like Sir Andrew? Is he worthy, do you think, of my exquisite child?"

"He seems a very charming young gentlemen," said Mrs. Cannon placidly.

"Does he charm you, Miss Gordon?"

I didn't dare answer; if I had opened my mouth I would have cursed him. After a moment he gave one of his harsh laughs.

"I'll have to accept Mrs. Cannon's verdict on Sir Andrew, then. Perhaps you have an opinion about the sister, Miss Gordon. Is she beautiful?"

"Yes."

"Dark or fair?"

"Fair."

"Older or younger than Sir Andrew?"

"I don't know."

"You're not very informative, are you?"

"No," I said.

"Then I suppose I'll have to go and decide for myself. See what lengths your taciturnity drives me to, Miss Gordon—I, who have not paid a social visit in more than a decade."

Mercifully. Mrs. Cannon caught the sense of the last remark, and came to my rescue.

"I'm not sure, sir, that the lady is receiving callers. Her health is poor."

"Yes, Sir Andrew said so. But she had strength enough to come here . . . Well, we'll see. That's all, Mrs. Cannon. Thank you Miss Gordon."

The first thing I did when I got back to my room was to reread Randall's letter. It sounded almost pleasant by contrast to what I had just been through. Randall was not subtle; Randall didn't administer sharp, poisoned stabs of malice. He simply told me, in good round terms, what he thought of me.

One thing was clear from the letter, despite its scolding tone. If I made the proper submission—if I was humble enough—Randall would forgive me. He didn't actually offer me the high honour of becoming his wife, but even that possibility was implicit. Naturally, I found the prospect even more repellent than I had earlier.

Late that afternoon, while I was crouching on the window seat staring dismally down into the courtyard, I saw a wagon enter the gate, and the servants unload parcel after parcel. Evidently Mr. Hamilton had been shopping in Edinburgh. I hadn't asked him to do any for me, so I forgot about the parcels as soon as they were carried into the house—until my door burst open. It was the same surly manservant who had brought my boxes the first night I came to Blacktower House. Now he flung a towering heap of parcels on to the bed and went away before I could say anything to stop him.

I knew, of course, that the parcels were not for me. But the rough handling had burst the paper wrapping of one, and through the rent gleamed something like summer grass with the sun on it. I opened the parcel. Then I opened the rest. And then I sank down on the floor and contemplated the riches before me.

One of the lengths of cloth was undoubtedly meant for me; it was a soft black wool that would drape beautifully, and could only be intended for a riding habit. Dress material, of course, was a very improper gift for a lady, from a gentleman, but only a prig could have taken the gesture amiss. Another of the dress lengths might have been mine—a pale-green dimity sprigged with white and yellow flowers. My summer wardrobe was painfully inadequate; I had few cool frocks. But somehow I hadn't expected Mr. Hamilton to notice that, or to realise that pale green is admirably suited to reddish hair. It was really a very pretty print. Surely, I thought, if I pay for them, I may keep the black and the dimity.

But the other materials . . . I shook my head as I lifted them, one by one. There was a length of emerald velvet that my fingers lingered on; it was almost as thin as silk, and must have been as expensive as the jewels whose colour it borrowed. I coveted that green velvet. My hair would shine like fire against it. And the deep-blue satin, the cream brocade sewn with silver threads . . . I had never cared for finery when I lived with father. Now I sat with the end of the velvet in my lap and stroked its softness reverently.

It was some time before I could bring myself to fold the velvet, and the satin, and the brocade back into their paper wrappings. But of course I couldn't keep them. Someone had made a mistake. Servants did not wear satin and velvet. Black wool, yes; sprigged dimity, perhaps. But the other materials must be meant for Annabelle.

I couldn't carry all three parcels, so I took the velvet and went to Annabelle's room. As I marched down the corridor, I had a sudden mental picture of myself in all those yards of heavy green. It would be a ball gown, made with the new hoops, bare-shouldered, and draped at one side of the bodice . . .

I stood in front of Annabelle's door for a good five minutes with the unwieldy parcel clutched to my breast, before I could make myself enter.

The good fairy had visited Annabelle too. Mrs. Cannon was with her; the two were exclaiming over the treasures littering the bed. I couldn't take them in all at once, but there was a length of pink, and a soft blue. All were shades which would suit Annabelle's pale colouring. Emerald green was definitely the wrong hue for her.

I marched into the room and threw my parcel down cn the bed, narrowly missing a heap of white egret feathers.

"The servants brought some of your parcels to my room by mistake," I announced. "Here is one; I will have James bring the others."

Annabelle rescued the feathers with a croak of dismay.

"What is it?" she asked fumbling at the paper with a child's greediness.

The wrappings fell away. Then there was an odd silence.

"That is not my colour at all," cried Annabelle in disappointment. "I hate that shade of green. Put it away, Mrs. Cannon. How stupid of my father."

Mrs. Cannon gathered up the emerald folds; but before she carried them off she looked directly at me. On her face was an expression I had never seen there before.

If Mr. Hamilton discovered what had become of his gifts he said nothing to me about it. I saw very little of him in the days that followed; it was as if we were both avoiding one another. I left the money for the black cloth and the dimity on his desk; the next day it had gone. It was a strange time, a waiting time, while I crept around the house on slippered feet, trying to see and not be seen, and Mr. Hamilton wandered from house to stables with his face set in a perpetual scowl. He wrote a good many letters, which I was not asked to copy, and received more than he had ever received.

Despite her promise, Lady Mary did not call again. She wrote, soon after Mr. Hamilton's return, to tell me that she had taken a cold and was confined to bed. I think she wrote to Annabelle too, but I didn't try to find out for sure. I was sick of spying and prying, and I had lost any hold I might have had on the girl's goodwill. She went downstairs without me now, under Mrs. Cannon's chaperonage, and once or twice she saw Sir Andrew—for he called again, if his sister did not. I felt sure that their affair was progessing beautifully in the sunshine of Mrs. Cannon's approval; and—I told myself repeatedly—the matter was not my concern. She could go to Sir Andrew, or to the devil, for all I cared.

I hadn't seen her for several days when I went to her room one morning in search of Mrs. Cannon. In sheer boredom I had taken to sewing. It was an art my father had never taught me, but I spent so many hours in my room now that I was becoming fairly proficient at needle-work. That day, though, I had reached an impasse with the bodice of my dimity dress. The pieces would not go together as they were supposed to go.

I expected to find Mrs. Cannon with Annabelle. They were usually together, concocting more finery with which to bewitch Sir Andrew, or discussing his charms. I tapped on the door merely as a formality, and went directly in. The sight I saw nearly sent me staggering back out of the door again.

Standing by the bed was Annabelle's maid, Janet. And beside her, supported by her brawny arms, stood Annabelle herself.

I stared, and rubbed my eyes, and stared again. Yes—she was standing, squarely on her little slippered feet. Janet's arms steadied her, but did not support her weight.

Before I could gather my wits, Annabelle began to shout.

"How dare you come in without knocking! Get out—impertinent, brazen woman!"

I was used to her epithets by now; their quaintness amused me, and didn't damage my feelings in the least. With a gasp, I sank into the nearest chair.

"Annabelle—how you startled me! I can't believe my eyes!"

Annabelle's face smoothed out and her eyes narrowed.

"I think it's wonderful—miraculous. But you mustn't tire yourself. Lie down and tell me how it came about."

Janet helped her back to bed; and, critical as I was of the big woman, I could find no fault in her handling of the girl's frail body. Janet and I had been antagonistic from the first, and now she seemed to resent my discovery even more than Annabelle did. As soon as she had put her mistress back to bed, she left the room without looking at me.

"Well, now," I said, having recovered my breath, "how long has this been going on?"

"Not long. I'm sorry I shouted at you; I wanted it to

be a secret."

"Then your father doesn't know. And Mrs. Cannon?"

"No, oh no. No one one knows but Janet—and you. Damaris, please—don't tell anyone yet. I do want to surprise them!"

"Yes, I understand. But, Annabelle, wouldn't it be better to consult a doctor before going on? I'm afraid you might hurt yourself."

"Don't be silly!" Her voice was sharp, but immediately she softened it. "How can I hurt myself? You gave me the idea, Damaris, when you said there was nothing wrong that you could see. So I thought then I'd try. At first I was afraid I'd fall, and that's why I didn't tell anyone. Later, I thought what fun it would be to see your faces when I came walking down the stairs all by myself."

She gave me a wide child's smile. I returned it, but inwardly I was in a turmoil. Her casual remark, that it had been my careless statement that stimulated her experiments, touched me to the quick. Even at the time I had regretted my words. And yet, now—I studied her closely, and she met my gaze with wide, imploring eyes. Not only did she appear to be unharmed, she looked better, healthier, and handsomer than I had ever seen her look. How could she hurt herself by such limited exercise? And wasn't the fact that she could do it proof that she might do so safely?

With rare good sense, Annabelle remained silent while I wrestled with my conscience. Her pale little face and pleading eyes were her best arguments, and she must have known it. I made her promise to be careful, and to tell me if she felt the slightest ill effect. But when I left the room, she had my promise of silence. Stupidity, poor judgment, sentimentality—I don't know which failing prompted my decision. But whatever my sin, I was to pay for it, soon, and bitterly.

All this time I kept working in the library. I was determined to have it in perfect condition when I left. However,

I took care to work only at odd hours, when Mr. Hamilton was sure to be out.

One afternoon, though, he caught me unawares while I was looking for a missing volume of a certain set on the gallery high above the room. He had just come in from riding. There was dust in his hair and on his boots; in his hands was a sheaf of letters, some opened, some not.

The shelves made a little alcove in the section of the gallery where I was standing, so he didn't see me. Common courtesy demanded that I make my presence known to him at once. Weakness kept me silent. I saw him so seldom; and seeing him, merely seeing him, was a need as vital as breath. So I watched while he seated himself heavily at his desk and laid the letters on its top. He separated one from the heap. It was a long letter, on several sheets of foolscap, and he read it silently to himself from beginning to end. A muffled sigh escaped him. He put his hands to his eyes and rubbed them, as if his head were aching.

I did wonder, a little, what was in the letter that had distressed him so, and then I concluded that he must have had bad news about his brother. But I don't think I really gave the matter much thought. It was more than I could bear to see him looking tired and unhappy. Arrogance became him; mockery was a weapon whose bite I could endure. But pity—that was too heavy a burden.

I was about to emerge from my hiding place when a servant knocked at the door and announced Sir Andrew.

I shrank back behind the shelves. If Sir Andrew caught me coquettishly playing hide-and-seek ... no, I would wait till he was gone.

He came in with his usual swagger, swinging a silver-handled riding crop, and smiling.

"Good day, Mr. Hamilton," he said, offering his hand.

Mr. Hamilton did not rise, nor take his hand.

"Sit down," he said curtly, indicating a chair across the desk from his own.

Sir Andrew's high colour faded slightly. He sat down

and folded one knee over the other.

"I have here a letter that concerns you, Sir Andrew," said the Master. Then he added, in a voice that chilled my blood, "If that is your name."

"What do you mean?"

"I have had inquiries made concerning you. The results were somewhat peculiar."

"What right do you have to make inquiries about me?"

"The classic, time-honoured right. You've been writing to my daughter, haven't you?"

Sir Andrew bit his lip. "I'm not ashamed of those letters. I've not tried to hide them."

"Haven't you? Yet Miss Hamilton denies receiving them, and I only learned of their existence by bribing one of my own servants. I'm afraid I'm forced to suspect someone of excessive secrecy."

"Are you intimating, sir, that my intentions to Miss Hamilton are not those of a gentleman?"

The Master's voice was like ice. "I intimate nothing. I don't care what your intentions are, or how you have carried on your correspondence. I am telling you that the letters must stop."

Sir Andrew rose and struck an attitude. "Mr. Hamilton! I do myself the honour of asking for your daughter's hand in marriage."

"I thought perhaps you would," said Mr. Hamilton equably. Then he laughed. "Sit down, you young fool. If you didn't look like such a consummate ass, I could almost admire your gall. Did you really think I'd give my consent to such a marriage?"

There was silence for a moment; a silence charged with passion. Then Sir Andrew said, in a voice so thick with rage as to be almost inaudible, "Why not?"

"Because my agents in Edinburgh were unable to find any trace of you in the places where you say you have been. Of course, if you can put them in touch with your solicitors, or the head of your doubtless distinguished family, I may be persuaded to consider the problem again."

"Solicitors be damned! Do you know who I am, sir?"

"No, I do not. That's the problem, isn't it? But I have my suspicions. I'm not notorious for devotion to my offspring, but even I will not hand the girl over to a penniless adventurer."

I ran forward out of my hiding place; the expression on Sir Andrew's face as he leaned forward terrified me. But the sound of my soft slippers was lost in the crash of his first as he brought it down on the desk, and both men were too inflamed to notice anything less than an earthquake.

"If you weren't Annabelle's father—" Sir Andrew choked.

"Miss Hamilton, to you."

"Sir, Miss Hamilton and I love one another!" Sir Andrew posed. He did look fine, with his broad shoulders squared and his head high. Looking down on the jeering face turned up to his, he added, "Can you honestly say that she will be less happy with me than she has been under your care?"

It was a hit, a palpable hit, as Mr. Shakespeare puts it. The Master's mouth tightened; the scar stood out across his cheek.

"Never mind that," he said curtly.

"No. It is of the utmost importance." Sir Andrew relaxed now. As he leaned across the desk, he looked like an earnest boy. "Mr. Hamilton, we have both spoken with too much heat. Of course you have every right to be sure of your daughter's choice. Your tone, however . . . But I won't make an issue of that. Give me a chance to satisfy your questions. I promise you—you will be satisfied."

Mr. Hamilton sat motionless for a time. He had not moved, under Sir Andrew's threats or Sir Andrew's wheedling. At last he said flatly, "Every man has a right to a hearing. Gather your evidence."

"Thank you," Sir Andrew straightened. There was triumph in his look, and some other emotion that was less pleasant. "You will hear from me. And I can promise you

—oh, yes, I can promise you—that you'll hear my request more civilly next time."

That was the Sir Andrew I knew best—spiteful and small. Without waiting for an answer he turned on his heel and strode out of the room. The door closed with a slam that rattled the pictures on the walls.

Still Mr. Hamilton sat motionless behind the desk. I looked at his face; then I shrank back on velvet feet into my hiding place. Not for anything in the world would I have let him know I had overheard.

For the next few days I avoided the library. Mr. Hamilton was in a strange mood; he stormed about the house like a thundercloud, berating the servants, quarrelling with Angus, and reducing Mrs. Cannon to tears on two occasions by his caustic comments on her management —which was, to be truthful, very slovenly. I had never seen him behave so; usually his rages were cold as ice or bitterly sardonic. I couldn't imagine what had come over him. It was unlikely that he could be fretting about Sir Andrew; that young gentleman was too negligible to matter. Either he was eligible as a suitor for Annabelle, or he wasn't; one way or another, the matter was easily determined. And, as Mr. Hamilton had admitted, his child's welfare didn't really concern him that much.

To me, his behaviour was decidedly peculiar. But although I tried to keep out of his way, I couldn't avoid meeting him altogether. Whenever we met, he stopped to talk; but, after asking a question or two, he would suddenly stalk away, leaving me in the middle of a word. Also, he had taken to calling me by first name. If he had ever shown any other sign of overfamiliarity I could have dealt with it, but his manner in general was as cool and abrupt as ever. On one occasion I encountered him coming up the stairs as I was going down. He stepped out, deliberately, into the centre of the stair so that I had to stop.

"Damaris."

"Yes?"

"Have you written to Cousin Randall?"

"No," I said. "I thought you wanted me to—"

"All right." He went on up the stairs.

Before long his erratic mood infected everyone in the house. The women servants were so nervous that they started and shrieked if one came on them unawares, and Mrs. Cannon took to peering cautiously out through a crack in the door before she emerged from her room. Only Annabelle seemed unaffected by the general strain, but then she never saw her father. I felt, myself, as if a thunderstorm were brewing. There was something electric in the air—some pressure, building up to a violent climax. I wished it would come. Anything, I thought, would be easier to endure than this constant, mounting tension.

But I was wrong. I never dreamed that the climax would come in the form it did. Certainly I had no premonitions, that afternoon when I saw Mr. Hamilton mount and ride out of the courtyard that I was within a few hours of one of the most shattering events of my life. I watched from my window as the Master rode off, very tall and straight and unusually formal in boots and riding costume. I was relieved to see him go. I had lost a spool of thread, and thought I must have dropped it in the library. Now I could search for it without running the risk of encountering him.

Before going downstairs, I finished putting in the sleeve of the dress I was sewing. The dimity was almost finished, and I wanted to wear it before the warm weather departed. It would be a pretty frock, I thought. I had made it with elbow sleeves, and trimmed it with green ribbons drawn from Annabelle's store of finery.

I kept a close watch on the time, and when an hour had passed I knew I had better go down and search for my thread before the Master returned. I was wearing low slippers, which made no sound on the stairs as I ran quickly down them. I opened the door and went into the library.

At the desk, with his head buried in his folded arms, sat

Mr. Hamilton. I stopped short, thinking I could retreat before he saw me; but he had heard the door open. He raised his head; and I stood motionless, with my hands against my breast.

Never, in his worst moments of anger, had I seen him look as he looked then. His face was absolutely colourless; even his lips were white. His eyes were as lifeless as dusty black stones.

I ran towards him. Perhaps I spoke, or cried out; I don't remember. I only remember what happened next. For as I reached the desk, his dead, dull eyes came to life, and the scar flamed out red across his cheek. He sprang to his feet, upsetting the heavy chair as if it had been straw. He put out both hands, as if pushing away some invisible horror.

"No," he said hoarsely. "No, not you. Go away."

I found myself on the stairs, pulling myself up by the handrail. When I reached my room I bolted the door. Later, after it was dark, Betty knocked and asked if I would come to supper. I said I had a headache.

I don't cry often, or easily. It would be better for me if I could weep as other women do, with fine calculation, and then wipe the tears away and be none the worse for them. That night, when the storm had finally passed, I was light-headed and sick with exhaustion. I got a fresh handkerchief from my drawer and, creaking like an old woman, went to the window and dropped on to the window seat.

Most of the other windows were dark. There was a light to the left from Annabelle's room; but it went out even as I watched. Far down at the other end of the wing I could see another lighted window. It might have been his; I couldn't be sure.

The wind pushed at the draperies and brushed my hot cheeks. It was a gusty night; little hurrying clouds ran along the sky. The moonlight flickered like a candle flame. Another of the frequent summer storms was coming.

Tomorrow, I told myself, I will write to Randall. The thought that had made me shrink only a week earlier now brought only a dull acceptance. Nothing moved me—nothing except the memory of the gesture with which the Master had put me away from him.

The wind rose, rattling the casements and blowing my hair about my face. It moaned in the pine trees beyond the court. But the sound was not loud enough to drown out a closer sound—a low tap at my chamber door.

Soft as it was, the sound brought me to my feet. It never occurred to me that it might be Betty, always solicitous about me. There was something surreptitious and sneaking about the sound, like the fumbling of blind hands. I knew the door was bolted; still, for a few seconds, I froze with alarm. Then I saw that there was something white under the door.

Some little time passed before I could nerve myself to go to the door and pick up the object. It was a note. I knew the handwriting.

"I must talk to you tonight," it began, without greeting. "But not in the house. Come to the Black Tower at once."

I read the note twice; at first I couldn't believe what it said. Brusque and peremptory as the message was, it was so much what I had hoped for, and never dared expect, that I doubted the evidence of my own eyes. His horror and revulsion had not been for me. They were caused by something else. He didn't hate me.

I tied a scarf around my head and changed my shoes. This took some time; I was still dizzy from my wild fit of crying. There was a way out of the house that did not necessitate passing through the courtyard—a corridor that led past the parlour into a seldom-used morning room, and through French doors into an abandoned rose garden. I didn't want to rouse anyone in the house or the stables. Secrecy was implicit in the note and in my own inclinations. A horse was not necessary to reach the Tower. It was a stiff climb, but I could do it in fifteen minutes.

I crept through the darkened house and out into the garden. Moonlight lay on a wilderness of untrimmed rose vines. The light vanished when a mat of clouds obscured the moon. The darkness then was so complete that I had to wait until my eyes adjusted. I could make out shapes, no more. But soon the moonlight came back, and I made my way out of the garden on to the path behind the house.

It was an uncanny night on which to be abroad. The air was warm but not still. The wind tore at my skirts and snatched my hair from its covering. Up on the heights above there was a great roaring, where the winds met and clattered together. The moonlight came, and vanished again. When it shone, it cast unearthly shadows, elongated and strange. When it was obscured by clouds, the darkness stifled the senses.

Tonight the Tower was in its proper element. In the fitful moonlight its scars were invisible. For a moment a mist came over my eyes and I imagined I saw it as it had looked in its prime—with the massive oak doors still in place, ruddy torchlight shining through the slitted windows, and the shouts of a crowd of rough Highland warriors within. Then I blinked, and the spell was gone. An empty shell, the grim pile loomed above me.

I came out on to the narrow ledge at the base of the Tower and looked about. The wind made such a noise that it was difficult to hear, and the moonlight was now hidden. Yet I was sure that there was no other human form in sight. Was I early for the rendezvous? Considering my laborious climb, that seemed unlikely.

I went to the gaping door of the Tower and peered inside. An unpleasant smell of mouldering wood met my nostrils. The Tower was roofless, but the height of the walls made the interior black as midnight. I hesitated, aware of an inexplicable reluctance to pass through the empty doorway. It seemed to me that there was something inside. There was no movement; no shape that looked human. But there was a sense of presence.

In a low voice I called him, by the name I had never ventured to use to his face. "Gavin..." The syllables echoed hollowly from the heavy walls. There was no other answer.

Suddenly I felt I must get away from the doorway. It was absurd; but I thought that something might come out of the door. There were wolves and other wild beasts in the high hills. One of them might have sought shelter in the Tower. But it was not a beast I feared.

Skirting the foundations of the Tower, I went around to the part of the platform that overhung the next glen. The wind struck at me like a club; for a moment I swayed, and reached out frantic hands towards the stones to steady myself. There was nothing below except empty space. Across the valley the outlines of the opposing hills were faintly visible against the sky; but the valley floor might have been a bottomless pit, swallowed in darkness.

As I stood swaying on the brink of the cliff something caught my eye. Almost directly below there was a small orange square of light. It must come from the window of the shepherd's shieling, which Mr. Hamilton had mentioned. Clutching my blowing skirts to me, I watched the small light, obscurely comforted by it.

I didn't hear any sound of footsteps in the howl of the wind. The instinct that warned me of their approach came from no physical sense; and it came too late. When I turned, a tall shape, featureless and black in the lesser blackness of the night, was already upon me. As I stared in dumb terror it collapsed in on itself, like a bladder when the air goes out of it, and crumpled at my feet.

I stepped back. I would have done anything to avoid the shapeless paws that seemed to fumble towards my skirts. But I had forgotten where I stood, I stepped back into empty air.

Briefly my flailing hands beat at nothingness. Then they caught on a rim of rock that edged the platform. The shock upon the rest of my body was terrible; I felt my fingers slip even as they caught hold. One hand loosened, and I made a wild upward grab, groping for something firmer. And I found it—not insensate rock, but the shape of a warm, living hand.

I remember even now the surge of joy that filled me.

Here was help, rescue—life. But even as I thought this, I realised that the unknown was making no attempt to return my clasp. My fingers twisted around a wrist, slipped inexorably down, along a palm that was as unresponsive as wood, and felt five rigid fingers, which did not curve to grasp my own. My right hand, still on the rock, was weakening. Soon its hold would fail. My feet dangled free in space. My only hope lay in that other hand. And it, except for its warmth, might have been the hand of a statue.

I thought of calling for help; but I couldn't spare the breath. So in deadly silence the drama was played out. My hand, surely, was more eloquent than speech. Its grasp was cruelly tight; but the owner of the other hand made no move, nor any outcry. I could see nothing. The moon was veiled; over me the rim of the cliff hung like a wall, and my eyes were too dim with terror to see anything even if there had been noonday light.

My right hand gave way, and for a moment I hung only by the failing grasp of my left hand on those stiff, denying fingers. Then, with a twitch so slight that it was scarcely felt, the fingers removed themselves. I fell into the bottomless pit of the valley.

The last of my breath came out in a shriek that sounded loud in my ears; but I suppose it couldn't have been heard more than a few feet away. I lost consciousness at once, from fright, so I felt no pain when my body struck the rock.

Rain woke me, gentle, inquiring fingers of rain on my upturned face.

I lay still while my senses came back to me. With the rain, the wild wind had died down. The skies, though still cloudy, gave off a dim light that let me see my surroundings. Directly above me was the edge of the cliff from which I had fallen. The Dark Tower seemed to lean dangerously over the rim, but it wasn't far away. I had fallen only a short distance. My feet had struck another ledge of rock that lay not far below the cliff. The ledge was so narrow that one of my arms dangled, unsupported, over its edge.

I brought the arm back, noting with idiot content that one limb at least seemed to respond to my directions. One by one I tested the others. My legs were stiff, and my back ached, but my body was intact. One side of my face felt bruised where it had struck the cliff, and that was all.

Painfully I got to my hands and knees on the narrow ledge. I couldn't climb straight up from where I was; the slope was almost vertical. But somewhere there was a path from the valley to the Tower. It was a dangerous path, but passable; and it must be near the ledge, since the shepherd's cottage was almost directly below. If the path could be reached from my ledge I was saved.

At first I could make out no trace of a path. The ledge widened, though, as I crept along it; and at its end I saw that the slope just above might be climbable. I started up, still on hands and knees. My heavy skirts gave my knees some protection from the sharp rocks, but they hampered my climbing. I knew I had been lying in the rain for some time, since all my garments were sodden with water. At first the wetness was pleasantly cool, but after a while my teeth began to chatter.

Time lost its meaning. The rain continued to fall, and I continued to crawl. When I pulled myself up on to the platform I wasn't even aware of having reached my goal. I continued to crawl, around the Tower and down the path towards the house. I didn't faint. Consciousness simply trickled out of me in a slow stream, and at some point, when the last drop of it was gone, my limbs stopped moving and I lay still in the mud and the rain.

CHAPTER 8

WHEN my senses came back I was in my own bed, in my own room. I knew where I was; but at first I couldn't understand how I had got there, or why I was so hot. I was covered with heavy blankets that weighed like stones. When I tried to push them off I found I was too feeble to move. I opened my eyes. Hanging above me, like a worried pink moon, was Mrs. Cannon's face.

"Thank the Lord!" she exclaimed. Then she said over her shoulder, "I told you, sir, she was not badly hurt."

"Can she speak?" The voice was Mr. Hamilton's.

"I'm too hot," I muttered.

"You are feverish," said Mrs. Cannon. "Small wonder; you were soaked to the skin. What were you doing out of the house in a storm, and at such an hour?"

"She's still too weak to speak," said Mr. Hamilton, still only a disembodied voice. "Give her that whisky, Mrs. Cannon." Then he said softly, "She must speak. I must know what she remembers."

"No whisky," I gasped. Memory was returning now, and with it a misery that drowned physical pain. "Leave me alone—go away!"

"I think not whisky, sir," said Mrs. Cannon professionally. "Betty, where is the broth I sent you for?"

"So you're here, too," I murmured, as the maid's face swam into view. "Quite a social gathering. How are you, Betty?"

"Oh, miss—I'm so glad you aren't dead!"

I laughed feebly, and choked on the broth she was trying to feed to me. Between my weakness and her agitation we made a pretty mess of the food, but when the warm liquid was inside me I did feel better. I could see Mrs. Cannon standing at the head of the bed, in an incredible dressing gown with writhing red dragons all over it. Behind her, in the shadows, was the Master.

"Now can she talk?" he demanded, when Betty removed the empty bowl.

By now I was feeling well enough to be angry. He wanted me to talk? Very well; I would.

I told the whole story, including the note which had taken me outdoors. At this point Mrs. Cannon gave her employer a startled look, but she made no comment. Betty was rapt. When I mentioned the black figure she jumped, and looked at me with bulging eyes. The effort of speaking exhausted me. When I was done, I let my head fall back on to the pillows and there was a long silence, broken only by the hiss of the fire as the raindrops touched it.

"I think," said Mr. Hamilton at last, "that you had better go to bed, Mrs. Cannon. Your patient will do well enough with her maid."

I didn't want to be left alone with him. I opened my eyes, and my lips, to protest, but Mrs. Cannon had already gone. Betty stood by the bed. I reached out and caught at her skirts.

"Don't leave me, Betty. Please don't leave me!"

"I'll not leave you, miss," she said steadily; but her eyes rolled fearfully towards Mr. Hamilton.

"You need not leave," he said coldly. "But stand over there by the door and don't turn your ears in this direction, or you'll be sorry for it."

Betty, scuttled away, with a last look at me that was meant to be reassuring. I could hear her breathing heavily at some distance.

Mr. Hamilton stood with his hand on the bed curtains, looking down at me. His face was grim but controlled. He drew up a chair and sat down.

"What are you afraid of?" he asked.

"I'm not afraid."

"Yes, you are. Do you think what you saw was a ghost?"

"That hand was solid."

"Yes . . . I sent you no note."

"You didn't?"

"No."

"But—I thought—"

"Never mind what you thought. How could you be such a fool as to go out at night, alone?"

I couldn't tell him the real reason : that love extinguishes common sense, and desire overrules caution. So I gave him only part of the truth.

"What should I be afraid of? No one would want to hurt me; I have no enemies."

His control slipped for a moment; the result was a livid glare. "God save you from your friends, then, if you have no enemies," he said violently.

"Amen to that."

"Listen—listen, and try to understand. It is possible to be an inconvenience, to be in someone's way . . ."

"If—someone—wants me to leave Blacktower House, he has only to say so," I said, trying to keep my voice steady. "This makes no sense. Do you want to frighten me? Is that why you speak so wildly?"

"Frighten you?" His hand darted out, towards the pillow—towards my face. "Damaris . . ."

His hand, in its black silk glove. I couldn't help it; I shrank away, with a gasp of fear, before it could touch me.

There was an unpleasant silence. Mr. Hamilton sat motionless, his hand still outstretched.

"Now it comes," he said. "You believe the black figure was I, that the hand that cast you off was mine."

I was paralysed, speechless. He read my answer in my face. He nodded, as if his neck hurt him.

"Of course you would think that. It's what you were meant to think, if you survived your fall. Damaris—the hand wasn't mine. I swear it."

"What good is your oath? You don't believe in God."

"I believe in some virtues, though. It's important that you believe this. How can I convince you?" He mused a moment. "Ah, I have it. The hand—the famous hand.

You held it for some time. Was it a right or a left hand?"

"How can I possibly remember?"

"Of course you can. You hung there, clutching it, for moments prolonged by terror. Close your eyes; feel it again. The wrist, the thumb and fingers, the palm. Do you feel it? Is it a right or left hand?"

"No—no! I don't want to remember . . ."

"The wind is howling, the moon obscured. Your feet hang over emptiness. Your hand—your left hand?— holds stiff, resistant fingers. Where is the thumb in relation to the palm? Right or left, Damaris? Which?"

I closed my eyes and turned my head from side to side, trying to resist the picture that forced itself back into my mind. The wind, the darkness, the terror of the abyss beneath my feet . . . I groaned aloud, but the voice said remorselessly, "Right or left? Which?"

"Right!" I shouted. I felt the perspiration burst out across my brow. "It was the right hand!"

"Are you sure?"

"Yes, yes!"

I began to cry. There was a rush of skirts and Betty dropped to her knees beside the bed, reaching out to wipe my wet face.

"Stop it, sir! How can you be so cruel?"

I tried to sit up then, fearing his anger for the girl.

"I'm finished," said Mr. Hamilton calmly. "Go back to the door, Betty."

She didn't move, bless her. Her eyes met mine, and I smiled at her.

"I'm all right, Betty. Do as Mr. Hamilton says."

I hated him thoroughly at that moment, even if he had been oddly gentle with the maid. As soon as she went away his eyes caught mine again, and there was no weakening of purpose in their dark depths.

"The right hand," he repeated, as if the interruption had never happened. "And you think it was mine. Look."

Holding both hands out before my face, he stripped the glove off the right one.

It was scarred, as I had thought it might be. There were deep healed grooves across the palm, like wounds made by a jagged knife. But that wasn't all. The hand had only three of its five fingers. The last two were only rough stumps, amputated below the first joint.

I looked at the glove, which he had flung on to the coverlet. Two fingers, and the thumb, were limp, empty shapes. The padding with which the other two fingers were filled rounded them out in to an uncanny imitation of flesh and bone.

"You said the hand was warm and ungloved," said the Master, without expression. "Even if you had mistaken that, you could not have mistaken cotton padding for flesh."

My eyes went back to the pitifully deformed hand, held rigidly in the full strength of the candlelight. It had been rigid; now, suddenly, the fingers began to tremble. Then it was gone. Mr. Håmilton rose from his chair and walked to the door. I heard him speak briefly to Betty, but I don't know what he said. There was a rushing in my ears and a fog before my eyes. I think I must have fallen asleep.

I was ill for a long time. When I awoke one morning, free of fever for the first time, I was weak as a kitten. The hand I put out to pull back the bed curtains was almost too frail to accomplish the task. But I managed to separate them a few inches, and saw blue skies outside my open window. The breeze that came in was sweet and cool, with autumn in its touch.

Footsteps came running. The curtains were pulled back, and Betty stood beaming down at me.

"Miss, you're better! Do you know me?"

"I ought to know you, when you've sat with me—how long, Betty?"

"Ten? No, eleven days." She counted on her fingers and nodded decisively. "It's September, miss."

"And there are great dark circles under your eyes. You must go and rest."

"I can now, miss; I was too worried to sleep before,

except in snatches, here on the cot. But you truly are better, aren't you?"

"Yes, much better. Thanks to you, Betty. I remember your being here; whenever I called, your hand was there, ready. I wish I could tell you—"

Her full cheeks turned red. "Now, miss, how could I leave you, with you so sick and afraid? Could you take something to eat now?"

She scampered out, evading my thanks, and when she came back with a loaded tray I didn't attempt to renew them. We understood one another. I told her again that she must go and rest, and she promised to do so when I had finished eating. I saw by the way she settled herself in a chair that she wanted to gossip a little.

"They're all glad to hear you're better, down in the kitchen," she informed me—with more courtesy than truth, I thought. "And I took the liberty of mentioning to the Master that you were awake; he was so glad. There were tears in his eyes when he thanked me for telling him."

I doubted the tears, and the thanks, but I didn't contradict her. It was a pleasure to talk to someone who thought the best of people. Mr. Hamilton had been attentive. His face, and Betty's, were the only coherent memories I had of the long nightmare of illness and fever.

"He has been very good," I said warily. "And how is Mrs. Cannon? And Miss Annabelle?"

"Both well. They've asked after you daily; and Sir Andrew and Lady Mary sent often to inquire. Not to mention Ian. If you weren't a young lady, and he only a groom, I'd be jealous."

"So Ian is a particular friend of yours? Well, I congratulate you. He is a fine man, from what I've seen of him."

"Oh, he is, miss! Not like the others here."

"They are a bad lot," I agreed. "Especially that old rascal, Angus."

"Ah, him! He was a sort trouble to me at first, the

114

reprobate. But since I've had my understanding with Ian he took that worry off me. He threatened to take a stick to Angus if he bothered me again."

This was a new sidelight into Angus's nasty character, but not one that I found surprising. I finished my soup and took up a piece of bread. Betty, who had been watching me hopefully, could contain herself no longer.

"Oh, miss," she burst out, "what was it you saw that night? Was it a ghost?"

"No, indeed. I touched a human hand."

"But the servants say there is a ghost that haunts the Tower. The ghost of a nun, miss!"

"Nonsense. What would a nun be doing here, in this stronghold of Protestantism?"

"Why, she broke her vows, miss. Ran off with a wicked young lord, she did, from her convent; and when he deserted her she hanged herself in the Tower. They say she walks. It's an ill omen for the Hamiltons when she does."

"The classic tale," I murmured. "Betty, I'll wager you never heard that until after I was hurt—now did you?"

"Well—no. But there'd be no reason to tell it until then, would there?"

Her mixture of superstition and common sense defeated me. "All I can tell you, Betty," I said, "is that the figure was not that of a nun. It was hooded and cloaked, yes. If you must have it a ghost, make it the ghost of a monk, for goodness' sake! But it was no ghost."

"Yes, miss," said Betty obediently. She grinned at me, and I saw that she delighted in the story. There was no use in disillusioning her.

"You're still mighty pale and thin," said Betty, shaking her head and abandoning a topic on which we were never likely to agree. "You'll have to stay abed for a time. But you're alive; I thought that night that you were a dead one, for sure. You gave me a turn, indeed you did—blood all over, and white as a ghost yourself, your pretty hair all wet and muddy, hanging down over the Master's arm—"

My exclamation stopped the vivid description. "He

brought me in?"

"Why, yes, miss. Did you think you'd walked in on your own two feet, in the state you were in? He found you on the path from the Tower, I'm told, lying in the rain."

A chill came over me, although the day was warm.

"I wonder . . ."

"What he was doing out of doors?" She finished the sentence for me. "He's often restless at night. Miss, you aren't thinking—oh now, remember what he showed you. It couldn't have been him."

By some strange alchemy the Master had won Betty's allegiance. I wished I could be so uncritically convinced.

Before I was strong enough to resume my duties the rowan leaves had turned red. It was autumn in the glen, a time of change. I went back to my work in the library, and found everything the same as it had been. Mr. Hamilton continued to avoid me; Mrs. Cannon slept; Annabelle was withdrawn and uncommunicative.

But there was a difference. The library was almost finished. My catalogue of the books was nearing completion, and the volumes themselves stood in neat rows, the bindings oiled and shining. My task was done. I could no longer delude myself into thinking that Mr. Hamilton needed a secretary. He had no more interest in scholarship than in Persian embroidery. His offer had beeen a sop to my vanity, a charity offered to a destitute kinsman. With his characteristic self-confidence, he had believed he was in no danger of succumbing to my attractions, and I had thought that I would know how to handle any such problem if it arose. We had both been wrong. He had succumbed, not to love, but to another emotion which I preferred not to name; and I was hopelessly caught. Every day it became more and more imperative that I make plans to leave, and every day it became harder to go.

If my plans needed any confirmation, I found it in a second letter from Randall, which arrived soon after I came downstairs again. It was black-bordered, so I was prepared for the news it contained, which was not a personal shock in any case. My aunt was dead. An apoplexy had carried her off, suddenly and painlessly, in the midst of a tea party.

The surprising thing about the letter was not the news it contained, but the altered tone of the writer. Randall asked me to come back to London. He promised me any sort of support I wanted, and assured me that I needn't marry him if I found the idea so repulsive. (I smiled at that; there was such a world of wounded vanity in the assurance.) But, he continued, if I would consent to be his wife, I could trust him to be prepared to overlook my mad behaviour. No reproaches would ever cross his lips after we were married.

I was softened, not by the offensive phraseology, but by the fumbling sincerity of the thought behind it. Maybe I had misjudged Randall. Now that my aunt was gone, living with him might be—might be possible. Perhaps it was better to marry without love, it was a decidedly uncomfortable emotion to live with. Hundreds of other women married for convenience, every day; and here was Randall, not even insisting on that sacrifice. I ought to have answered the letter at once; its kindness demanded acknowledgment, if not acceptance. But I didn't answer it.

Mr. Hamilton went off to Edinburgh soon after that. He was due to return the afternoon Lady Mary and Sir Andrew called for the first time since I had been ill. They came to inquire after my health—so they said.

The lady hardly gave me time to say I felt recovered before she burst out, "My dear creature, you have no idea how your adventure has set the village on its ears. Nothing else is talked of in the alehouse—or so my faithful spy tells me."

"They must have very little else to talk about," I said.

"That's true. But you must admit it is a delicious story. Was the apparition really a skeleton wrapped in a cloak?"

She laughed aloud before I could answer; I suppose my

face spoke for me.

"No, that would be too delicious. What *did* you see?"

"Nothing, except the shape. No features at all."

Sir Andrew, who had been nibbling daintily on the handle of his riding crop, remarked, "Yet you must have speculated, Miss Gordon. Who can it have been? Who could have behaved so inhumanly?"

"Why, I think perhaps there was no real harm intended," I said slowly. "The figure never touched me; I was not pushed."

"No, but you weren't helped. There was a moment during which the unknown might have pulled you to safety; and did not. At least," Sir Andrew added casually, "that is the version of my bucolic friends."

"Yet even that may not be so bad as it sounds. The unknown may have been injured or ill; he collapsed at my feet like someone overcome. Or there may be other reasons which elude us."

I don't know what prompted me to leap to the defence of the hostile figure in black. Perhaps I was following the habits my father had tried to teach me, in seeing every side of a question. At least I was speaking the truth when I added, "After all, Sir Andrew, why should anyone want to harm me? I have no enemies; there is no one whom I threaten or offend."

"Are you sure?" Sir Andrew asked softly.

I knew he was quizzing me again; and once again I was fool enough to forget myself in answering what sounded like an implicit accusation.

"I can tell you one thing," I said firmly. "Mr. Hamilton has proved, beyond question, that it was not he whom I encountered. There can be absolutely no doubt of that."

With a loud sigh Lady Mary sank back against the couch, one white hand pressed against the laces that covered her bosom.

"I am so glad!" she exclaimed. "So glad to hear you say that!"

We were all silent for a moment. Lady Mary, leaning

back with closed eyes and a smile curving her mouth, seemed occupied in calming some palpitations of the heart that had set her laces aflutter. Sir Andrew's silence was reserved and enigmatic. Mine was, frankly, the silence of bewilderment.

"Forgive me, Miss Gordon," said Lady Mary at last. "You must think me quite mad. But since we last spoke, I have become as fierce a defender of your employer as you. The tales I have heard distress me terribly."

"You have met Mr. Hamilton?" I asked stiffly.

"Oh, yes. I confess, he attracts me very much."

"He—he never said that you and he had become acquainted."

"Oh," she murmured, "I expect he doesn't always speak of matters that are important to him."

At that moment I knew I disliked Lady Mary immensely. She chattered on, apparently quite unaware of the fact that we had become mortal enemies.

"I don't know Gavin—Mr. Hamilton, that is—well enough yet to question him," she said brightly, "but one day I intend to find out the truth about those silly rumours."

"You mean the stories about his wife?"

"Yes." She leaned forward, her blue eyes glittering. "It is suggestive, though, isn't it, that there are no possessions of the lady still in the house? Or is that a lie, like the other tales?"

"No," I said listlessly. "I suppose he couldn't bear to look at her things after she died."

"Perhaps. And yet such action smacks louder of hate than of love."

I was about to reply when Sir Andrew, lounging near the door, made a warning movement. When Mr. Hamilton entered, the lady and I were sipping tea in demure propriety, and Lady Mary was in the midst of a remark about the weather.

He was plainly taken aback at seeing us all so cosy together. The small check in his long stride and a quickly masked frown might not have been noticed by a casual observer. I noticed them.

He bowed over Lady Mary's extended hand and bowed *at* me. I sat back quietly in my corner of the divan, like the governess I hadn't wanted to be, and kept still. Sir Andrew, for some reason, was also untalkative. The other two, the lady and the gentleman, filled the room like actors on a stage. Mr. Hamilton knew the polite banter of society. He had never employed it with me; but he countered the lady's witty comments brilliantly. His voice was the old cool mocking one, but now and then there was a flash from his black eyes that was not at all cool.

I tried to tell myself that he was not deliberately ignoring me. But he had eyes for no one but her. When she rose to go he took her hand again, and it seemed to me she let it linger there.

"I'm for the village," said Andrew, returning to life with a suddenness that made me jump. "Can I hope for your company, sir?"

"I think not, no."

"A fine brother is he not?" said Lady Mary, smiling. "He leaves me to return alone—and through that very wood, Miss Gordon, where you had your strange adventure. I vow, I think the place must be haunted. What shall I do, Andrew, if a bogle or brownie jumps out at me?"

Mr. Hamilton glanced at me when she mentioned my adventure; his expression was vague, as if he didn't see me.

"Why, I believe I must go along," he said slowly, "to protect you from the brownies."

From my window I watched them go. The lady was mounted and waiting when the groom brought out Mr. Hamilton's stallion. When they rode side by side out of the gate, I couldn't help but admit that they made a striking couple.

I hadn't planned to follow them; such an idea would have shocked me a few months earlier. But as soon as they were out of sight I tore off my dress and put on my riding habit. Within five minutes I was in the courtyard asking Ian to saddle Flame.

It wasn't the first time I had ridden her since my fall. She had behaved seraphically ever since, but Ian had never accepted the obvious explanation of her bolting. He helped me mount without speaking, but as I turned away I thought I heard him mutter : "Aye, it's unco strange !"

The Master and Lady Mary were out of sight when I left the courtyard, but I knew the path they would take. I let Flame walk; I had no desire to catch up with them. It was an exquisite day for riding. The rowans stood like scarlet banners against the sombre green of the pines. The heather was turning brown. To my left the burn plunged forward towards the mouth of the glen, over stones green with lichen.

I was aware of these things with only half my senses. The blue mountain ridges beyond the glen, distantly clear in the transparent air, touched my awareness like old friends, but I was more intent upon my own unpleasant thoughts, and even more unpleasant errand. What had I sunk to since I came to Blacktower House? Now I was hiding, prying, spying on two people who had every right to be free of me and my inquisitiveness. The thought made me writhe internally, but I kept on going.

I came upon them so suddenly that only their preoccupation with each other kept them from seeing me. They had dismounted within the little copse of fir trees and were walking side by side, talking earnestly. I brought Flame to a stop, and the amiable animal at once began to crop the grass. Then, dismounting, I peered cautiously through a screen of fir branches. No, they hadn't seen or heard me. Flame's slow steps had been muffled by the needles that lay thickly underfoot.

I was too far away to hear what they were saying, and I felt, not shame, but keen regret. If I were to be that most despicable of creatures, an eavesdropper and spy, I wanted at least to be a successful one. But if I couldn't hear, I could see, and it was apparent that they were not gossiping casually, nor admiring the beauties of the autumn landscape.

Lady Mary was doing most of the talking. The Master listened, with a word or a nod from time to time. Both faces were sober. Once the lady smiled briefly; another time she put her hand on his arm. He didn't respond to either gesture, but walked beside her staring down at the carpet of pine needles.

My eagerness to hear almost betrayed me. I was leaning forward, one hand braced against the trunk of a tree, when the hand slipped and I stumbled forward with a crackling of branches. I let myself drop to my knees and crouched there, my heart beating wildly, as I continued to watch through the screen of bushes.

The lady whirled about, her hand reaching for his in a gesture so intimate and so familiar that I felt the breath catch in my throat. Mr. Hamilton also turned, staring at the bushes behind which I crouched.

I closed my eyes and prayed. I mustn't be caught there, in such a humiliating position. It was no more than I deserved, perhaps, but it was more than I could endure. If one of them came closer I would run to Flame and ride away.

When I opened my eyes again Mr. Hamilton was shaking his head, reassuring her. It had been the wind (I could almost hear his words) or an animal in the underbrush.

After a moment they resumed their discussion, but now it had a more hurried air, as if they didn't want to risk another interruption. Lady Mary no longer smiled. She appeared to expostulate, and he to resist. They stood facing one another, only inches apart. He shook his head. His denial angered the lady. Her face hardened and she answered so decisively that her yellow curls bobbed.

Then, as I watched, shamelessly, I got my punishment for spying—as fine a punishment as any wrathful deity could have invented. Lady Mary's face softened and broke into a smile. She held out her hands to him. I hated her thoroughly then, but I could hardly hold back a gasp of admiration at her unearthly beauty. She had flung off her hat, and her soft curls lifted in the light breeze. Her cheeks were flushed and her eyes alight; she was poised so daintily on tiptoe that she scarcely seemed to touch the ground. Mr. Hamilton hesitated; but only for a second. He caught her in his arms, with a sudden strength I knew very well. The two black-clad forms melted into one and he bent to kiss her upturned, smiling face.

CHAPTER 9

NEXT morning there was frost on the heather. From my window I saw it glistening like a fall of diamonds on the russet ground. Kneeling on the padded window seat in my favourite position, I folded my arms on the high sill and rested my chin on top of them. The wind from the distant hills was no longer cool; it was cold, and I shivered as it struck my skin through the flannel of my nightdress. I welcomed the cold. It seemed to strike cobwebs from my mind, and sweep into corners where dust had gathered.

What was I to do?

I had known the answer for weeks. Now I admitted it openly. I must leave Blacktower House at once. There was no longer any hope, any excuse for lingering.

I closed my eyes, and vivid as a painting, the scene in the pinewoods came back into my mind. The sunlight slanted through the green boughs and the breeze whispered in the branches; and the two interlocked figures stood motionless, caught in a furious embrace.

Today was Friday. Every Tuesday Ian rode to Castleton with the mailbag. The next time he went, I must have a letter ready for him to take—a letter to Randall, telling him ... What precisely was I going to tell him?

Three days later, on Monday, I still couldn't answer that question. It was raining again that day, and the house was as cold and dreary as a tomb. I should have been in my room, writing to Randall. Instead I wandered through the house like a distracted phantom, from library to drawing room, up to my own room, and back to the library, as if I hoped to find a solution somewhere outside my own mind.

I ended up in the entrance hall, which had plenty of space for pacing the floor, and walked up and down studying the portraits on the walls—all of them dark and badly in need of cleaning. The monotonous mutter of the rain was audible even through the heavy oak door. I thought of going up for my shawl; the hall was damp and chilly. Then I started, as the heavy iron knocker outside fell with a crash.

None of the maids was in sight, so I went to open the door. I assumed it must be Sir Andrew knocking; no one else would brave such weather, and I hated to leave even him outside in the wet.

I had to use both hands to pull the great oak panels towards me. A man was standing on the steps. When he saw me he removed his hat, and a cupful of rain spilled off the brim and splashed into his face. He was soaked to the skin; his face was as wet as if he had been bathing, and the ruins of a handsome moustache dripped forlornly into his open mouth.

I didn't recognise him at first. He was out of place, as wildly incongruous in this setting as Charlemagne.

His frown deepened as he watched me hanging, all agape, on the door handle. "Are you going to leave me standing in the rain, Damaris?" he demanded.

"I—I beg your pardon, Randall. Come in."

He entered, splashing at every step.

"Good God, Damaris, this is really too bad of you! Of all the isolated, abandoned spots—! How will I ever get back to Castleton tonight? I'm drenched. You know what my colds are like; I sneeze and suffer for weeks—"

"Well, you can hardly blame me for the weather, Randall," I reminded him. "Of course you'll have to stay here tonight. Wait a moment and I'll see about a room for you."

I left him with his mouth ajar, standing in the middle of a rapidly spreading puddle. Mrs. Cannon was sleeping when I burst into her room, but my news roused her at once. Another gentleman in the house! Gentlemen required service. They could not be expected to wait for anything they wanted. When she was stirred up, she could move quickly. In a short time there was a fire blazing in one of the guest rooms and fresh sheets on the bed, and one of the menservants had been sent to fetch Randall's bag and tend to his horse. I went back to the hall, where I found my cousin standing like a statue of Indignation, in the exact spot where I had left him. I showed him to his room. Then I went back downstairs.

Now that the immediate necessities were settled, I had time to wonder if I had been dreaming. To find Randall dripping on the doorstep was only one step less incredible than finding myself transported instantaneously to London. I seriously doubted my own senses, and I went so far as to tiptoe out into the hall and stare questioningly at the puddle on the floor where he had stood.

Then it occurred to me that I ought to be upstairs tidying myself—brushing my hair, or changing my frock. The dress I was wearing was one of my oldest London costumes, frayed at the cuffs and yellowing at the collar. My hair, as was usual in moments of stress, had come undone and was hanging down my back.

I bundled it unceremoniously into its net, brushed a bit of lint off my skirt, and went into the drawing room. And there I sat, hands folded in my lap, frayed cuffs uppermost, and waited.

Randall was a long time in coming. I ordered tea from Betty, who had guided him downstairs, and then braced myself for the inevitable lecture.

Randall went directly to the fire, where he stood warming his hands; so for a few moments I was able to study him unobserved. I had to admit that he made a good appearance. He was tall enough to carry his extra weight easily; it showed to disadvantage only in his full cheeks and in his hands. Most of his head was adequately covered by light-brown hair. He had it trained quite neatly over the balding spot on top. In his dress, he was beyond criticism. His coat and dark trousers were so immaculate it was hard to believe they had just come out of a portmanteau. The coat looked new, and so did the gold stickpin in his cravat.

My inspection had to end there. Randall turned, clearing his throat in a manner I remembered only too well.

"Well, Damaris."

"Well, Randall?"

"I confess, I hardly know how to begin. Do you realise what people are saying about you?"

"What are they saying?" I inquired politely.

"You have completely ruined your reputation. It is known in London that you came here with—with that man."

"Are you referring to Mr. Hamilton?"

"To what other man could I refer?" asked Randall, looking surprised. "Of course I know he is heir to a peerage. But all the same, Damaris, he has a particularly unsavoury reputation. And this nonsense of being his secretary—"

"Are you implying that I have ever been anything else?"

"I imply nothing." Randall's tone was lofty. "I know you too well, Damaris, to doubt your innocence. I make allowances for your youth, your inexperience—and for a certain boldness of character, which, if I may say so, I always believed your lamented father was reprehensibly lax in restraining."

"Indeed?" I murmured. Randall ignored the warning in my voice, which was very soft.

"No, I don't blame you. I do blame Mr. Downey; I am seriously displeased with him for allowing you to escape in this fashion. But let that pass. I don't blame you; but others are less charitable. Your reputation—"

"Oh, curse my reputation! Do you never think of anything but what the world thinks?" I bounded to my feet. He had solemnly advanced upon me as he spoke, and when I stood up, my face was just below his. "Have you come here to rate me and lecture me? If so, you can turn around and go back again! When I think that only today

I meant to write to you—meant to tell you I was coming back . . . How could I have forgotten your bigotry, your stupidity, your—"

Randall put an end to my tirade in a most unexpected fashion. He seized one of my gesticulating hands and pressed it to his breast. I was so astonished that I sat down, pulling Randall to his knees. He remained in that position.

"You wrote to me? You said you would come to me? My darling girl—"

"No, no," I said weakly, trying to extricate my fingers from a grip that was squeezing the bones together. "I didn't write. I meant to, but . . . Randall, you are not yourself. What are you doing?"

"Something I should have done a long time ago," he said tenderly, capturing my other hand and crushing it till I almost screamed with pain. "What a beauty you are when you're in a temper, Damaris. My little sweetheart . . ."

I had never appreciated how luxuriant his moustache was. The long ends were tickling my nose. Just in time I stifled a shout of laughter, and made my face as stern as I could.

"You are hurting my hands," I said severely, "and ruining your trousers. Do get up, Randall, before someone comes."

Neither severity nor ridicule touched him. The moustache came closer; the expression on the face behind the moustache was almost unrecognisable. I resigned myself to being embraced. I thought I might be able to reason with him better once he had got that out of his system. It was at that moment that the door opened and Mr. Hamilton entered the room.

He stopped in the doorway, staring, and I am sure I didn't blame him. Randall's grip had frozen on my hands; I couldn't free them. Nevertheless, as he knelt at my feet, my hands locked in his, I spoke in my most composed voice.

"Mr. Hamilton, pray allow me to present my cousin,

Mr. Randall Gordon, of whom you have heard me speak. Randall, my employer, Mr. Hamilton, Master of Dunnoch."

True breeding, they say, tells in the end. Randall got up, releasing my hands. "How do you do, sir," he said with magnificent aplomb.

"Your servant, sir," said Mr. Hamilton, in an icy voice.

They were almost of a height, although Randall was broader and thicker than the Master. The latter was dressed in his usual costume, kilt and hose, and jacket over a not too clean white shirt. He wore no cravat; his collar was open; and his hair was wet. If a stranger had been asked to decide which of the two was the heir to a great peerage, he would never have chosen Mr. Hamilton. After one long look, Randall's hand went to his cravat in an infuriating little gesture.

"You must pardon my unwarrantable intrusion, sir," he said. "I came from London in response to my young cousin's request, and I had hoped to escort her back to Castleton tonight. But I hadn't realised that your property lay so far from the town. I fear I must crave your indulgence for tonight."

Mr. Hamilton listened to this speech with perfect gravity. Only once, when Randall referred—misleadingly —to my "request," the Master's eye shifted to my face, and as quickly went back to Randall's.

"Don't speak of indulgence, I pray," he answered. "I hope you will do me the honour of remaining for several days."

"Sir, I thank you." Randall bowed.

"Your servant, sir." Mr. Hamilton bowed.

It was all very silly; but I didn't feel like laughing.

"Has Mrs. Cannon prepared a room for Mr. Gordon?" asked the Master, aiming the question in my general direction, but without looking at me.

"Thank you," said Randall, before I could reply. "I have been made very comfortable."

"Then I hope we may count on your company until the

end of the week, at least."

"Sir, I am reluctant—"

"Miss Gordon cannot return to Castleton on horseback. There are her boxes, for one thing. You must have the coach, and I regret to say that it is unfit for use at present. By Saturday the wheel should be repaired."

There was no reason why I should have doubted this statement. Yet I did. I hadn't even seen the coach since the day we arrived; for all I knew, it might have collapsed completely. But I had come to know the Master's voice, and there was a note in it that sounded flat and unconvincing. I gave him a curious look, which he pretended not to see.

"Besides, continued Mr. Hamilton blandly, "Miss Gordon has friends in the neighbourhood whom she will wish to take leave of, and who would regret not being able to bid her farewell."

Randall nodded complacently. The statement was reasonable, in terms of the world he knew. He couldn't imagine how wildly incongruous it sounded to me.

No doubt Mr. Hamilton had cause to congratulate himself on his ingenious excuse about the coach. The weather gave no cause for delay; the next day was cold and bright, and the roads dried to a hard, half-frozen crust. Somewhat to my surprise, Randall made only conventional protests about staying. Mr. Hamilton was exerting himself to be entertaining. He showed Randall the house, the horses, and the countryside. We dined *en famille* (but without Annabelle) in the draughty hall, and after dinner the gentlemen retired to a billiard room, whose existence I had not even suspected, or they played chess in the library. One night they went down to the village. It was very late before they came back, and I heard them coming from a good way off. One of them singing; the voice was not a baritone, but a florid tenor, which I had never suspected Randall of possessing.

All this astounding activity on Mr. Hamilton's part made my own resolution easier to follow—of not allowing myself to be left alone with Randall again. I was beginning to think kindly of him, even a little sorry for him; perhaps he was not the complacent stick I had thought him. He was very courteous to his host, and very gallant to me; but still ... The memory of his red face close to mine still sent a shiver up my back. What I would do when we were alone together in the coach, or back again in London, I refused to think. I managed to build up a thick shell between myself and my thoughts during those days. There were too many things I didn't dare think about.

One day at tea time, when we were sitting hypocritically in the drawing room enjoying that meal, Sir Andrew arrived. At least Mr. Hamilton and I were hypocrites. Both of us behaved as if the pleasant afternoon ceremony were habitual, whereas, of course, we had never taken tea together until Randall came. It was all for my distinguished cousin's benefit—and he took it for granted. I was willing to make the effort, but I really wondered at Mr. Hamilton's consistent affability.

However, he wasn't so affable to Sir Andrew, although there was no hint in his manner of the contempt he had shown the young man during their tense interview in the library. I concluded that Sir Andrew had proved his case, and identified himself. If he was not as yet Annabelle's accepted suitor, he was at least acceptable. I didn't doubt for a moment that Mr. Hamilton would have tossed him out of the front door personally if he hadn't produced his credentials.

I poured a cup of tea for Sir Andrew, who looked as if he would have preferred another beverage but didn't have the courage to ask for it. He had brought me a note from his sister containing an invitation to—of all things—a ball to be held at Glengarrie on Friday. "Just a small informal affair," Lady Mary wrote. "I had hoped to introduce you, dear Damaris, to some of my old friends who have come to visit. Now, alas this must be in the nature of a farewell party." The invitation concluded by including my "distinguished cousin" in the group.

"Please thank Lady Mary for me," I said. "But I must decline the invitation. We are leaving so soon, and I really have no suitable dress."

Randall stopped stroking his moustache and stared at me. "Don't you mean that you have no dress that has not been worn, Damaris? Ah, the charming illogic of women! Lady Mary will excuse you for wearing a frock twice."

Already he was behaving as if he were responsible for me and my belongings. It offended his pride to think that I had no ball dress. Well, I was sorry, but there was no reason for me to be ashamed of the truth.

"I have no suitable frock," I repeated. "Nothing that would be proper for an evening party."

I really believe that Randall was on the verge of asking to inspect my wardrobe when Mr. Hamilton intervened. He was leaning against the mantel, balancing his cup in one hand. "Annabelle has enough fabric to stock a shop," he said quietly. "I'm sure you can find something on her shelves that could be made into a dress."

His eyes met mine, and I saw green velvet reflected as if in a mirror. That fabric had been meant for me, and he knew that I had rejected it.

"I couldn't do that," I said.

"Certainly not," Randall agreed. "Damaris needn't depend on Miss Hamilton's kindness. I will ride into Castleton tomorrow. A white muslin, I think, is always appropriate for a young lady."

Mr. Hamilton said nothing. He continued to watch me, a faint smile contorting his mouth. It was unnerving to realise that he could read my private thoughts so plainly. Obviously my attempt to avoid the ball was doomed. I must be dependent on the charity of some man for my dress. My only choice was between Randall and the Master. I boiled with anger which I couldn't show.

"You can't possibly ride to Castleton and back tomorrow," I said in a stifled voice. "I'll speak to Annabelle."

One opponent having been conquered, Mr. Hamilton

turned to the other. "You force me to expose Annabelle's little surprise, Mr. Gordon," he said smoothly. "She had hidden away this fabric as a gift—a birthday present—for Damaris. As a matter of fact, I haven't told the poor child yet that her dearest friend is leaving. It will hurt her sadly. But if anything will mitigate her grief, it will be the joy of seeing Damaris in her birthday offering."

"I see" said Randall, who thought he did. "In that case, of course . . ."

"I knew you would sympathise." Mr. Hamilton turned to Sir Andrew, who was concealing his yawns of boredom behind his cuff, and began to talk about hunting. Randall listened, with the air of a man whose hall is littered with trophies, and I poured out a cup of tea whose steaming temperature matched my own.

My birthday is in March. Randall, of course, had forgotten the date. The Master had never known it. He had no scruples at all about gaining his ends, even when the end was as unimportant as this. Poor Annabelle, grieving over the loss of her dearest friend . . . birthday offering . . . it was enough to make one gag. If Randall hadn't been such a fool he would have seen through the pretence, I thought unjustly. I saw through it, but what I didn't see was the reason behind it. Why should the Master care whether I went decked proudly in emerald velvet, or went out of his house as I had come, in dusty cotton?

When I went to Annabelle's room to inquire after the velvet, I knew immediately that she had heard of the ball at Glengarrie. I half expected an explosion, or at the least a demand that she be taken there. To my surprise she mentioned the subject quite calmly.

"You'll need a dress," she said amiably. "Look in the wardrobe, and see if there is something suitable."

I found the fabric at once, atop a heap of gauze and *peau de soie*. Annabelle offered it to me, with a remark to the effect that it was really not her colour.

All this was so unlike the Annabelle I knew that I began

to be dimly suspicious. "Wouldn't you like to go?" I asked, turning with the heap of soft green in my arms. "You're so much better now. How is your secret coming along?"

Annabelle's pale lashes drooped to veil her eyes. "Very slowly. I can't walk yet. But I know I must be patient."

"Oh, yes, the weakness of years can't be undone in a day. But I think you might be carried in the coach quite easily. Wouldn't you enjoy watching the dancing?"

"Watching? No, indeed!"

She spoke sharply, and I thought then that I understood. Of course it would be hard to sit like an old lady muffled in shawls while other women enjoyed dancing and compliments. I forgot my suspicions. And when Annabelle asked if I wouldn't make the dress in her room, so that she could watch and make suggestions, I agreed at once. Poor child, I thought, is all her life to be spent in watching other women dress for balls?

CHAPTER 10

I WAS half hoping the dress would not be finished in time, but it went together as if under a magician's spell. Mrs. Cannon was a skilful seamstress, and Annabelle had enough pattern books for a dressmaker's shop. I was appalled at the pattern they selected; it had a skirt wide enough to cover six women, and hardly any bodice. I was sure there wouldn't be enough cloth for that skirt; but when we spread it out, on the carefully swept floor, it was like a sweep of emerald grass. There was enough material, and to spare.

On Friday morning we had the final fitting. When I looked at the figure reflected in Annabelle's tall mirror I could hardly believe it was I. The green skirt billowed out in a graceful bell shape, supported by the new-style hoops which Mrs. Cannon had presented me with. The velvet was a lovely shade; it varied from bright emerald to shadowy darkness according to the light. The bodice left my arms and shoulders almost completely bare. I tugged at it, and Annabelle laughed, and showed me pictures in her books of ladies with even less cover.

Friday afternoon after tea Betty came to help me dress. She went after me like a French maid dressing a courtesan; I expected her to demand mare's milk for bathing. Ian fetched the water for my bath. It wasn't part of his usual duties, but I suspected that he was finding excuses to work inside the house nowadays. I looked out of the window most of the time he was in the room; and I heard one or two little soft sounds that showed he and Betty were quick to take advantage of my tact.

After I was bathed, Betty asked if she might do my hair.

"I've looked at the pictures in Miss Annabelle's book," she explained earnestly, "and I've found a lovely one. Oh, please, miss, may I try it?"

"Of course," I said, smiling at her excitement. "You can't do a worse job of it than I do. I usually bundle it into a net."

She sat me down before the dressing table and went to work. First she brushed my hair until it crackled and clung to her hands. Then she began to twist and braid it. I was amazed at her skill. When she had done I had a high crown of twisted braids, and three long curls over one shoulder. Then she went out and came back with what appeared to be a handful of fresh flowers. I gave an exclamation of surprise and bent to look at them. They were flowers—white silk roses with green stems cunningly covered and leaved with the same velvet as the dress.

"Miss Annabelle gave me the roses," said Betty, beaming. "And I trimmed them."

"They are lovely," I exclaimed, as she set them skilfully in the waves of my hair. "Betty, you are wasted here. You might be a great lady's personal maid."

She took a long time to dress me, enjoying the fun of it. But at last the final rose was set in place, the last curl was arranged, and the sweeping skirt settled to her satisfaction. Betty left, with a lingering glance of pure love at her creation; and I stood, stiff as a stuffed figure, before the mirror.

I was alone now, and it was the last night. For four days I had supressed all thought of the future. But now I thought : This is the last time. I will never look in this mirror again; never watch the fire die in my hearth, or see the dawn break through my window. Tomorrow I leave, forever—leave the house and the view of Ben Macdhui's purple slopes and the gorse turning gold in September; leave Betty, my friend, and Toby, and my little horse Flame; leave the Master.

"I can't stand it," I said aloud.

The sound of my voice startled me; it seemed to come from someone else. Certainly the cracked, stifled tones couldn't have emerged from the creature in the mirror.

She was a girl of copper and ivory and emerald shadows, slim as a dryad above the billowing skirts. Her eyes looked green; I had always thought mine were grey. I stared curiously into the mirrored eyes, and for a moment they darkened, as if something deep down behind them were struggling to come up, and out. I put out my hand to push it back. The girl in the mirror looked very well, with her green eyes and calm mask of a face. I would take her downstairs and show her to all of them; and no one, least of all Gavin Hamilton, would guess that she was not I at all. I turned, awkwardly in my billowing skirts, and went down the hall to say good night to Annabelle.

She clapped her hands delightedly at the sight of me. She looked unusually pretty that night; even vicarious pleasure seemed to excite her. As I turned and postured for her benefit, I thought wryly that Betty and Annabelle seemed to be enjoying my debut immensely. That was just as well; someone ought to enjoy it.

I said good night to Annabelle, and went towards the stairs.

The men were waiting for me in the drawing room. There was a tray with decanters and glasses on the table. Randall was sprawled in a chair near the table, a half-filled glass in his hand. He looked up when I entered, and I thought, for a moment, that he was going to drop his glass. He stumbled to his feet and stood gaping; his mouth was half open and his lips shone wet in the lamplight.

Mr. Hamilton, in his favourite pose near the fireplace, made no move at all. He wore Highland evening dress, and looked like a chieftain from the Forty-five. His coat was green velvet, matching the green of the tartan; there were ruffles at his wrists and silver buckles on his shoes.

Randall came towards me and kissed my hand. He did it very awkwardly. He wore evening dress, black broad-cloth and a frilled white shirt. A diamond stickpin glittered among the ruffles. As he straightened, still holding my hand, I caught a strong reek of brandy. Father never drank spirits, only wine. The smell of brandy always bothered me, but that night it seemed more offensive than ever. Or perhaps it was not the brandy so much as the clasp of Randall's plump fingers and the possessive glitter in his eyes as he looked down at me.

From a long distance off, I heard Mr. Hamilton's voice. "The carriage won't be here for a few minutes," it said. "Randall, offer Miss Gordon some sherry."

Randall had to release my hand then. I sank down into the nearest chair with my eyes fixed on the green velvet folds of my skirt, and tried to steady myself. It was going to be worse than I had thought. Green velvet—in my dress, in his coat. I would never see green velvet again without remembering.

Randall brought me the wine and I took it eagerly, remembering how, once before, it had nerved me to face a distasteful interview.

Randall filled his own glass once more, and the amber liquid slopped over the rim on to the rug when he dropped heavily into a chair facing me. "A toast!" he said, slurring his words. "To the beautiful Miss Gordon—may her name always be the same!"

He chuckled happily and drank. I don't know whether Mr. Hamilton joined him; I couldn't see him from where I was sitting, and there was only silence from that part of the room.

Randall came up out of his glass and took a deep breath. "I was thinkin' of something," he announced owlishly. "Now what was it?" He looked for inspiration into his glass, and brightened. "I remember. The beautiful Miss Gordon, eh? You two—why so formal? We're all cousins, ain't we? Use first names. Damaris, meet Gavin; Gavin meet Damaris. Come on, shake hands all 'round."

He made a grab for my hand, and missed; and then Mr. Hamilton emerged from his retreat and stood between us.

"It's time to leave," he said.

"Shake hands," Randall repeated, blinking at him.

"I will," said Mr. Hamilton coolly. He grasped Randall's hand, simultaneously removing the glass my charming cousin was nursing. Then he turned to me. "Come, Damaris."

In the hall we found Mrs. Cannon, wrapped in a fantastic pink taffeta cloak, and she and I got into the carriage together. Her coming had been a last-minute decision. Annabelle had mentioned, casually, that the old lady was eating her heart out because she would not see the festivities, and had added, equally casually, that my situation really demanded the presence of a chaperone. I didn't care what my situation demanded, but I thought Mrs. Cannon ought to have her simple pleasures, so I arranged for her to come.

The Master swung into his saddle and Randall climbed laboriously into his. He looked ridiculous, in full evening dress on horseback. I think he had meant to ride with me in the carriage, until he found that Mrs. Cannon would make a third. I hadn't thought about that when I invited her; now I realised that virtue does, sometimes, have its advantages.

I took my place in the carriage and arranged my skirts; they covered most of the seat. When I looked out of the window I saw Betty, huddling her arms under her apron, peeking out at me from the shelter of the balustrade. I smiled at her. Then, all at once, without premeditation, I heard myself saying, "Look after Miss Annabelle, will you, Betty?"

She nodded obediently, though she looked surprised. She was no more startled than I was. I settled back in the carriage, wondering what had prompted me to speak so.

We jolted over the rough road, under brilliant moonlight and through patches of dark woods. For a wonder, Mrs. Cannon was wide awake and talkative. She chattered on about the party, and dear Lady Mary, and delightful Sir Andrew, until I could have boxed her ears. But, in a way, I was glad of her babble because it kept me from thinking. Thinking about tomorrow, when Randall and I would be sitting in this same carriage on our way to London.

We saw the lights of Glengarrie long before we reached

the house. It seemed to float atop the low ridge like a ship, lit by a ghostly luminescence of moonlight beams and candle glow. The doors stood open, and Sir Andrew was at the top of the steps waiting for us.

Randall handed me out of the carriage and then assisted Mrs. Cannon's bulk to descend. So when I turned to mount the steps to the terrace, I found myself on Mr. Hamilton's arm. We went up the stairs together, not speaking. The worn velvet of his coat sleeve was soft under my hand. Sir Andrew greeted us and passed us on; and inside the hall, under a blaze of candles from a sconce overhead, the hostess stood.

Lady Mary wore blue, which clashed hideously with my green. She swept forward, hands outstretched and a smile lighting her face. There were blue ostrich plumes in her fair curls and a necklace of diamonds and sapphires around her throat. Hanging earrings made little blazes of light on either side of her face.

Only one note in her costume was jarring, out of place —a big heavy brooch of rough silver set with a smoky yellow cairngorm. The piece caught my eye at once, it was so large and was set so prominently among the ruffles at her bosom. It was obviously an heirloom of some age. The silver had been polished, but the black in the deep cuts of the design had resisted cleaning.

Then I realised that Gavin Hamilton, at my side, had gone rigid. Under my hand his arm was like a bar of iron.

"What is it?" I asked in a whisper.

"Nothing."

He removed his arm from mine and took the slim white hand Lady Mary held out to him. But by then I knew where the brooch had come from.

After that, the finest social gathering would have been a failure for me. And this gathering was not really very elegant. Some of the awkwardness couldn't be helped. The house was rented and the furniture worn; by this time of year all the flowers were gone, and fresh ones couldn't be imported so far. A proper orchestra for dancing would have been hard to come by, and ours consisted of an old man who played a violin and a blowsy-looking lady at the piano. To their unmelodious strains we danced. I had the first dance with Sir Andrew, and Gavin took out his hostess. This left Randall to the attentions of a lady in a low-cut, rather dirty rose frock, whom Lady Mary had introduced to him.

There were a dozen couples in the set, and, as we stood waiting to take our place, I said to Sir Andrew, "What a sizeable crowd! I didn't know the neighbourhood could produce so many people of dancing age."

"It can't. Imagine. In this whole district we found only two families worth knowing. Duncan has four blooming daughters and Easton one; they are not very worthwhile acquaintances, but at least they are of our class. Most of the guests, however, are friends of Mary's and mine."

The couple ahead of us finished their turn and I joined hands with Sir Andrew. We moved sedately down the floor in time with the squeaking of the violin, and resumed our places.

"A pity this is to be our last meeting," he said. "You're very handsome this evening, Miss Gordon. Festivities become you."

"And you. You are all aglitter with excitement."

"Well, our excitements here are limited," he admitted, with a rueful shrug. "My friends in Paris would laugh to see me at such a rustic display; but, I assure, you, it was the best we could do."

I danced next with Randall, and then with Mr. Hamilton. Unfortunately this last dance was a waltz, not one of the set figures we had been performing. He held me impersonally, at arm's length; neither of us spoke. But every moment of it was misery for me.

As soon as the waltz was over Lady Mary came up to capture Gavin, and to introduce me to a Captain Dubois, with whom I danced next. He seemed old to be one of Sir Andrew's friends, although that was how he had been presented to me; I didn't care for his hard, lined face or the clumsiness with which he tried to ape polite manners. As the evening wore on, I began to think that Sir Andrew's friends were an odd assortment. There were only two ladies in the group—if they merited that title; their gowns looked elegant across the room, in dim light, but on closer inspection I could see that their laces were mended and their flounces soiled, and that the glow on their blushing cheeks was not the bloom of nature. The gentlemen were equally shabby. They all had military titles, and they might actually have been soldiers, if one could judge by their weatherbeaten faces and gruff manners. Indeed, although they bore different names, they were oddly similar in appearance; tall and short, fair and dark, all six had a look in common—a shiftiness about the eyes, a hardness about the mouth.

I was relieved when, a waltz being announced, my hand was sought by Mr. Duncan, one of the Scottish gentlemen from near Castleton. He had grey hair and a portly figure, but the candour of his blue eyes was refreshing, after the faces I had been studying. He, too, it appeared had noticed the motley crew.

"A queer lot, aren't they?" he said, with a disparaging glance at Major Green, who had just stumbled by with one of the Duncan daughters in his embrace. "I'm a wee bit sorry we came. But Sir Andrew is a bonny mon, and his sister is verra lovely."

And you, I thought, have four marriageable daughters. But I liked the old gentleman, although he was waltzing relentlessly on my feet, so I said, "I had the same impression of the guests myself. But I thought perhaps I was being too critical."

"Na, na. You've no' the experience, but a lady's instincts never fail. Now I've been abroad maself, and I ken the type. Hangers-on, adventurers, and their ladies—I'll wager there's no' a genuine commission among the lot of them. Captain This and Major That—bah."

"But," I said slowly, "what can they be doing here?"

"Oh, they'll be friends of the young gentleman. It's no'

uncommon for a lad to pick up such trash in the fashionable world, and he's a lighthearted, trusting body."

"I'm surprised that Lady Mary allows such people in her house."

"Lady Mary's a verra indulgent sister. I grant, the lad needs a firmer hand. I've no doubt he'll get it, once Gavin enters the family."

I hadn't missed a step, although Mr. Duncan was not the world's easiest partner. I missed one now.

"You think . . ."

"Oh aye. You saw the brooch? Wi' the Hamilton's, it will be the announcement of a betrothal."

"I saw the brooch. But I didn't know it meant that."

Flattered by my interest, Mr. Duncan ventured on a sweeping turn. By a miracle, for I wasn't paying much attention, I avoided his stamping boots, and the old gentleman was flushed and beaming when we finished up in time with the conclusion of the music.

"You're a bit pale," he said, peering at me kindly. "Would you be the better for some air?"

"Yes. Please."

As we went towards the French doors, I saw Gavin talking to a heavy, middle-aged lady—Mrs. Duncan. Sir Andrew was nowhere to be seen. Randall, somewhat the worse for wine, was standing with the rose-clad damsel, who seemed to have taken his fancy. She was laughing up into his face from behind a tattered fan, and Randall was endeavouring to brush away the screen with the tip of one wavering finger. His was not the only flushed, hot face in the room. The wine had flowed freely, and several of the so-called officers were unsteady on their feet.

The air outside was cold, but refreshing after the reek of the ballroom. I folded my arms across my shoulders.

"Tell me more about the brooch Lady Mary is wearing," I said.

"Aye, the brooch. It was a plaid brooch once, ye ken; the Chief of Dunnoch bore it. After the Forty-five, when the family was near wiped out, some fule of a boy gave it to his betrothed, as if it were a lady's trinket, instead of the badge of a warrior. Since then it has been the betrothal gift of a Hamilton to his bride. Gavin had it from his mother. He was the favourite son, though not the eldest; Alan never cared for the old ways."

"I see."

"It pleases me sair to see the lad thinking of marriage," the old man went on thoughtfully. "It's a lonely life he's led all these years, casting off his friends when they would have helped him. But they're a fine proud lot, the Hamiltons; proud as Lucifer."

A cool wind stirred the bare branches of the willows. Shivers of cold ran up my bare arms, but I ignored them. In a voice I tried to make casual, I said, "The loss of his wife was a grievous blow to him, no doubt."

"That's as may be." Mr. Duncan's voice was gruff. "A blow, maybe. A blessing in disguise, I say."

"What do you mean?"

" 'Twas doomed from the first, that marriage. He took her secretly, against the wishes of his family. The daughter of a playactor she was, and with a reputation none too savoury. But there—she was bonny, and he—well, he was no' sae bad in his looks then, and the heir to Dunnoch, after Alan. No one expected Alan to wed, puir timid body that he was."

I hadn't expected to feel sorry for the woman who was once Gavin's wife. But I couldn't help but pity the young lovers, who had nothing against them but the girl's lack of family. Naturally, Mr. Duncan would share the prejudices of the older generation.

"Did you know her, after he brought her to Blacktower?"

"What, call on a drunken playactor's daughter?" Mr. Duncan hesitated; then he admitted, shamefacedly, "Maself, I might have gone, for Gavin's sake and old friendship. But Mrs. Duncan would have none of it. And, ye ken, they kept to themselves."

"Sixteen years ago . . . and you never knew her. Why

are you so harsh with the poor lady now?"

"I've no cause to be harsh with the dead," he answered slowly. "But—I've known Gavin since he was a bairn. I saw him change, from a laughing laddie with never a hard word for man nor beast, and the gentlest hands on a horse, into—what he is today. It was a transformation—black magic no, less. And it was she who changed him. But you only know him as he is now. You'll not understand."

I did understand. The few, simple words had created a picture so vivid that I could almost see it; perhaps I had always suspected that it had been there. We stood in silence, Mr. Duncan already regretting his impulsive words, and I seeing a phantom, bright against the blackness of the night—a dark-eyed, laughing boy with gentle hands and a clear, unscarred face.

When the shadow fell between us, we both started. Gavin stood in the French doors. If he had overheard, he gave no sign.

"Aileen is ready to leave, Duncan," he said calmly. "She asked me to find you."

Mr. Duncan fled, after the most perfunctory of farewells. I remained where I was, leaning against the balustrade, and Gavin joined me. He was carrying something over his arm; now he unfolded it and draped it around my shoulders. It was my shawl.

"Thank you," I said. "Do you want to leave now?"

"When you're ready. But we may have trouble removing Cousin Randall from the mad pursuit of pleasure. When I last saw him, he was in the supper room gorging himself."

His voice was the same—harsh, sardonic. The hand that lay on the balustrade beside mine wore the ugly black glove. I shivered, but not with cold. The shining phantom boy was gone. He had been gone for almost sixteen years.

"So," said Gavin, breaking the silence, "tomorrow you leave."

"Yes."

"What are your plans?"

"I have no plans."

I couldn't see his face clearly in the shadows, but I thought his eyebrows lifted in a familiar, mocking gesture.

"Cousin Randall has plans—enough for both of you."

"He can keep them to himself," I answered shortly, drawing the shawl closer about me and preparing to go in. Gavin's hand stopped me.

"Wait a moment. I want to talk to you."

"What is it?"

"Am I to understand that you havn't revised your original impression of Randall? Since you summoned him here to your rescue, you ought to be civil to him, at least."

"I didn't summon him. You know that."

"Yes, I know. But that makes his gallant gesture all the more romantic. Not duty, but love, called him over the mountains to your side."

I no longer wanted to cherish sentimental memories of Gavin's youth. I wanted to slap him. I framed a withering retort and prepared to deliver it; but, to my consternation, out came words I had never planned to say.

"Why are you saying these things?" I whispered.

He turned so that I saw only the back of his head.

"I don't know. Because I'm only human, I suppose. No, Damaris, don't go in yet. I wanted to know whether you had any alternative to Randall, and whether you wanted an alternative. Don't—don't worry. I'll speak with you tomorrow morning, before you leave."

"Why not tonight?"

"For reasons of my own which I find good and sufficient," he said curtly, without turning.

It was too much. I could feel my self-control cracking.

"Your reasons—always yours! Don't you ever think of anyone but yourself? Are other people only objects, chess pieces, to be moved to and fro according to your whims?"

He turned, putting out his hand. "Damaris—please don't—"

"Please don't!" I mimicked him savagely. "Why don't you let go, and say what you really think? I intend to! Just for once, I mean to have the infinite satisfaction of speaking my mind. Oh, I know I have no reason to reproach you. You've always been the perfect gentleman, haven't you?"

"Be still," he said, in a voice that shook despite his efforts to control it. "Someone will hear you."

"I don't care! So, I'm not to worry, am I? Have you made arrangements for me? You're no better than Randall —passing me about like a piece of furniture, or a horse, or—I hate you both! Oh, God, if I were only a man and could—could—"

"That, my dear, is a wish I can't share," said Gavin and I finally identified the emotion that shook his voice. He was laughing.

I forgot where I was and who I was. I forgot everything but my rage. Words came into my mind that I never realised I knew, and I lifted my clenched fists to strike at him. He took me by the shoulders and shook me until my hair came unbound and hung down my back.

I was crying by then, but they were tears of rage, and when he pulled me into his arms I tried to bite them. He stopped my mouth with his, in a kiss that drew blood; he caught my flailing hands and twisted them behind me. And even while I raged, and struggled, and writhed, some hidden, shameless part of me revelled in the struggle, and in the way he subdued it, breaking my body and my will to his.

When at last he raised his head I lay against him, spent and shaking, and, as my agonised breath quieted, I could hear him speaking in disjointed phrases against my hair.

"You wish you were a man, do you? That would be a waste—a terrible waste. Do you let Cousin Randall kiss you like this? I hope not. It's a shameless way to behave, Damaris . . . Damaris?"

"What?" I murmured, against his shoulder.

"Cousin Randall. Do you let him kiss you like this?"

"I don't let him kiss me at all."

"Good. See that he doesn't." His arms tightened. "Randall can't have you. You belong to me. How do you like that, you fiery feminist?"

I replied, but not in words. For some moments the conversation was too chaotic to be reported.

Finally I withdrew—not far—and asked breathlessly, "Are you convinced now—that Randall need not worry you?"

"I should be." He laughed softly. "But men, Damaris, are irrational animals. When I think of you and Randall together in the carriage tomorrow—by heaven, I'll tie the fellow to a horse with my own hands."

Even in the circle of his arms the wind grew colder. "The carriage," I repeated, falteringly. "But—you don't mean to send me away . . . not tomorrow . . ."

"You must go. Tomorrow." His mouth brushed mine as gently as the wind. But I felt his will, unchanged, inflexible.

"You can't. You can't ask me to leave you."

"You must go. Tomorrow."

The cold was not only in the air, it was inside me. I tried to draw away from him.

"Then—you're playing with me. You do mean to marry her."

He had resisted my efforts to withdraw. But at those words his arms loosened. "Marry—her? My God, Damaris, what are you saying?"

"I knew it," I said, watching his face, with its clear-cut look of disgust. "I knew there was something. What hold has she over you, Gavin? Why did you give her the brooch? Or did you give it to her?"

The moon hung over the dark treetops. It was cold and remote; a dead, silver world. The pale beams shone on his face. I watched the play of emotion across it, and saw it twist, finally, into a look of agonised mockery.

"Yes. I gave it to her."

"Why?"

He let his arms fall and turned away with a groan. "Damaris, you mustn't ask questions."

"Is it because of your wife?"

"What do you mean?"

148

"Oh, Gavin, can't you ever trust anyone? Don't you know the tales they tell in the village, about how your wife died? Lady Mary knows them. What else does she know?"

"My wife," he repeated dully. "Is that what you think, Damaris? That I killed her?"

"No, no! You couldn't do such a thing."

"But if I had?" His voice was very quiet. "How would you feel about me then?"

"It doesn't matter what you do," I said; and I knew I spoke the naked truth. "Or what you've done. I'll go on loving you till the day I die."

He drew a deep, shaken breath, but made no move to touch me.

"Trust me, then, just for a little while. It won't be long, I swear; and then—"

He stopped, staring past me out into the pinewoods. The fine beauty of the night was passing. Veils of cloud obscured the moon, and the wind was bitter cold. I shivered, even in my shawl. Then I saw what Gavin had already seen; a shadow dragging itself slowly out of the shadow of the pines.

Gavin vaulted the low balustrade and ran towards the stumbling figure. It struggled upright, and then the moon came out from behind the clouds and shone on the staggering body of Ian the groom.

I gathered up my skirts and ran towards the steps at the end of the terrace. When I reached them, Ian had collapsed on to the ground. Gavin knelt beside him, supporting his shoulders. The fallen man's broad chest heaved in and out like that of a winded horse. Along one side of his face was a long dark streak, like a scar. I looked again, and saw that it was dried blood, from a cut along the hairline.

The groom's eyes were closed when I came up; but as I dropped to my knees beside him he forced them open and caught at the arm that supported him.

"Miss Annabelle," he gasped, fighting for breath. "They've—taken her!"

CHAPTER 11

I FOUND my handkerchief and wiped Ian's face. It was streaming with perspiration, despite the chill of the night.

"Who has taken her?" I asked.

"The one they call—Sir Andrew."

The effort took all the breath he had husbanded, and he fell to panting again.

"Good heavens—have you run all the way here from Blacktower?" I exclaimed.

"Aye. The blackguard—loosed the horses. Donald—was in his pay."

"But—" I tried to sort out my tumbled thoughts. "But Sir Andrew is here."

"Have you seen him recently?" Gavin spoke for the first time. His voice was calm, but I recoiled at the sight of his face. "No, I think he left soon after the first dance. Ian, lad, I must know a little more. Save your breath as much as you can. Did Miss Annabelle go with him willingly?"

Ian nodded.

Gavin's face was stone hard. "But how?" he muttered. "We have the coach, and she—"

Ian plucking at his sleeve. "She was walking, master. He mounted her on horseback—and they rode off."

Then I remembered, and went sick with regret and shame. "Oh, Gavin—she was trying to walk! She has been trying for weeks. And I knew, and didn't tell you!"

He glanced at me coldly. "No time for that now. So she could walk. But I think that trip, on horseback, will be hard for her. How long ago, Ian? Were the two of them alone?"

"I dinna ken—the time. There was anither mon, a stranger—he struck me down—when I fought with Sir

Andrew. I lay for a time—not long—then I came here."

"An hour," Gavin muttered, "or two. But they must go slowly. There may be time ... Take care of him, Damaris."

He was gone, running fleetly towards the front of the house. Ian struggled to his feet, pushing at the hands with which I would have restrained him.

"Na, mistress. I'm no' hurt. Only winded—and that's passing."

He followed his master, and I followed him; so we were in time to see what was happening at the front terrace. A broad beam of light spilled out through the open door where Lady Mary stood, bidding farewell to her departing guests. An antiquated carriage stood at the steps, and at its window I saw the lined face of Mrs. Duncan. Her husband already had his foot in the stirrups of his horse.

Gavin picked the little man up and set him aside. In one movement, so wild and beautiful that it sent my heart up into my throat, he swung himself into Mr. Duncan's saddle and turned the horse with a force that brought it up on its haunches. Then he was off, pounding along the road to Blacktower.

Poor Mr. Duncan was still standing on one foot, staring, when the horse and rider disappeared into the darkness.

"What? What?" he stammered, as I ran up to him.

"Oh, Mr. Duncan, you must help! Miss Annabelle has eloped with Sir Andrew. Mr. Hamilton has gone after them."

Then I saw the mettle of which the Scot is made. Mr. Duncan—fat, middle-aged, scant of breath—turned without another word and pelted away towards the stables at the back of the house. He flung a word of command over his shoulder at his coachman, and the carriage rolled away with Mrs. Duncan's astounded face still framed in the window.

At the door Lady Mary stood still as a statue. Then she came down the stairs towards me, walking with slow grace.

"Do I hear aright?" she asked. "What has my brother done?"

"He has stolen Annabelle," I said. "A gentlemanly act towards a neighbour."

"There must be some mistake. The groom is lying."

I gave her a look of scorn, but didn't bother to contradict her. She had known all about the plan, I felt sure; she, of all people, would have noticed Sir Andrew's absence during the evening. In fact, I suspected that the ball had been designed for that very end. And Annabelle had made sure, with a subtlety that spoke of someone else's suggestion, that Mrs. Cannon was away from the house. Janet was the only one left to attend to the girl, and Janet was surely open to bribery. No doubt she had been in Sir Andrew's pay from the first.

Mr. Duncan came galloping around the corner of the house, mounted on one of Sir Andrew's horses. He had two others by the bridle. He drew rein by the steps just as the other guests, aroused by the noise, came out on to the terrace; and, with unerring aim, he called to the only two of them who might help him.

"Easton—Mr. Gordon! Sir Andrew's away wi' the lassie and Gavin after them. There'll be murder and worse if we canna catch them before he does. Hurry!"

There was a moment of shocked silence and then a babble of exclamations. Randall came rushing down the stairs to me. His face was still flushed, but he seemed almost sober.

"Good heavens, Damaris, is this true?"

"Yes, I fear so. Ian brought the news."

"But I thought Miss Hamilton was an invalid," said Randall.

"So did we all, and we were wrong. Oh Randall, don't waste time! Mr. Duncan is right. Gavin will kill him. Please hurry!"

"It's the most damnable thing I ever heard of," muttered poor Randall, wiping one hand across his hot forehead. "Oh, very well, Damaris, if you want me to go. But I must see you home first."

"No time for that," called Mr. Duncan, who had taken command of the expedition. "Here are the carriages. Easton, put your ladies in, and send them off home. Where's the old body who came wi' you, Miss Gordon? Get her inside, in God's name, and be off wi' you."

I ran up the stairs and seized Mrs. Cannon, who was blinking and shaking in the doorway, quite overcome by it all. I propelled her down the stairs at an undignified trot, and shoved her into the carriage amid a whirl of petticoats.

"My cloak!" came a wail from the dark interior; but I paid no heed.

"In with you," I said to Ian.

He tried to protest, but I paid no attention. I thrust him also into the carriage. I think he stepped on Mrs. Cannon, for I heard her shriek. Then I turned to Randall.

"Hurry, hurry!" I said again.

Easton was already mounted, and as I shoved Randall towards the third horse, Mr. Duncan also bade him make speed. I didn't wait to see them go. I climbed into the coach and shouted at the coachman. With a jolt the heavy vehicle lumbered into motion. Within a minute the three horsemen streamed past, overtaking us, and I heard the beat of galloping hooves before the sound was lost in the thunder of our own rapid progress.

I put my head out the window, at the risk of being brained by a branch, and looked back. I caught one flash of the scene, miniature and brightly lit, like a scene on a puppet stage—Lady Mary, her hair an aureole of bright gold, standing like a doll at the foot of the steps, while her motley guests crowded behind her in their tawdry laces and faded satins. Then the trees engulfed us and the scene vanished.

Never has a night passed so slowly. The minutes dragged by and the hours seemed like days. At first I found sufficient occupation in settling the disorganised household at Blacktower House. I got Mrs. Cannon into bed and out of my way, made sure that Ian was taken care of, and then tried to get a coherent story out of Betty.

She was oddly embarrassed, and reluctant to talk to me. I couldn't imagine why, for I had already discovered that it was her vigilance that had discovered the plot, and I was ready to praise her to the skies. But when I insisted that she sit down she perched on the edge of her chair, twisting her hands in her lap, and keeping her face averted. It took me a long time to find what the difficulty was, and then I understood her reluctance.

She and Ian had arranged to spend the night together. He was in her room when she went down to check on Annabelle, and that was why she had been able to summon him so quickly, before the eloping pair left the house.

When she realised that I was going to accept this part of the story without comment (who was I, after all, to censure her?) she relaxed and spoke freely.

She had been strongly affected by my request to "look after Miss Annabelle." The very meaningless of the words fixed them in her mind, and they didn't leave even after she and Ian (here she blushed furiously) were together in the darkness. At last, moved more by irritation than by any other impulse, she had gone tiptoeing out to listen at Annabelle's door.

She found Sir Andrew there, with Annabelle, hooded and cloaked, in his arms.

She got out one scream before Sir Andrew, dropping Annabelle unceremoniously into a chair, leaped on her and covered her mouth. But the alarm had been given. Ian came rushing down the stairs. Seeing her struggling with an intruder, he had leaped to her aid.

"He would have had the rascal," said Betty, weeping with the memory, "but for the other man. He was on the lower stairs. He came on Ian like a fury and struck the poor lad down."

With Ian out of the way and the other male servants

(who were not worth much in any case) snoring in their own part of the house, the rest was easy. The miscreants had bound Betty to a chair and gagged her; then they had simply walked out.

"He carried the lassie down the stairs," Betty whispered. "She looked at me over his shoulder, and laughed. Her arms were about his neck and she kept giving him little kisses on his cheek. I never thought Miss Annabelle had so little heart! She must be a wicked girl."

"She knew you would come to no harm," I said feebly.

"Ah, but with Ian lying on the floor in his blood and me choking on that dirty cloth they put in my mouth—No, it was wicked!"

"None of the other servants tried to stop them?"

"Why, miss, they're off in the back of the house; I doubt that they heard anything. I only saw that wench Janet. She was in with them; she went along behind Miss Annabelle.

"I thought so. And the other groom?"

"Oh, aye, he was in it too."

Ian, merely stunned by the blow, soon recovered and freed Betty. After ascertaining that she was unhurt, his first thought was to warn his master. He ran down to the stables, but found them empty, and the courtyard gates wide open. Donald, the second groom, was counting a pile of silver coins by the light of a lantern. When he saw Ian, who must have presented a fearful spectacle with his bloody head and enraged face, he did not stay to talk, but followed the horses out of the gateway and into the night. So Ian had set out, like the hero he was, to run to Glengarrie.

"You should be very proud of him, Betty," I said. "And you—your fidelity is beyond praise. I had no reason to expect you to look after Annabelle. I don't even know why I said that."

"You have second sight, miss. Something told you she would be in danger."

"Come now, Betty," I said, glad of a chance to smile at

some event that terrible night, "you aren't a Scot; surely you don't believe in the superstition of the second sight."

"Oh, miss, it's not superstition. Ian told me of his grandmother—"

"It is always the grandmother," I interrupted, smiling. "Never mind, Betty. Second sight, or instinct, or whatever you wish to call it, it served us well tonight. At least —I hope so."

I sent her to bed, and sat alone in the drawing room. The slow hours dragged on; the candles guttered and grew dim. I had opened the curtains and flung one window wide so that I might hear the first sounds of someone coming. The air was bitter cold and the darkness so profound that it seemed to overflow into the room like a thick black fog, lying in folds on the floor and piling up in corners beyond the feeble light of the candle flames. Huddled by the dying fire, I lost track of time. But it was still pitch black outside the windows when I heard horses approaching.

I staggered to my feet, my limbs cramped with long sitting, and ran to the window. Strain my eyes as I might, I could see nothing. The slow hoofbeats came nearer—up to the door—and stopped. I ran to the door and tugged at the bolts. My fingers were stiff with cold, and with fear. There were only two horses. Three men had followed Gavin; three horses had preceded him. Where were the others? And—which of them had come back?

There was no sound outside the door, no knock, no voice requesting entrance. The bolts seemed glued into place. At last they yielded, and I flung the portal wide.

Lady Mary stood on the stairs.

She looked like a fairy woman in her hood and cloak of green, with her cold, fair face. A man behind her held a lantern; in its light the green-yellow folds of the cloak shone like leaves with the sun on them. I recognised the lantern bearer as one of the mock-colonels I had met at the ball. I started to close the door.

"Wait." Her voice was imperious. "Will you leave me

outside on such a night?"

"I'll not have that man in the house."

She laughed. "Go around to the stables, Jack," she ordered her companion. "The young lady has taken a dislike to you, it seems. Stay—give me the lantern, lest you set the place afire."

He muttered sullenly, but obeyed. Lady Mary held the lantern high, so that its rays fell on her face and mine.

"Well, Damaris Gordon? Are you afraid to let me in?"

In silence I stepped back, and she entered.

I led her into the drawing room and crouched by the fire. I was chilled to the bone by those brief moments at the open door, but the lady, laying her light cloak aside, seemed unconscious of the cold. She went at once to the window and stood looking out. Her slim figure was rigid; it was as if she commanded the night to produce some sign. At last the slender shoulders slumped, and she turned away from the mute darkness with a little sigh.

"Sit by the fire," I said, moved to pity despite my dislike. "You must be cold."

"Not from the air." But she came and stood holding out her white hands to the coals. "Where are they now, do you suppose?"

"I can't even guess. I wish I could."

There was much we might have said, so much that neither of us could begin. One picture filled my mind, so sharply that it seemed printed on the white painted walls. Mr. Duncan and the others had been ten minutes behind, and Gavin rode like a centaur. He would catch up with the fugitives before the others could arrive, and what then? There had been murder in his face when he rode away from Glengarrie, but they were two to one. At this moment Gavin might be lying dead beside the lake. In my mind that was how I saw him, with his face upturned towards the stars and blood staining the ruffles of his shirt, while Annabelle and her lover rode on through the pass to safety.

So we sat together while the hours dragged by on leaden feet—two women who had no cause to love one another, yet bound together by a common fear. The first pale streaks of dawn were in the sky before we heard the horses coming home.

I got to my feet, and found I could move no farther. My limbs felt frozen. The hoofbeats came closer; there were many of them, it was the right party now. Lady Mary sat motionless, staring into the dead fire as if she had heard nothing.

At last I heard the voices, among them the one voice for which I was listening. Relief weakened me so that I had to catch hold of a table or I would have fallen. The outer door opened, and slammed. There was a tramp of booted feet in the hall. Then Gavin came into the drawing room, carrying his daughter in his arms.

She was so limp and wan that I thought she had fainted, but when he deposited her in a chair she sat up and opened her eyes. They didn't look at her father, but went, like iron pulled by a magnet, to the man who had entered the room after them.

At the sight of her brother, Lady Mary leaped up and ran to him. They did not embrace, but merely clasped hands. Then she stood beside him, facing Gavin. It was a rather gallant gesture. They might be united in mischief, but united they certainly were.

Randall followed Sir Andrew into the room and closed the door. He was much the worse for wear. His fine black broadcloth was grey with dust; his cravat was twisted under his ear, and his hair stood straight up on end.

"I feel like one of the devil-ridden peasants in the fairy tales," he muttered, rubbing red-rimmed eyes. "Damaris, you might pour me a glass of brandy. What a hellish ride!"

"Where are the others?" I asked, going to the sideboard and taking out a decanter and glasses.

"I sent them home," Gavin answered. "And General Marlborough, or whatever he calls himself, with them. He'll be all the better for a few days in the cellar at Duncan's place."

"You have no right to imprison him," said Lady Mary calmly.

"No?" Gavin tossed the word over his shoulder, without looking at her. "I see no one capable of preventing me."

"I warned you, Gavin—" she began.

He cut her off with a violent gesture of his hand.

"Be still! You warned, and you promised, and you lied —as I might have known you would. I'll not trust your word again."

I poured drink for all of them, thinking they must need a stimulant. Gavin took the glass I handed him and offered it to Annabelle.

She struck it out of his hand. The liquid spilled in a tawny flood and the glass fell, shattering, on to the floor.

"Charming," said Gavin ironically. "I begin to suspect, Annabelle, that my paternal efforts to save you from the classic degradation were not welcome."

She shot him one dreadful glance, and Sir Andrew, clearing his throat, stepped forward.

"Mr. Hamilton, I resent your words. Your daughter and I—"

"Were fleeing to the nearest minister of the gospel. I'm damned sure you were. Save your speeches, you young swine, until my daughter is out of the room. Randall—"

Randall gave a start and juggled the glass, which nearly fell from his fingers. He had been staring at Annabelle with a mixture of astonishment and—yes, it was admiration. I had forgotten that he had never seen her.

"Yes, Gavin?"

"I regret more than I can say that you have been dragged into this noisome business. Will you do me one further service? I have business with Sir Andrew. If you would carry my daughter to her room—"

"Certainly. A pleasure."

Randall advanced, grinning self-consciously, and then froze as Annabelle began to shout.

"I'm not going to my room! I'm staying here! I'll leave

159

this house; you can't keep me; this is Scotland, not black Africa! Do you think you can lock me up like a prisoner, in this day and age? Do you think you can keep me from the only happiness I've ever known? I love him! I will marry him, I will, I will, I will—"

Gavin struck her across the face.

The blow was slight, and had the desired effect, of cutting off her now unintelligible shrieks. Still, it was an unattractive action. Sir Andrew stepped forward, flexing his arms, and even Randall emitted a little cluck of shocked surprise.

"Take her up, Randall," said the Master. "Damaris, show him the right room."

Randall circled his victim cautiously; but she had now collapsed into a sobbing huddle of pink silk, and he could lift her up without provoking any further hysterics. I led the way up the stairs, and, at my direction, Randall put her gently on her bed. The room was cold. I had forgotten that Janet was gone. I would have to tend to the girl myself.

"Light the fire, will you, Randall?" I asked, and began to strip off Annabelle's slippers and stockings.

Randall did as I asked. Then he tiptoed towards the bed and stared in fascination at Annabelle's face. She lay limp against the pillows, her features shrunken amid a tangle of yellow hair. But from the look in Randall's eyes I realised that he was seeing a Sleeping Beauty.

"Is there anything else in which I may serve you, Miss Hamilton?" he asked.

"No," I said, knowing she wasn't going to answer him. "Go to bed, Randall, do. You must be exhausted."

"Yes, I am," he said sulkily, remembering his grievances. "Damaris, this is all your fault. What are we doing, embroiled in this mess? You should never have come here, I told you so."

"For pity's sake, Randall—go to bed!"

I turned my back on him and began removing Annabelle's dress. Randall vanished.

I had begun to suspect, long before that, that I would never love Annabelle. Still I couldn't help but see her point of view. As I wrestled grimly with stays and petticoats, getting no help at all from the limp shape that was Annabelle, I had to admit that, in her eyes, we had behaved like ogres. Why shouldn't she have the young idiot if she wanted him? I didn't—and don't—hold with the feeble doctrine that any sort of husband is better than none. But for a romantic noodle like Annabelle, the doctrine might well be true.

By the time I finished putting her to bed I knew that she was only pretending to be unconscious in order to inconvenience me. I was perspiring with the effort of moving her about, and I shoved her between the sheets rather unceremoniously. The last rough jerk wrung a childish *"Ow!"* from her, and I couldn't help laughing. It was a strained, miserable laugh, but it relieved my feelings.

"Annabelle," I said, taking her limp hand in mine, "child, don't be too hard in your thoughts. Why didn't you tell your father how you felt, instead of running away like a little fool? Now you've only angered him."

"I had to run away. He wouldn't let me marry Andrew."

"Why not?"

She shrugged angrily. "Oh, he said something—some lie—about Andrew not being a gentleman. As if I cared!" Her mouth curved in an odd little smile, and the tip of her tongue crept out between her lips. I dropped her hand, feeling strangely repelled. "The real reason he won't let me marry Andrew is because he hates me, and always has. He doesn't want me to be happy."

"He doesn't want you to be miserable!" I said angrily. "He knows what's best for you. Sir Andrew is a—a rascal!"

She studied me dispassionately. "What a fool you are, Damaris. You love my father, don't you? You believe everything he tells you; you fawn on him like a dog. Well, after today you won't see him ever again. That hurts, doesn't it? Try telling yourself it's all for the best; why don't you?" She laughed—an ugly sound that went through me like a knife. "Oh, I know how you feel. But I've got hope; I'll get to Andrew somehow, and soon. Nothing can keep us apart! But you—you're going away. You won't see him again. Not ever!"

She wasn't hysterical; I couldn't slap her. But I couldn't sit there and listen any longer, either. The words did hurt, although I knew they weren't true.

My hand was on the doorknob when she spoke one final sentence that sent the blood rushing into my head, "Andrew is a better swordsman; he studied in Paris."

I spun around.

"What are you saying?"

"Fool, fool, fool!" She lifted herself up in bed and spat the words out. "What did you think would happen, after the things he said to Andrew? Why do you think he sent you away? What do you suppose they're doing down there, *now*?"

CHAPTER 12

WITHOUT waiting to hear more, I ran out and down the stairs. The drawing room was deserted. I ran back up and pounded on Randall's door. A sleepy muttering finally answered me.

"Come at once," I called. "Something terrible is happening!"

I heard the bedsprings creak as he arose, swearing, but I couldn't wait for him. I had to find them. Already it might be too late.

There was a shuffling of feet behind me. I turned. Angus stood at the head of the stairs.

I seized him by his coat sleeve. The fabric was so greasy my finger slipped. "Where are they? You know; I can tell by your face."

"Aye, I ken," said Angus, grinning.

"Where? Tell me!"

"I'll not," said Angus, and spat.

I could feel my face change. I don't know what it looked like, but the effect must have been startling. Angus cringed away from me and swallowed his smile.

"Down there," he muttered, pointing.

At the end of the hall, a heavy oak door shut off the West Wing from the older house. I wrenched it open and ran, my feet echoing on the dusty wooden planking of the long corridor.

Then I heard voices. They were hard to locate, and I began trying one door after another. The third one opened on to the minstrel's gallery, high above the Great Hall. The gallery faced east; through the high windows streamed the light of dawn, transmuted into sickly saffron and pale scarlet by the stained glass. The colours cast an eerie glow over the two men who stood facing one another in the centre of the hall.

They were almost of a height; Gavin topped the younger man by less than an inch. His back was towards me, but I could see Sir Andrew clearly. He was posing again. One hand rested on his hip, and the other twirled his moustache.

"That is my final offer," Gavin said, as I came on the scene. "Do you accept it or not?"

Sir Andrew hesitated, glancing around the room as if in search of an answer. Neither of them had heard me enter. The balustrade of the gallery was so high I had to stand on tiptoe to see Gavin, who was almost directly below me. Then, from a spot I couldn't see, came another voice.

"He rejects your offer, as you call it," said Lady Mary. "Gavin, don't be a fool. You have nothing with which to bargain."

"You forget Annabelle. I'll sink her in the pool before I'll let him have her."

The passionate contempt of his tone turned me cold. Sir Andrew went white, and then crimson.

"How dare you speak that way to me?" he demanded.

"Why, I think I've been quite restrained up till now," said Gavin in a lazy voice that was utterly offensive. "I've not called you any of the things I'd like to call you. Coward—cheat—liar—"

In spite of my dislike for Sir Andrew, I couldn't help but admit he was responding well to what could only be deliberate provocation.

"I will give you one chance to withdraw those words," he said, flushing.

"I withdraw nothing."

"Then you leave me no alternative. One of my friends will call upon you."

I had never realised how young Sir Andrew was, until I saw how he smiled with satisfaction at his grandiloquent words.

"Oh, no." Gavin leaped atop the carved oak chest by the fireplace. When he jumped down he held a fencing foil in each hand. "We'll settle the matter now. These blades are dusty, but they will serve."

Sir Andrew recoiled a step. Oh, I'll give him his due; I don't think he was afraid. But at that moment he was the civilised man, and Gavin the barbarian. In his archaic dress and pleated kilt, with a naked blade in each hand, the Master looked like one of the savage horde who had followed the Stuarts howling a battle cry.

"Unless," he said deliberately, "you are afraid."

Sir Andrew's lips writhed in a snarl, but still he didn't move. Then Lady Mary came into view, advancing slowly, with her azure, rose-trimmed skirts billowing around her.

"Go on, Andrew," she said. "This may be the best way after all."

My paralysis broke. "Gavin," I cried. "You're out of your mind. Stop it!"

"Go to your room," said Gavin, in a voice he might have used to his dog.

The gallery was small; there were no stairs down into the hall. I would have to go back and down and around to reach them, and by the time I traced that lengthy path they would have begun.

Gavin held out one of the foils and Sir Andrew took it. I knew, by the way his hand fitted itself around the hilt, that Annabelle was right; he did know how to fence. I looked at Gavin's black-gloved fingers, on the hilt of his own weapon; and then I remembered that two of those fingers were only cotton. Dear Heaven, I thought wildly, he can't hold a foil in that hand; Andrew will disarm him with the first pass. I gathered up my skirts and turned to run.

The doors at the far end of the hall creaked and swung open. Through the crack peered Randall's sleepy, inquisitive face.

"Good morning," he said, blessedly inane. "Is something wrong?"

"God Almighty," said Gavin furiously. "You, too? Is this a stage performance? Get out of here, Randall."

"Randall, stop them," I cried, tiptoeing. "They mean to fight."

"So I observe." Randall closed the doors carefully behind him and advanced into the hall. "Gavin, are you out of your senses? Duelling is outlawed in this civilised state, whatever the custom may be in such places as France. You may incur a legal charge."

I groaned aloud. It was the most halfhearted plea for reason I had ever heard.

"Lady Mary," Randall continued, bowing, "do help me put some sense into these two."

"You are a gentleman, Mr. Gordon," said Lady Mary, turning the full magic of her smile and her eyes upon him. "You heard the terms Mr. Hamilton used to my brother earlier. Now that you're here—why don't we let them get it out of their systems?"

She laughed gently, reducing the whole affair to a sparring match between two angry little boys, and Randall's chest expanded visibly.

"I expect you're right," he said, fingering his cravat. "A little exercise, just to calm them . . . I'll stay, to ensure fair play."

"Fair play? Do you think this is a game?" Gavin pulled off his coat and threw it on the floor; with one impatient hand he wrenched his collar open. "Come sir, *en garde*. Let's be at this before the rest of the household arrives."

Andrew bowed. He removed his own coat and stood waiting.

I picked up my skirts and fled. There was only one way to stop them now—to put myself physically between them.

My velvet skirts weighed like lead, when I would have flown. Once again, I came near regretting my sex. If I had been a man I could have run unhampered along the unending corridors, and descended the stairs in three bounds. If I had been a man I could have stopped them —and I would have stopped them, instead of muttering and looking pompous, like Randall! They were mad, all of them, with the strange masculine insanity that prefers bloodshed to reason, violence to talk. Gavin's sullen arrogance, Sir Andrew's impudence, and Randall's pomposity—I don't know whch I hated most.

I fell on the stairs and rolled down half the long flight before I could stop myself. I was up again, and running, almost before I stopped rolling. The door under the stairs resisted my strength; I swung on it with my whole weight until it gave, with a shriek of rusty hinges. Rust on the hinges, rust on the sword blades; they had not been used for years. The boy had been in Paris; they had academies there to teach the art of fencing, the French regarded it as brave and chivalrous.

Even before I reached the hall I knew I was too late. There was no mistaking the sharp ring of steel on steel.

The sun was above the mountains now. It made a dazzle in the hall, and turned the slender steel blades into wheels of fire.

Gavin was still on his feet; more, he was holding his own. They must have crossed swords as soon as I left the gallery, for both of them were already breathing hard. Sir Andrew moved carefully, as if a first, unsuccessful attack had taught him to respect his opponent. They circled warily, the movements of their feet matching like steps in a dance. Forward and back; left and back. The blades touched coyly, with a gentle chiming sound.

Then there was a flurry of movement and a bright musical crash whose echoes rang among the rafters. Sir Andrew bounded back, his shoulders hunched; and Randall, clearing his throat, lifted one arm.

"Halt!" he called. "First blood!"

Gavin gave him a sardonic look, but lowered his point obediently. Sir Andrew, head bent, was examining a narrow trickle of red on the fine lawn of his shirt sleeve. Randall started forward, but the boy waved him back.

"It's only a scratch," he muttered.

"Still, sir, you are wounded. I think the demands of honour are met."

"Honour be damned," said Gavin, almost before Randall

was finished speaking. "Again, Andrew—unless you've thought better of it."

I turned to the woman who stood near me, watching the scene with detached interest. "Hasn't this gone far enough?" I asked. "If Andrew refuses to go on, there won't be any more fighting. You can stop him, if you will."

Her head pivoted on her slim white throat. She didn't look at me, but at some ineffable vision in the air beyond me; and the look on her face turned me cold.

"Oh, no," she said gently. "I've no intention of stopping him."

Sir Andrew was turning back his cuff to keep the blood from trickling down on to his hand. There was still time. I darted forward.

Lady Mary's hand shot out and ringed my wrist. There was the strength of a man's in her slender arm. I struggled, plucking at the long pale fingers with all my strength; but the moment's delay had been enough.

The blades rang together. There was a difference in the sound, and in the men. Their movements were quicker and more violent. The steel chimed like a carillon of bells. Gavin's dark hair curled damply on his forehead; he tossed it back with an impatient jerk of his head. Five minutes...ten. They seemed like as many hours. Gradually Gavin began to lose ground. His feet never lost their precision, but step by step they retreated.

I stood still, held by the woman's delicate hand with its iron fingers, and by the deadly beauty of the duel. The muscles of Sir Andrew's back and sword arm moved with an animal's refined grace under the thin cambric of his shirt. It was hard to believe that the responsive agility of the two bodies was designed for murder, or that death could hang on anything so beautiful as the two slim, shining blades.

Sir Andrew advanced, forcing the pace, and Gavin turned. I could see Sir Andrew's face now. His moustache had lost its curl; it veiled a mouth set in a humourless white grimace. His eyes were narrowed to slits.

Gavin leaped back to escape a vicious thrust which he was unable to parry. The blade passed within inches of his left side. Perspiration streaked his face and ran down his bared throat, soaking his shirt. Back, and always back. He was moving clumsily now, and was wholly on the defensive. He didn't try to attack; it was all he could do to parry Sir Andrew's thrusts. The fifteen years between them were telling. Sir Andrew was breathing hard, but his arm seemed tireless.

Then the end came. Gavin's sword arm drew back, in a gesture so awkward that even a novice could see the danger he was in. It left his right side completely exposed. I gave a stifled shriek and fought the restraint of Lady Mary's hand; and as I cried out, Sir Andrew's blade went home.

For a moment—surely not more—while his foil was sheathed in flesh and muscle, he was weaponless and off guard, and in that moment Gavin's blade completed the circle it had begun. He went back, and then forward, all in one movement, tearing Sir Andrew's sword from the wound and extending his body in a long lunge that made arm and sword one line. The line ended in Andrew's breast. I saw the tip come out through the boy's back.

For the space of a long heartbeat spectators and duellists were frozen. Gavin's body was still extended in the deadly grace of the thrust, and Andrew stood upright like a beetle impaled by a pin. Then Gavin withdrew. Over Andrew's face came a look of childish surprise. His eyes were still open, inquiring, as he started to fall.

Lady Mary made a sound deep in her throat. When I looked at her I saw that her proud face had crumpled like wet paper. With a shriek of "Andrew! Andrew!" she darted towards him, and was in time to throw her arms about his shoulders as his body folded. She went down with him, dragged by his weight. His head lay on her lap as she crouched on the dusty floor, with her rumpled skirts making a bright blue pool of colour around her. She pressed her hands to his pale cheeks, moaning.

It was a terrible sound. It pierced the heart. I went to her, walking on limbs that felt wooden and weak at the same time, but before I could touch her Randall brushed me away with a brusque, "This is no place for ladies, Damaris!" Later, this comment was to strike me with ironic amusement, but then it seemed uncommonly apropos. I looked down at the wounded man. He didn't look wounded; he looked dead. There was no colour left in his face, it seemed to have concentrated in the crimson stain on his breast. He looked very young, like a boy asleep. I forgot that, a few minutes earlier, those closed eyes had been as sold and feral as an animal's. Lady Mary's sobs wiped out my former dislike of her. There was pity and anger in my heart as I turned from the victim to the murderer.

Gavin's scar stood out like a fresh brand. Save for that fiery mark his face was as white as his shirt. His right hand was still clenched on the sword hilt; the other clasped his wounded arm, so tightly that the cambric of his shirt bulged out above the black-gloved fingers. His eyes were riveted on his fallen opponent, and on his face was an expression of bitter regret.

Under that look my anger melted. "Gavin, Gavin, don't be grieved. Perhaps he can be saved."

"He can be saved. The thrust was too high. Too high." Gavin flung the blade away with a savage movement that sent it clattering across the flagstones. "The devil take me for a blundering fool—it was too high!"

"You—*meant* to kill him?"

His eyes focused on my face, and I shrank away from what I saw in them. "Good God, are you still here? Get out. Take your jackanapes of a lover, and go."

"Go where, Gavin?"

"Castleton, Edinburgh, London, I don't care where. Just get out."

"You want me to leave Blacktower House," I said stupidly.

"At last you grasp my meaning." He blinked, and I

thought he swayed a little. But the whole room was suddenly unsteady; the floor swung to and fro under my feet.

"This is no place for you, Damaris," he said less violently. "It's not a place for any decent Christian soul."

"Wherever you are is the place for me," I said desperately. I was past caring whether I was overheard, by Randall or Lady Mary. At my words Gavin's face smoothed out and hardened. The corners of his mouth, twisted by the scar, lifted in an unpleasant smile.

"By God, I believe you took me seriously last night," he exclaimed. "I've underestimated my own talents!"

I felt the blood draining out of my cheeks, but I was incapable of speech. I stood staring dumbly at him while his eyes raked me from head to foot with an intolerable amusement.

Then he said, "Stay, if you want to. But in justice to both of us I ought to remind you that I never mentioned marriage."

I raised my hand and struck him across the face. He staggered back a few steps at the blow, as he had not done under Andrew's thrust. The marks of my fingers took shape, redly, across the pallor of his unscarred cheek. His smile did not alter.

I turned, blindly, and found myself staring at Randall's crumpled shirt frills. He had heard then—heard everything. I didn't care. I didn't even care when he took my arm in one fat, possessive hand, and pulled me against him.

"The boy's not badly hurt," he said, in a voice that oozed satisfaction. "Get some of the servants, Damaris, to carry him upstairs."

"He'll find no shelter in my house," said Gavin coldly.

"He'll have to find it, whether you like it or not," Randall said, with a sneer. "If you pack him off he may die, and if he does—by heaven, I'll see you before a magistrate charged with murder, sir! Don't worry, we'll all be out of your hospitable house as soon as we can—eh,

Damaris?"

Gavin's brows came together in a scowl, but he did not reply. Randall ostentatiously turned his back and, towing me with him, returned to the little group on the floor. I went without demurring. It was rather pleasant to have someone to tell me what to do.

"Take care of the lady," Randall said in my ear. "Poor thing, she is quite distraught. Small wonder!"

She urged them on, I thought, but I didn't say it. What difference did it make, to try to allocate the blame for what had happened? They were alike, the three of them —brutal, murderous, false. Still, she was a woman, and she was near collapse. The face she turned up to me looked as old as Mrs. Cannon's.

"He will live," I said gently. "Come with me now, while the servants tend to him."

She rose obediently, stumbling like a feeble old woman. There was no bellpull in the hall, so I went to the door, put my head outside, and shouted for Angus at the top of my lungs. I thought he would be about—horrid old ghoul that he was—and when he made his appearance I gave the necessary orders.

Angus pushed rudely past me and looked on the scene of battle.

"He's no deid, then," he remarked in a disappointed voice.

"No one is dead," I snapped. "Get the men to come at once."

"Och, aye, the men are here," said Angus calmly. "They was all watchin', like maself."

I turned away from him in speechless disgust. Lady Mary would not come with me; she would not leave Andrew. So we waited until the men lifted him on to a small mattress in order to carry him easily. He was still unconscious; his golden lashes were like silk against his cheeks. There was a terrifying amount of blood on his white shirt, but since Randall and Gavin had both diagnosed the wound as not necessarily fatal, I assumed it looked worse than it was. I wasn't really much interested.

As the others crowded around the impromptu stretcher I saw Gavin making his way to the door. He was supporting himself with one hand against the wall, and his feet were unsteady. Something twisted painfully inside me, like a bad tooth coming back to life after sleep. I made myself turn away. He was no concern of mine. He had made that eminently clear.

It was Randall who tended the boy's wound, his hands moving with a competence that surprised me. Randall had his virtues, undoubtedly. It was a pity that none of them interested me.

There was nothing I could do for the lady, except have a cot moved into Andrew's room. She refused to leave him or to look at anything but his pale face. So we left them there together.

When we were out in the hall, Randall let out an enormous sigh. "What a mad night!" he said unoriginally. "You have plunged us into adventure, Damaris—with a vengeance!"

"I wish you would stop harping on my part in all this," I retorted. "Heaven knows it began innocently."

"Oh, of course." Randall patted my shoulder. "Well, we can't leave today, as we'd planned. That's out of the question, with the place in such a turmoil."

"We can't leave this house until Sir Andrew is out of it," I said.

"What?" Randall gasped for a moment. Then, displaying more mental quickness than I had expected, he stammered, "Do you really think Hamilton would ... Damn it all, Damaris, I don't like the scoundrel myself, but he wouldn't—"

"I didn't mean that," I said, knowing that I lied. "But half the servants have run away, and most of the others are worthless; Mrs. Cannon is of no use at all. With two wounded men and an invalid girl in the house, I can't simply walk out and leave them. If anything should happen—"

"Two? Oh, yes, Hamilton managed to get himself punctured, too. I'd forgotten. But, hell's bells, Damaris, it wasn't much of a wound; he walked out on his feet, didn't he?" Randall wrestled for a moment with his conscience, or some other organ; his face grew longer, and finally he groaned dismally. "I suppose you're right. If something *did* happen, and the story got about, our part in it might be misinterpreted—only by malicious people, mind you, but still—oh, hell!"

"I'm sorry, Randall. Get some sleep. You're tired, I know."

"Gad, yes. Might as well go to bed. Maybe this time," he added, with a wry humour which was new to him, "I'll be allowed to stay in it for a few hours. Good night, my dear. Or good morning, rather."

He kissed me on the cheek, rather absently, and ambled off down the hall scratching his head. With an emotion that was almost affection I watched his big awkward figure until it vanished around the turn in the corridor. Poor Randall; he did the best he could. To blame him for being insensitive and a little stupid was to damn him for being himself and not another man. If only he were someone else's husband, I thought, I might get to be quite fond of him. Just then, though, more than anything else, I envied him. He was going to lie down and go to sleep, untroubled by any emotion more grievous than vexation. I rather doubted that I would be able to sleep.

At least I could take off my dress. It weighed on my weary limbs like armour, and I hated the sight and feel of it. Someday—after I was Randall's pampered, wealthy wife—I would have another ball dress; perhaps even a velvet dress. But not green velvet.

I was turning into my room when I realised that the fourth door down from mine stood open. Someone was in the opening. The figure was hidden, but two thin pale hands were clamped around the doorframe, so tightly that even the nails were white.

I reached the girl just in time to keep her from falling.

174

As my arms went round her, her knees gave way and she fell heavily against me. She turned her head from where it lay against my breast, and looked up at me, her eyes enormous in her pale pinched face.

"Is he dead?" she whispered.

"No, oh, no! He's not dead, nor even badly hurt. Who told you?"

"No one. I heard them coming up the stairs. I was waiting . . . I saw him when they brought him up. Oh, God— I thought he was dead!"

She turned her face into my bosom and began to sob.

I had been through too much that night to be much moved by her tears. I half led, half carried her back into her room, and put her into her bed. Then I pulled away the hands she had lifted to her face and looked directly into her eyes.

"If he had been killed," I said, "it would have been your fault. You brought this on—you are the cause of it. If you hadn't tried to run away . . ."

She looked up at me, the tears still wet on her cheeks. "One of the reasons I hate you is because you're such a hypocrite. You know why I had to run away. My father was planning to send me to Edinburgh today—with you and Randall."

I stopped short in the midst of pulling up the pink satin coverlet.

"I didn't know! He never said a word to me."

"Well, he was. And now he can't." She grinned. "You can't go today, the place is in too much confusion. And before you can go I'll think of something else."

I finished tucking in the covers. "Do as you like," I said. "I haven't the faintest interest in you or in your father."

Once I was outside the door I wiped the perspiration from my face—perspiration that was not solely the product of exertion. So he had meant to send her away. I believed her, congenital liar that she was, simply because it was the sort of thing he would do. And that explained all the things he had said on the terrace at Glengarrie—the kisses, the words that melted my very bones. He couldn't send Annabelle away unless I went with her. My departure had been part of his plan all along.

I stood in the corridor, now bright with morning sunlight, and listened. There was not a sound, not even from behind Annabelle's closed door. I might have been in an abandoned house. The hall was bitter cold, despite the sunlight. The wet spot on the bosom of my dress, where Annabelle's tears had soaked in, felt like ice. There was another damp patch on the skirt; evidently I had slopped water from the basin I had carried to Randall for his surgical efforts. The front of the dress was grey with dust. Along the hem was a third patch of wet, darker and more matted than the others.

I went on down the hall, dragging a little, to do what I knew must be done. No one else would do it; no one else had even thought about doing it. From my early investigations I knew where the Master's room was located. I didn't even knock. I just turned the handle and walked in.

I had been wrong. Someone else had seen Gavin's face when he dragged himself out of the Hall. Angus, the faithful servant, had come to tend his wounded master.

Gavin was slumped in a chair, his head thrown back and his arms hanging. He seemed to be unconscious, for which I was devoutly thankful. Evidently he had reached his room, and the chair's support, before he collapsed; and Angus, instead of putting him to bed, had left him in that painful and impractical position. The old man had unbuttoned his shirt and dragged it off one arm and shoulder. When I walked in he was digging at the wound with a cloth so soiled and tattered that it might have been one of the housemaid's discarded dusters; the fingers that held the cloth were closer to water just then than they had been for months. Angus's ministrations had not improved matters noticeably; Gavin's bare arm was streaked with blood and dirty water, and a horrid-looking puddle had formed under his dangling hand.

I had thought I was too tired to feel anything again;

but I went for Angus like a fury. "Get hot water," I ordered, snatching the filthy rag from his hand. "Hot, mind you! And a sheet from the linen room. Hurry, you scoundrel!"

He gave me a scowl and a muttered curse, but he obeyed. I knelt down on the floor and lifted Gavin's arm on to his knees. I forgot about the puddle until it was too late, and then my limbs refused to lift me again. The dress was ruined in any case. . . .

There wasn't much I could do until Angus got back, but I found my handkerchief and wiped off most of the dirty water. Gavin was still wearing those damnable black gloves. The right one was soaked with water; I stripped it off and looked at the ruined hand, with its scarred stumps. No, not ruined; it had served him well that day, if not so well as he had hoped. Moved by some obscure impulse, I took his other hand, the one I had never seen ungloved, and freed it of its covering. There was no mark on it.

Finally I heard Angus's deliberate, shuffling steps in the hall. He was walking even more slowly than usual. I said nothing, but waited in formidable silence until he had deposited a basin of water and one of the best linen sheets on the floor beside me. Angus's only virtue was that he didn't make me feel I had to talk to him. But I waited until he was out of the room before I went to work.

Having watched Randall with Sir Andrew, I knew what to do, although I was awkward enough, heaven knows, and the water in the basin was boiling hot; but Gavin made no move or sound the whole time. Then I looked up and met his eyes, open and aware, and I was so startled that my fingers slipped from the end of the bandage.

"I didn't know you were awake," I stammered.

"I thought you'd run off in virtuous horror if I spoke, and on the whole, I prefer your ministrations to Angus's."

"Thank you," I said.

"It's not a great compliment. You're as clumsy as he is, and I'm sure you detest me as thoroughly. But your sadistic impulses are less well developed."

I finished tucking in the ends of the bandage. "I'll help you to bed," I said. "Try to stand."

He didn't like that; he would have preferred to walk by himself, arrogant and independent. But he was weaker than he thought, and he had to lean rather heavily on my shoulder. I ought to have enjoyed seeing him humbled, if only physically. I tried to tell myself that I pitied him—he would have hated that. Instead, like the meekest of his servants, I helped him to lie down, took off his boots, and covered him with a blanket.

Either he had exhausted his invective or he was tired of baiting a dumb stone that never responded, for when I was finished with him he pretended to be asleep. I knew the closed eyelids were only pretence; I could see conscious will in the hard, angry line of his mouth. His head was turned on the pillow so that the smooth, unscarred cheek was towards me. That night he had tried to murder a man, and he had failed only because his skill would not serve his intent. He had taught his own child to hate him, and had shamefully misused me. But as I stood looking down at the pale, rigid profile, the words I had spoken on the terrace at Glengarrie came back to my mind :

"No matter what you do, no matter what you've done —I'll go on loving you until the day I die."

CHAPTER 13

"Miss! Miss Damaris! Please wake up."

I was dreaming of fire and blackness. The fire was the thin flame of the candle held by Betty, who was shaking my shoulder urgently. The blackness hovered beyond the light; outside my windows night still lingered.

"What is it?" I muttered sleepily.

"I'm to pack for you, miss, at once." Betty's eyes, reflecting the flame, were wide with excitement. "You're to leave in an hour!"

I sat bolt upright. "What? Who says this?"

The Master, miss. And Mr. Randall." Betty put the candle down on the table and darted towards the wardrobe. Someone had infected her with haste; she tore my dresses from their hangers with rapid hands.

"But I can't leave! Mr. Hamilton is not yet well, and Sir Andrew—"

"Sir Andrew's gone, miss. Back to Glengarrie. Mr. Hamilton packed him into the carriage last night after you went to bed, willy-nilly, helter-skelter, and sent him off with the lady. He says you're to be away before dawn, and Mr. Randall's already packing."

The room was cold. No fire had been lit. Outside, the wind howled and knocked at the casements. I drew the covers up around my shoulders and watched, shivering, like someone in a dream, as Betty dragged my portmanteau out of its corner, blew the dust off the top of it, and began packing my dresses.

It was three days after the duel—Tuesday morning. Sir Andrew had lain abed, an unwilling and begrudged guest, all that time, and Lady Mary had stayed beside him. Her meals had been taken to her; I hadn't so much as seen her since the fatal morning. But I hadn't thought the boy would be well enough recovered to be moved, even by carriage. Not that Gavin would have cared about that. What scheme had he afoot now?

There was a brusque knock at the door, and Randall burst in, without waiting to be invited.

"Still abed?" he shouted. "Make haste, Damaris. What will you wear? It's bitter cold. This wool dress, I think, and your heaviest cloak. Good God, what drab clothes! We must see to that when we reach London."

"Randall, sit down for a moment and talk sense. What is happening?"

"We're leaving," he said. Then he added, with a gesture that stopped my incipient protest, "No, I don't know why our charming host has taken it into his head to evict us so suddenly. But it suits me admirably. I want to get out of this madhouse as soon as possible. I'd never have stayed if you—"

"Never mind that. Did you know he was planning this?"

"Ye gods, no! Not till an hour ago when he stalked into my room like a monk out of a horror tale, and bade me stir myself. But I didn't object." Randall laughed sarcastically. "No, indeed!"

"Sir Andrew is gone, then?"

"Yes." Randall stopped pacing and stared at me with the dim bewilderment of a child. "By heaven, Damaris, I've never seen such a thing—utterly heartless, I call it. As soon as you had gone to bed last night, Hamilton ordered out the coach. The boy wasn't in such bad shape," he admitted grudgingly. "Walked down on his own two feet, at any rate. Then into the carriage and away!"

He began to pace again. "Hurry, can't you?"

"I can't dress with you standing there," I muttered.

Randall gave me a blank look and then started. "Oh, gad, to be sure. I'll leave then."

I dressed hurriedly, my teeth chattering with cold. Betty, after packing my things, brought my breakfast. I couldn't eat, but the hot tea warmed my numb body a little. It had no effect on my frozen brain.

I hadn't finished buttoning my boots when Ian came for my boxes. He was dressed for out-of-doors, in heavy gloves and a coarse woollen cloak with a hood, such as many of the peasants wore.

"Are you going with us?" I demanded.

He nodded, woodenly. "I'm to drive the coach, mistress. We'd best hurry. I dinna like the look of the sky."

There was no sun that morning. When I reached the courtyard I entered a dead grey world, curtained in heavy clouds. The wind was like a knife, even in that sheltered place. I went quickly towards the shelter of the coach, and then stopped short. The coach was occupied. Mrs. Cannon's astounded pink face was at the window. Beyond her, I saw Annabelle's profile.

I stepped back, pulling the blowing folds of my mantle closer around me. I should have expected it. This had been Gavin's aim all along.

The door of the house banged, and Randall came out. He glanced at the threatening sky and groaned. "Snow before noon, I'll be bound. And I'm to ride! How the hell—"

A groom came up, leading his horse, and Randall, cursing, heaved himself into the saddle. Ian made his appearance with a heavy box, which he hoisted atop the coach and strapped into place. I thought his face looked grimmer than usual. But my mind was working slowly that morning. I had my foot on the step of the carriage before I thought of something.

"Ian," I said, "how long will it be before you get back here?"

"A week, mistress. I'm bidden to stay in Edinburgh."

His wooden face did not change expression, but the eyes that met mine implored.

"Has Betty friends among the other servants?"

"There's hardly a one left, mistress. Only two of the kitchen wenches in the house—and Angus—"

He was standing by the horses, holding the long reins. I went to him and put my hand on his arm.

"Ian. What is going to happen here?"

"I dinna ken, mistress. But he's sending them all awa' —yerself, and the young lassie and the auld one, and maself. It's as if—"

He stopped, as if afraid to say more.

"Yes," I said. "Betty can't stay here. I'll see what can be done."

Before I could go back to the house the door slammed open again and Betty came running out. She wore a dark cloak with a hood pulled tightly over her curls and she was carrying a box.

"Oh, Ian—miss—I'm going, too," she exclaimed, running up to us. "I'm to be the young lady's maid. Oh, Ian—"

She clung to her lover, and briefly his bare dark head bent over hers in a gesture of rough tenderness.

"Into the carriage with you, Betty," I said, trying to smile and finding it oddly difficult. "Hurry. We'll be leaving now, I think."

Ian, handing his sweetheart into the coach as if she were a fine lady, glanced at me. "The Master wants to speak wi' ye first, mistress."

I didn't want to speak to him. I didn't want to see him, or hear his voice—that low, harsh voice that was so unforgettably like no other man's voice. But I could hardly insist that Ian drive on. So I stood by the coach door and waited. Randall, still muttering, was riding slowly back and forth to keep warm. At last the door of the house opened again. The wind snatched it, massive as it was, and flung it back against the wall with a crash. Gavin came out.

He was bareheaded. The wind lifted his dark hair and stirred the pleats of his kilt. There was no sign of the sling he had worn for three days, but his arm was supported by the plaid, which was drawn across one shoulder and fastened with a plain silver brooch. He walked like Satan through the wrath of heaven, with a long, free stride and arrogantly poised head; and I wondered how many years it would take to wipe that picture of him out of my mind.

"What do you think of the sky?" he called to Ian, now on the box.

Ian shook his head and the Master nodded.

"You must force the pace. Get to Dunkeld before the snow, if possible."

Then he turned to me. His eyes didn't meet mine; they went from my mouth to my hair and off to the side.

"With luck you'll reach Dunkeld this afternoon, Edinburgh tomorrow. You'll stay at the home of my solicitor there. See that he gets this."

I took the package he handed me. It was small, bound with tape, and might have contained letters. With it was a heavy leather purse.

"The purse is yours," Gavin said.

I opened my lips to protest, and Gavin laughed.

"Scatter the contents between here and Edinburgh, for all I care," he said brusquely. "Or give it to a society for protecting wayward serving maids. That would be quite in character for you."

"Good-bye," I said, "Mr. Hamilton."

If he answered, I didn't hear the words. I pulled my hood closer, to hide my face, and turned to get into the carriage.

Something brushed my arm. It might have been the wind, but it seemed too gentle. I turned again; but Gavin, face lifted, was frowning at the sky, which seemed to frown back at him. Something small and white, like a feather from the tiniest of birds, came to rest on the blackness of his wind-tossed hair.

"Get in," he said, without looking at me. "The snow is beginning."

Four hours later we had left the glen, through the Gorbals, and were galloping along the main coach road towards Castleton. I had found the journey to Blacktower exhausting, but this was sheer torture. Ian was forcing the poor horses to their best speed, and we were tossed about on the rutted glen road like peas in a hard pod. I almost envied Randall on horseback, even with the wind biting at his nose. Once through the Gorbals the road had improved, but Ian took advantage of it and urged the horses to an even faster pace. I could understand his haste. Although we kept the windows tightly closed, the cold grew more intense and the heavy grey of the skies was like twilight. The snow still held off. Isolated dainty flakes drifted lazily down, melting on the windows; but there was as yet no heavy fall.

Annabelle was beginning to show the strain of the jouncing ride. I paid no attention to Mrs. Cannon's perpetual sighs; she was so well padded that she couldn't suffer much. But I was worried about the girl; for all her recently improved health, she was pale and drawn. I had to admire her fortitude. She hadn't uttered a word or a complaint since we started. I leaned forward to speak to her.

"It won't be much longer, Annabelle. We'll stop for dinner, and I'll make sure you have time to rest."

She glanced at me and then, with cold deliberation, turned her face away. I didn't blame her. No doubt she thought her poor young heart was broken. I knew it was still intact, or she couldn't have been so angry. When something breaks, all the contents spill out; there is nothing left inside but emptiness.

I leaned back, trying to get some support from the padded seat, but it bounded away from me with each turn of the carriage wheels. Against the dark window Annabelle's profile was as hard as stone, and oddly adult. She no longer looked like a child. She looked like—my mind fumbled for an elusive memory. I thought it must be an impression of her father that haunted me; but when I compared the features of the girl across from me with the ones printed eternally on my mind, there didn't seem to be any real resemblance.

A sudden gust of wind blew a handful of white flakes at

the window glass. Looking back, I could see Randall trotting along after the carriage. At least I assumed it was Randall; in shape it was only a huddled bundle, its face concealed by shawls and scarves. It looked intensely miserable.

I retreated into my corner and returned to my contemplation of Annabelle's frozen profile. Yes, there was a familiar look about that outline. I had seen that same expression, on her face or his, before; but the memory slid, fishlike, through the meshes of my mind, and wouldn't be captured. It was a trivial thing; but I welcomed trivialities just then.

The motion of the coach was terrible. I began to feel ill. My head throbbed and there was a constriction around my chest, like a gradually tightening band. My eyes grew heavy. I was so tired that even the jolting of the carriage couldn't keep me awake. My eyes closed. . . .

And the memory slid slyly into the emptiness of half-sleep.

It jarred me awake and brought me upright and breathless to the edge of the seat. My hands went to my throat and plucked at the fastening of my cloak as if it, and not my own thoughts, were choking the breath out of my lungs. Oh, impossible, I thought wildly. And yet—

If it were true, it would explain so much! The coming of the Elliotts to Glengarrie and their strange hold over the Master; the black moment on the windswept cliff, when I clung for my life to an invisible hand; oh, yes, even Angus's enigmatic laughter, and the sad old song. . . .

No. The song at least could have no meaning. That would be too monstrous. The picture was bad enough without it—not so much because of what had happened, but because of what was going to happen. Gavin's determination to send us all away took on a new and terrible significance. What was he planning? I had no doubt that he had some scheme in mind. What could it be? There was nothing he could do now, except. . . .

"Oh, no," I said aloud. "Not that . . ."

Mrs. Cannon rolled her eyes at me, but Annabelle didn't even turn her head. She had heard me, though; the muscles of her cheek twitched, and then froze again. I wondered how much she knew. Not much, surely—perhaps nothing at all. For one wild moment I considered telling her the truth—or what I thought was the truth. I dismissed the idea at once. She wouldn't believe me.

The next minutes were among the worst I ever spent, as I wrestled frantically with possible solutions. Ian? Randall? Certainly not Randall; he would laugh incredulously, or shrug his shoulders. Ian might go. But then who would drive the carriage? And even if he went, I wouldn't know what was happening. I would have to go on enduring all the anguish, fear, suspicion, and utter helplessness.

"Miss—are you feeling ill?"

I had thought Betty was asleep. I followed her worried gaze, and saw my hands writhing and twisting together like frightened animals. With an effort I made them quiet.

"No," I said. "No, I'm all right."

And it was true. As I spoke, the answer came. I knew what I had to do.

The time after that, before we reached Castleton, was almost too short. I had to plan, so that I might accomplish my deception as quickly as possible. It could be done, if I took care.

Soon the houses of Castleton appeared, and the horses slowed, wringing a grateful sigh from poor Mrs. Cannon. We rolled into the courtyard of the inn and stopped. We had been travelling for six hours; it was noon.

I was out of the carriage almost before the wheels stopped turning. The wind enveloped me like icy water. My mind was working clearly now, and I didn't feel the cold. But the weather was of immediate concern. I looked anxiously at the sky. My face prickled under the melting fingers of the snow, but the lovely, treacherous stuff was still falling lightly. It lay like a dusting of sugar on the dead brown heather. The clouds still lowered. They seemed slightly less dark ahead, on the road to Dunkeld.

Behind us they had gathered sullenly. I knew that snow must already be heavy on Ben Macdhui.

Ian climbed down off the box. His face was bright crimson with cold, but he smiled cheerfully at me and then helped the other ladies out. All the while I could hear Randall, who thought no one was listening, swearing strange and wonderful oaths.

The host was waiting for us and he soon got everyone settled: Mrs. Cannon and Annabelle in a private room upstairs, and Randall in the inn parlour, toasting himself before a fire. I made sure he saw me climb the stairs after the other ladies; but I didn't go with them. I found an empty guest room and rang for a servant. When she came, I ordered paper and ink, and sat down to write a letter.

The letter had to be convincing. I didn't think Randall would follow me; he had Annabelle to consider, and his own comfort. Yet I must make sure. My letter was a masterpiece. I read it over, thoughtfully. Then I dipped my pen once more and added a final line. "I have been Mr. Hamilton's mistress since I came," I wrote—with, I thought, admirable brevity.

That ought to take care of Randall. He would never try to get me back. He would rub his hands and say "Good riddance,"—and, most probably, discover that Annabelle was as lovely as she was rich.

I folded the letter and wrote Randall's name on the outside. Then I called the servant back.

"This is for the gentleman downstairs," I said. "But you are not to give it to him until he asks where I am, or until they are ready to go on."

She said she understood. To reinforce her understanding, I opened the purse Gavin had given me. The sight of its contents stunned me. There was enough money there, in banknotes and gold, to keep me for a year. I took the smallest of the notes and gave it to the girl. Her mouth opened in a great "O", and I was sure she would remember my instructions.

I waited a few moments after she had gone, and then

crept down the stairs. The door of the inn parlour was ajar; Randall was still stamping and swearing. When his back was turned I slid softly past the door and out into the stableyard.

The horseboy had tended our horses and was sound asleep in a pile of straw. I had to stir him with my toe before he woke, and when I told him what I wanted he gaped foolishly and scratched his head. An older or more intelligent servant might have remonstrated with me. The boy didn't care. I assured his cooperation by the same method I had used with the girl, and a few minutes later I was riding away from the inn.

I took the precaution of avoiding the main road until I had left the village. Once on the highway I gave the horse his head, and we set out at a rapid pace for the mountains. They seemed very far away. Six hours away, by carriage. A rider might take less time; but at this time of year dark would be falling by four o'clock.

I realised, then, the utter ruthlessness of desire. The odds were all against me; there was nothing in my favour. The weather, my female constitution, my poor horsemanship, even the time of day, all made failure a foregone conclusion. Yet none of them dismayed me; none even roused a doubt in my mind. Only one thing mattered : to reach Blacktower House before it was too late.

It wasn't long before I encountered my first difficulty. This horse was not my placid Flame; he was a big shaggy beast with a back as wide as a table and a trot that rattled my very bones. He had been dragged out of his warm stall into the snow, and he wanted to go home. I had to keep kicking him to make him trot, and finally he stopped and stood with head sullenly lowered, refusing to move.

I, who had never touched an animal in anger, broke a switch off a pine and beat the animal's flanks. The horse reared. I stuck like a burr. Then I hit him again. But I think it wasn't so much the blow as the knowledge of my determination that started the animal into a fast walk.

My spirits lifted; I patted the horse and told him I was

sorry. I didn't want to urge him into a gallop. I knew I had to hoard his strength and mine. But we hardly seemed to be moving; the mountains were no nearer. I turned my head to see how far we had come.

The village was gone. The high road stretched back like a grey ribbon. On it, riding fast, and closing the distance between us, was a solitary horseman.

I dug my heels into the beast's flanks and screamed at it. The animal responded with a suddenness that jerked me back in the saddle. He was no beauty, but he certainly could run. The wind whistled past my ears and tore the hood from my head. My hair loosened and streamed out like a banner.

Exhilaration seized me, and I called aloud to the horse and laughed. Speed, speed, that was what I wanted! When I turned to see if the rider was gaining, the wind whipped my hair across my face, blinding me. I was confident, dizzied with the mad rush of wind. He would never catch me! But I was surprised at Randall—at his horsemanship, and his impetuosity.

The rider tricked us, or we would have won. I heard a long shrill whistle from behind, and my horse slowed, pricking his ears. I dug in my heels and called to him; but the other horse loomed up beside us and a hand shot out and snatched the reins. Sick with despair, I looked at the rider.

It was not Randall. It was Ian.

He was so angry that he spoke to me as he might have spoken to Betty. "Ye fule of a woman," he shouted, right into my face. "What ails ye, to do such a feckless thing? Why not cut yer throat an' be done wi' it?"

"How did you know?" I asked placatingly.

"Betty. She knew sommat was amiss, an' watched ye."

I knotted my hair into a loop, not an easy task with my stiff, gloved hands, and pulled my hood back into place.

"Did you tell Mr. Randall?" I asked.

Ian scowled. Then he shook his head.

"Ian, I must go back! Something is wrong; something

189

terrible is going to happen. You must believe me—" The words died in my throat and I peered incredulously at his averted face. "You do believe me! You think so, too. Ian, what do you know?"

"Naught," he muttered. "The Master told me naught."

"Then why didn't you tell Randall I was gone? Why are you sitting here arguing with me now, instead of dragging me back? You know—"

"Hush yer haverin'!" He glared at me. Then he burst out, "Aye, I suspicioned sommat was amiss. All the summer I've watched the Master fight some black trouble, but I dinna ken what." Never articulate, the groom struggled to find words to express his emotions. Then he leaned forward and said intensely, "Mistress, ye maun go back. Nay, dinna argue! I'll tell ye this—five years back I lived i' the village wi' ma stepfather—if ye can call it livin' wi' naught but black bread to eat, and a beatin' every day. The Master caught the auld blackguard at me one day. He thrashed him within an inch o' his life and took me up to the House to train for his groom. Dinna ye believe I'll do my best to aid him? Wi' the help o' God and all good fortune maybe I can reach the House tonight. If ye come, neither of us will get there."

"We'll go together. And we'll get there." I lifted my reins.

"Mistress, dinna ye believe me?"

"Yes, I believe you." I reached out and caught his hand in both my own. It was hard and strong. "And if you ever need the last drop of my blood, it's yours, for what you're doing. But don't you see that I must go with you? I'll keep any pace you set."

Ian scowled at me and I stared back, trying to make my determination visible in my face. Suddenly, to my utter astonishment, the corners of his mouth quirked in one of his rare smiles, and he reached into his saddlebag and handed me a bundle. In it was a coarse woollen cloak, a thick shawl, and Betty's mittens.

"She said you'd not be made to see reason," he

remarked resignedly.

I put the cloak on over my own, and tied the shawl on my head. At any other time I would have thanked him; now there was no time, and no need for words.

"Who will drive the coach?" I asked.

"I spoke to the ostler at the inn. He's a canny mon, and will take them to Dunkeld—unless the snow worsens. Mistress, the snow—"

"I know. We must hurry."

Those were the last words either of us spoke for hours. Ian took the lead, keeping the horses at a steady walk. The road slid past in a blur, mile upon mile without change. I might have fallen asleep except for the cold, and the wet of the snow against my face.

At intervals Ian stopped to rest the horses. I raged at the time lost, but knew it was necessary. He chose halting places that were sheltered from the wind, behind rock outcroppings or in the shadow of pinewoods. We both dismounted and walked about stamping our feet to restore the warmth to them. The horses stood with heads bowed breathing heavily. Under other circumstances my heart would have smitten me for driving them so hard, but now I was as merciless with them as with myself.

As the afternoon raced on, our stops became more and more frequent. The landscape was rocky, our way steep. The road beneath the plodding hooves was no longer grey, but smooth white. The snow was only a thin layer as yet, but it was dangerous. Twice the iron-shod hooves slipped on ice.

I strained my eyes, always, to find familiar landmarks. It was hard to see with the wind driving snow—now hail-like, icy pellets—into my face. And always, always the air grew darker. Night was almost complete when I saw, through slitted eyes, that just ahead the road plunged in between jagged rocks before soaring up to disappear over a steep rise. We had reached the Gorbals; the mouth of the glen was only two miles away.

When we got to the gorge the going was easier. It was

a relief to lift one's face and feel only cold, not the sting of snow which had become hard as sleet. The wind was now a distant force, howling wildly through the branches of the pines above the cliffs. The light was entirely cut off; I couldn't see at all. I loosened my reins to let the horse follow its head and came up beside Ian before I knew he had stopped. We were at the foot of the rise. Snow had trickled down the slope and outlined the path whitely against the surrounding blackness.

"Go on!" I said.

As soon as we reached the slope I knew there would be trouble. The stuff under the horses' feet was not snow, but ice. My animal slithered and slipped; I could feel his flanks quiver through the wet skirts of my dress. That should have warned me. Still the disaster seemed to come all at once, like a lightning flash. There was a mingled shriek from man and horse ahead, a crashing fall, and then the most dreadful of all sounds, the screams of an injured animal.

I fell, rather than dismounted, from my own horse. The gallant beast stood still, though he was trembling in every limb. When I reached Ian, he was kneeling beside his horse.

"Are you hurt?" I cried.

Ian didn't answer. His hands were busy under his coat. The last of the light from above shone dully on the object in his hand. He leaned forward. The cries of the injured horse rose to a pitch, and stopped.

I stumbled away a few steps, and caught the rough trunk of a tree for support. The next thing I was aware of was Ian's hand on my arm. In silence he drew me down the slope and lifted me back on to my horse. Then he took the reins and turned the animal's head. We started back towards the mouth of the gorge.

I bowed my head and clutched the pommel with hands that had lost their power to feel. For the first time, my hagridden anxiety to reach the house was dulled by another feeling—remorse. My folly had killed the horse; it might have killed Ian. And yet we were too close to give up now! Only two miles to the mouth of the glen, then down its length to the house. But those two miles would be slippery and treacherous with snow.

I looked down at Ian's bent head as he stumbled along beside me. "Are you hurt?" I asked again.

He shook his head, with the slow motion of a man too exhausted to speak. He was lying; I could see that his stumbling walk was due to more than fatigue. He had hurt his leg or foot, how badly I didn't know.

Soon we were out of the shelter of the rocks, and now wind and snow flung themselves on us in a wild fury. I couldn't imagine where Ian was going, and, except for his sake and that of the horse, I didn't care. We had not passed a house for miles. But Ian plodded on, leaning more and more heavily on the support of my stirrup, and at long last I saw, through the pine branches which now surrounded us, the yellow square of a lighted window.

The hut was a low, small place, huddled up against a steep rock slope. That was all I could see of it through the storm. Ian had to pound against the door for a long time before it opened, but then rough, hospitable hands pulled us inside and put us down before a roaring fire.

The inhabitants of the hut were five in number—a shepherd and his wife, and a cow and two black-faced sheep, who stared curiously at us over the bars that separated the stable from the single room of the house. The two humans were obviously just as curious at finding us out on such a night. But the instinctive courtesy of their class kept them from questioning me, and although Ian seemed to know them, the poor lad was in too much pain to be talkative. His knee had been badly wrenched. As I watched the flesh swell and turn purple in the warmth, I marvelled that he had been able to walk on it at all.

The good wife insisted that I take the single bed; she dragged it nearer to the fire and piled it with rough home-spun blankets. She and her husband retired to the loft and Ian, his knee tied up in a revolting mess of sheep's fat, was bedded down in the stable. I went in to say good night to him, and to make sure he was comfortable.

He looked up at me, his face still white with pain, and his eyes tormented. "Mistress, I did ma best."

"I know."

"Tomorrow—when th' horse is rested—I'll go on." He put out one big hand and touched my sleeve gently. "Mistress, dinna worry yerself. Naught can happen tonight, up there."

"I know," I said again. "Don't you fret, Ian. You did everything a man could do."

I left him no more reassured than I was myself. Even if the storm stopped by the next morning he wouldn't be able to go on. He would be lame for days. And one day might be too late. It would take more than snow and storm to keep Gavin from—whatever he meant to do.

I lay down on the bed. I didn't expect to sleep, but merciful nature took its toll of my exhausted body, and I fell at once into a heavy slumber.

Something woke me, while it was still night. From the weariness in my limbs I knew that I had slept only a few hours. The house was still, except for a rattling snore from above. The fire, thriftily banked, had died to a bed of glowing embers that gave little light. Wrapped in the rough wool blankets, I stared drowsily at the crimson coals. A desperate, illogical need tugged at me, commanding me to go back to the house, which was so near, yet so unattainable. Sleep was out of the question. I slid out of the blankets and went to the window.

The storm was over. Racking clouds fled before a keen wind, and behind them I saw a cold, pure circle of moon. The silver rays fell on the blanket of snow that covered the ground and frosted each twig of the dark pines, outlining their shapes against the ridge. Nothing moved. The exhausted world slept after its travail.

A stream of cold air blew in around the window frame, but I couldn't tear myself away from the strange beauty of the night. The hut was very near the steep wall of the ridge; I couldn't see its top. I craned my neck as far as possible; and there, sharp against the moon-washed sky, was an outline I knew, though it was high and far and shrunken by distance. The Tower.

I remembered a spring morning under its wall, and Gavin's voice: "...the cottage of one of my crofters. I have walked that path myself...."

On the heels of that memory, clear as a voice crying for help came the silent command that had led me forward all day It was stronger now. "Hurry, hurry...come back, come back."

I turned from the window and began to dress. My cloak, spread before the fire, was dry, though sadly crumpled. The insides of my boots were still wet. I took the goodwife's shoes, which she had left at the foot of the ladder leading to the loft. They were big enough to hold four of my feet, but I stuffed them with rags and laced them tight around the ankle. I put on my own cloak and Betty's and tied the hood tightly around my face with her scarf.

It took me some time to find the start of the path. In fact, I'm not sure I ever did find it. I crawled and stumbled among the rocks at the foot of the cliff until I came to a spot where climbing was possible; then I climbed. The wife's shoes weighted my ankles like lead. Often I slipped on the icy rocks and slid back as far as I had come. The cold edges of the stones tore at my hands, slashing the gloves to ribbons as I crawled upward, winding my way back and forth across the sheer face of the rock.

Midway in the climb I lay at full length against a smooth slope of ice and tried to catch my breath. When I looked down I saw the black pines far below, and a faint trail of smoke from the chimney of the hut, now hidden among the trees. That sight nerved me to go on.

The rest of the climb was a merciful blur. My arms and legs moved mechanically, until I fell at last into a deep cover of snow on the platform at the base of the Tower and lay half buried in the cold whiteness. My hood had fallen off long before and my wet hair cushioned my cheek. I would have stayed there, and fallen into the deadly sleep of cold, if that insistent, silent command had not still hammered at my brain. Dizzily I raised my head and looked about.

The moonlight was so bright that it made a diamond glitter on the snow. The Tower's foundations were black as pitch against it. Then I saw something that swept the sleep away from my eyes. At the base of the Tower, near its northern corner, a form separated itself from the foundation shadow and came towards me. It came so quickly it seemed to float over the snow. It wore a dark hooded cape. I lifted myself on my hands and stared as it came up to me. Within the depths of the hood I saw Gavin's face.

CHAPTER 14

My senses became hazy for a little while, and when they came back to me I didn't know where I was. The place was warm and dark and sheltered. My wet dress and cloak were gone; I was wrapped in a coarse woollen garment that itched against my bare arms. Gavin's arms were around me, and his face was against my hair.

For a time I lay still against his shoulder, mindlessly content. My eyes were beginning to adjust to the darkness; I saw a hint of rough stone walls and a low ceiling. There was light somewhere—a dull red glow, like a tiny fire. Then I saw another light—two globes of shining luminescence, a few inches off the floor.

I let out a gasp, and Gavin's head lifted. He laughed softly, and said, in a muted voice, "It's only Toby. He makes a good watchdog. It was he who heard you crashing about in the snow outside."

Toby sauntered over to me, licked my face thoroughly, and then sat down on my arm and began to purr. My strength was coming back, and with it, my memory.

"Lady Mary," I said. "Where is she? Have you—have you—"

"Don't talk so loudly." Gavin laid me back against the floor and sat back on his heels. "I don't know where she is at the moment. What do you mean, 'Have you?' Have I what?"

His voice was so reasonable that I felt a shamed doubt.

"I thought—I was afraid—"

"Ah, I see. You thought I intended some mischief to the lady. My dear girl, the chances are much greater that she will do me some mischief. Damaris—how on earth do you happen to be here?"

I pulled the covering closer about my bare arms. I could

see its pattern now. It was Gavin's plaid.

"I rode back, from Castleton," I said. "Ian came with me, but in the Gorbals his horse slipped and broke its leg. We had to go back to the herder's hut."

"Where is Ian now?"

"Asleep, down below. When I saw the storm was over I decided to climb the path. You showed it to me one day, remember?"

"Yes, I remember. So you decided to climb—on bare rock and ice, and at night. Damaris—"

His voice broke off, and after a moment of silence I asked, "Where are we? I don't know this place."

"A cell in the foundations of the Tower. This is my base. I'm sorry it's not comfortable, in spite of the brazier. I can't risk a fire, you see. This damned moonlight has complicated all my plans."

"What plans?"

My eyes were used to the gloom. I saw him make an impatient gesture with one hand. Toby lifted his head and stared, and then relaxed and resumed his purring.

"What plans?" Gavin repeated. "I'd prefer not to discuss them, not with you. And in any case they are in rags and tatters now. In God's name, Damaris, I thought I had you out of the way. Why did you come back?"

"Something happened—before we reached the inn. I was looking at Annabelle—"

"Annabelle," he interrupted. "I hope to heaven she, at least, is on her way to Edinburgh. The package I gave you—you didn't bring it back with you?"

"I left it for Randall," I said. "With a note."

"Will Cousin Randall be dragging himself up the cliff next?"

"Not he. By now he is doubtless toasting his feet before a fire in Dunkeld. He wouldn't follow me—not after he read my note."

Gavin made a little sound which might have been a laugh. "Yes, I can imagine the sort of thing you might have written. Did you tell him why you were coming back?"

"I gave him a reason, of course. It was not the true one."

"What is the true one?"

I hesitated. Now that the actual moment of challenge and revelation had come, I couldn't make myself say the words. "Tell me first what you are doing. Why did you send us all away? What are your plans?"

Somewhat to my surprise he answered without further equivocation. He settled himself back against the cold wall and stretched his long legs out. "I sent Annabelle away so that that little swine Andrew shouldn't get her. She's utterly besotted; if he beckoned she'd be off to the nearest parson. Since he is cunning and she is now ambulatory, the only sure way of preventing the match was to get her out of the way. Randall's coming was a godsend. I knew he'd get her safe to Edinburgh; he's the dogged, stupid sort of fellow who sticks to his instructions. Once there, my lawyer, who is an old family friend, will take care that she makes no mistakes."

His unusual loquacity made me uneasy. Like myself, he was skirting around the fringes of the real danger. He didn't want to talk about it either.

"Annabelle—I can understand that. But why did you send me away?"

"I thought I made that plain," said the Master.

"Oh, you did. Very plain." I swallowed something that stuck in my throat. "But if you had wanted me to go for another reason, you still might have acted as you did."

He leaned forward, so suddenly that Toby gave a low growl. His hands clasped over mine. "Damaris, I'll take you back down the cliff. It's not so bad going down."

"If you'll stay with me—and not come back here."

"Damn you for a stubborn, senseless wench! All right, Damaris; it will have to be said, sooner or later. What did bring you back?"

Strange, how hard it was to tell. And yet he was right; it had to be said.

"It was in the coach," I began for the second time. "I was looking at Annabelle. Her face reminded me of something. For a time I teased myself by trying to see you in her, but I couldn't pin down that impression. Then, all at once, I did pin it down. It wasn't you I saw in her face, Gavin. It was Lady Mary Elliott."

Gavin sat motionless, without speaking. The silence was so profound that Toby's purring sounded like a roar.

"She's your wife," I went on, in a voice that was strange in my ears. "She didn't die in London, or drown in the loch. She ran away that day fourteen years ago, out through the pass. I think perhaps you believed she was dead. You hadn't seen her, had you, until she came back this summer, under a false name?"

Still Gavin did not speak. I could hear him breathing heavily, like a man in pain.

"I don't understand it all," I said. "I suppose she decided to come back after your nephew died, and you became the Master of Dunnoch. But surely she couldn't expect that you would take her back. And this business of Andrew and Annabelle, that must be a trick. Her child and her brother—"

Gavin stirred.

"He's not her brother."

That did surprise me. I gaped at him as he continued, with rising passion. "She says he is her cousin. It would be bad enough to have Annabelle marry into the same witch's brood that produced my incomparable wife; but even that is a lie. It sickened me beyond endurance to see her dallying with her mother's worn-out lover."

"You must be mistaken," I said horrified.

"No, I'm not. Mary had no brothers or sisters. This rascal is only the last of a long line. She loves him, though; in her own queer way she is as besotted with him as Annabelle. My God, Damaris, I thought you must have seen it."

"No. No, I didn't."

"I hoped," said Gavin, in an expressionless voice, "that

I could kill him when we fought. It's easier to kill in the heat of a fight than in cold blood. . . . His death would have broken Mary's will. I could have dealt with her then. But I'm too old; I failed. I've lost most of my skill in fencing."

"Killing is no solution. There must be some other way out."

"But there isn't. Not now." Gavin laughed; the sound jarred in my ears. "I'm caught in my own net, Damaris. Or, rather, I planned too late. Why do you think I'm skulking here like a cornered rat? I've got to kill Andrew before he kills me."

I made an incredulous sound, and Gavin swept on.

"You saw that motley crowd at the ball the other night, I'm sure. Friends of my dear wife's—cut-throat adventurers, the dregs of England and Europe, brought in to ensure that the odds were in her favour. I don't believe she meant murder at first. But when I saw that crew, I knew. Men of that type don't work for nothing, and she has no money of her own to pay them with. The income from the Dunnoch estates is almost fifty thousand a year, Damaris. My brother is a dying man. And when I'm dead, it all goes to Annabelle."

Even in my worst imaginings, I had not anticipated this. I shook my head in dumb protest.

"It seems fantastic to you," Gavin said gently. "Shall I tell you the whole story, Damaris? You know the important part of it now—the part I moved heaven and earth to keep from you. Will you hear the rest?"

His hand found mine. I let it rest there.

"Yes," I said.

"I met Mary Malloran," Gavin began, "when I was eighteen. Her father was the schoolmaster at Castleton— at least that was his profession that summer. God knows what he had been before; he would chant Shakespeare while in his cups, which was often, and at other tmes his vocabulary was pure thieves' cant. But Mary was different —prim and dainty and beautiful. Guess where I met her,

Damaris. In church. Isn't that charming? The first time I ever saw her she was sitting in a front pew, and her face stood out among the weatherbeaten faces of the villagers like that of a goddess. All through the sermon I watched her like a man in a dream—her half-averted face, with a cheek like Aphrodite's, her soft golden hair in the dusty sunlight—oh, I was lost before I ever touched her hand or spoke to her.

"The affair developed quickly. Like the adolescent fool I was, I told myself that it was one of the classic romances —the coming together of twin souls, who need no time to know one another. It was a glorious summer. We met clandestinely, under the pines; she picked wild flowers while I watched her hands and burned to hold them. I see now that what possessed me was not love, but something simpler. Just to be near her made my breath go short and my hands tingle. But she was clever. She let me kiss her— I'll spare you that, Damaris—but when I would have pressed her further, she wept and withdrew and said I didn't honour her. The end of it was, of course, that I married her. It's easier to do in Scotland, you know. There were no banns, no witnesses; only the pastor at Dunkeld, where we rode together one fine day in September.

"We spent one night together and then I went back to face my father with the news. I thought he'd have an apoplexy. He stormed and raved and actually slashed at me with the riding crop he was carrying. I was nimble and thin in those days, and I managed to keep out of his way until he cooled down. Which he did, at last. Damaris, you would have loved him. He was the kindest man on earth under all his bluster. He might have cut me off without a penny. Instead he gave me Blacktower House to live in and a small income. I never saw him again. He died the next year; and I always wondered if my behaviour had shortened his life. . . .

"Mary and I came here to live. We were royally cut by every family in the neighbourhood; none of the ladies would call on old Malloran's daughter. He had relapsed into permanent alcoholism soon after we were married and died shortly afterwards, but the taint was still on Mary. She didn't seem to care that no one came to see us. I lavished jewels, clothing, finery on her; I spent every penny of my little income trying to please her and worked like a bailiff on my own lands trying to get more to spend. Then Annabelle was born, and she seemed to be happy. I know I was. . . .

"About a year after the child came, we had the first blow. My shy recluse of a brother fell in love, married, and got his lady with child, all in the space of a few months. I saw the change in Mary after that, but, God help me, I didn't understand it. I thought our quiet life, which satisfied me, was beginning to pall. She was irritable and cross, even with the child. Once I saw her slap the little thing for tugging at her dress. We began to have quarrels. They weren't lovers' quarrels; they were violent, ugly battles where she threw bric-a-brac at me and did full justice to her father's vocabulary. I think my ardour began to dull even before that. She was basically a stupid woman, you see; clever and quick, but shallow. But she had other talents, and after every battle, when our passions were at their ugliest, she would throw herself at me, and . . . I'm sorry, Damaris.

"Well, I was caught, and so was she; there was no way out of the marriage. I began to invite friends of mine to stay—not the local gentry, they were still lofty about Mary, but friends from my university days, and from London. They didn't bring their wives, of course. But Mary brightened up with company, and for a while we got along better.

"The spring Annabelle was two we had a man staying with us who was one of my oldest friends. He had been a few years ahead of me at St. Andrews, a brilliant scholar and athlete—I was proud when he condescended to me. He was a handsome devil, too—something in the style of Mary's latest. Mary took to him at once. They played and sang duets together in the evening while I sat in the shadows and watched, all unsuspecting. I suppose I didn't care enough to be suspicious.

"The final blow to Mary's hopes came while Jack was here—a letter from my brother announcing the birth of a healthy male child. The letter stripped away my title and bestowed it on a puling infant. I didn't care, Damaris. But after the letter came, Mary went to her own room for the rest of the day and came down looking different. She was very gay that evening, laughing and singing. She danced with me, while Jack played a polka; and later, when we had gone to bed . . .

"I had to go away the next day to talk to some of our crofters at the other end of the glen. I took my agent with me. There was some problem with the rents, and we didn't get back till late in the afternoon. It was a grey, misty day, with rain threatening. When I walked into the house, I knew something was wrong.

"The house servants had disappeared—all but Angus. The house was very still. Usually one could hear Annabelle chattering or crying (she was a whining child, I remember) in the nursery, or Mary would be playing the piano or scolding the servants. When I saw Angus's wicked grin, I was sure that something had happened. I think I even knew what it was.

"Angus told me. 'Yer wife's off wi' the Southron, Hamilton,' he said, and laughed so hard his face turned red. I could hear him laughing as I ran through the house towards the stables.

"You may ask why I pursued her. I didn't love her. But there was pride, and anger, and outraged friendship—and Annabelle. I'll admit I never was a doting father, but she was my child—or so I thought then—and I wasn't going to let her bitch of a mother have her.

"The saddle was still on the horse I had ridden. I was on his back and out of the gates before the groom stopped gaping. The first drop of rain fell as I left the courtyard. It kept on, mizzling and misting, as I galloped on.

"When I came out of the woods I saw them on the road

that passed the pool. Mary's horse must have picked up a stone, because they were going far too slowly for safety. They heard me coming. Jack looked back. I heard him cry out words that were lost in the distance, and then the brave soul gave his horse its head and rode like a madman for the pass. Wasn't that a vile thing to do—to abandon her to my rage after seducing her away?"

Gavin stopped to clear his throat; he had grown hoarse with talking. He didn't expect an answer, and I made none. I could tell that the worst of the story was yet to come.

"Mary saw me, too," he went on, in a flat, expressionless voice. "She struck at her horse, and it tried to gallop. But I was gaining fast and she must have realised she couldn't get away. The next thing I saw, through the mist was that she had pulled the beast to a stop. Something fell from her arms on to the wet gorse. It looked like a bundle of clothing, but I knew what it was even before the child's bright hair emerged from one end of it. Mary's horse trotted off, and there stood my daughter—two years old —shivering and rubbing her bruises, and crying out after the mother, who was riding away from her as fast as she could go.

"I forgot all else, Damaris, but the pool. The edge of the water was ten feet away from the child, and a two-year-old has no more sense of danger than a worm. In my horror I did the worst thing I could have done. I began shouting, at Annabelle, and set spurs to the horse. She turned and looked towards me. You know what she must have seen— a furious apparition, shrieking and bellowing at her, thundering down upon her on a huge horse. She let out one little squeak of terror—I heard it very plainly—and ran straight for the pool. I was so close that my hand brushed the tail of her frock as she went in.

"You know what the current is there. It took me time to get off my boots and coat. I didn't bother with the rest. The water was bitter cold. When I came up for air I saw the bright tail of her hair only a few feet away. I caught her by the hair and dragged her into my arm. When I saw her face I thought she was gone. The hair hung down over her features like seaweed. One strand lay across her eyes, and they were wide open, staring sightlessly. I realised later that she had simply lost her wits through fright. But then, all I could think was that I must get her body back for burial. Somehow it was important that I should not let the water take it.

"I had been able to keep myself afloat easily; I was a strong swimmer. But when I tried to strike out for land, I felt the water tug at my body, and I knew the current had caught us. I struggled with the deadly undertow as I have never struggled, before or since; but I was like a child in a giant's hand. Slowly, despite all my efforts, we were drawn towards the centre of the pool, and then down towards the falls. Nothing could survive a fall from that height over the rocks; I knew our only hope was to reach the island in the middle of the pool. It was then that I hurt my hand; you'll have some idea of the strength of the current when I tell you that it tore my grip from the jagged ridge I had grasped, and took part of the hand with it.

"I didn't feel pain then. The shock was too great, and I had more urgent matters on my mind. I did manage, at the instant before I lost hold, to fling Annabelle's body up on to the rocks. Then the current dragged me away; I had a flashing glimpse of her mop of hair and wet pink frock, draped over the stone like sacking. That is the last I recall. They found me later on another islet farther down the loch. I suppose I cut my face then, but I have no memory of it. The searching party from the house didn't find us until almost dark, and it was much later when I came back to consciousness and learned that my daughter still lived, and that I no longer had a whole set of fingers on one hand. Angus swore later that two of them were hanging by a shred of skin, and that he had simply cut away the remainder. But I've wondered, since. . . ."

The words trailed off into silence, and he sat for a time staring into the coals in the brazier. Then he looked up and said, startled, "Damaris, my darling, you're shaking. This cursed cold hole—"

"I'm not cold," I said, "not in my body. . . . Gavin, I've never heard a more terrible story."

"Do you remember the first night you came, when Davey sang the song that enraged me so? It was too close for comfort, Damaris."

"You can't press a resemblance too far. Your—your wife didn't intend harm to the child. She only let Annabelle down to delay you."

"Oh, Damaris, there's not a female in the animal kingdom that would throw her cubs to the hunter in order to win freedom for herself! The stable cat will fight a dog for its young; the doe will run into the hunters' guns to lead them away from the fawns."

His analogy was not really fair; but when the heart is involved, logic goes out of the window.

"And you didn't hear of her again until this summer?" I said quietly.

"No. I made no attempt to find her. I had such a horror of her. I never wanted to hear her name or see her face. And I came to have the same horror of the child. Annabelle grew more like her in appearance every day."

"So that's why you're so unkind to her."

"Yes. I marvel that you didn't see the resemblance earlier. To me, it shrieked aloud to be seen. Of course Annabelle isn't handsome as Mary was—is, even yet. But the colouring, the features—"

"I think I was misled by the portrait," I said. "It was that of some ancestress, then. Annabelle took it for her mother and cherished it as such." I explained to him about the miniature.

He nodded. "You're right. Worse than the physical resemblance, though, was the development of Annabelle's character. I saw nothing of myself in her—only her mother's selfish grasping, her tantrums, her stupidity. I began to wonder if she was my child at all. This performance with Andrew—my God, Damaris, it was like mother, like daughter—a man, any man, like a bitch in—"

"You're wrong," I said. "She was in love with Andrew. But never mind; tell me about this summer."

"Well, after Mary heard of my nephew's death, she made her plans. She had had a series of protectors, and had done well. This boy is pleasure after business, I think. She can hardly keep her hands off him."

"And yet she was willing to hand him over to Annabelle!"

"Only as a last resort." His voice was bitterly amused. "The initial idea was for her to take her old place back."

"As—your wife? But not even she could think—"

"Her egotism is boundless. No doubt," he added indifferently, "she had a pitiful tale prepared. She did make one or two attempts to reassert her former fascination, but my response was not what she had hoped. However, the real barrier to her plans was you."

"I?" I said incredulously; and then I understood.

"Naturally, she assumed that I wanted you—and she was right, Damaris. Being a woman of feeble imagination, she further assumed that you were holding back, as she would have done, for the position of legal wife. A spot of blackmail seemed in order. The fact that I already had a wife was known only to her and to me, and she didn't consider me the man to be stopped by a small thing like bigamy."

"But you were."

"Oh, I confess the thought entered my mind," he said, with assumed lightness. "But I couldn't risk it—not with you, and the way I felt about you. For months I fought against my love for you, and when I finally had to face it, I did what I should have done years ago—I set lawyers to work trying to trace my legal wife. I would have celebrated if they had found she was dead. In lieu of that unlikely joy, I meant to start divorce proceedings when they located her. Then, I thought, I could speak to you. I would have the title, at least, to offset the scandal of divorce and of my deformed face and body."

I rose to my knees, letting the plaid fall away from my body, and held out my hands to him.

"You want me to humble myself again," I said. "You know I'm shamelesss—I don't care if you have ten wives and forty scars. Is that what you want me to say? It's true. Only don't send me away again. Come with me now, down the path, back to Edinburgh."

"Stop it, Damaris! I can't."

"Why not? We'll go to Edinburgh and do what you planned at first, before she came. Gavin, please—if you can't get free of her, I'll—I'll stay with you anyhow. Or —were you lying when you said you wanted me?"

His hands shot out and caught my bare shoulders, the fingers biting into my flesh with bruising force. He pulled me down across his knees. Then he caught himself, and his hands loosened. I pressed myself against him and wound my arms about his neck.

"Won't you come?" I whispered.

"You don't play fair, Damaris," he said, against my hair. "Dear heart, you don't have to bribe me. I've waited a long time for this; I won't have it here, in this filthy hole in the ground. Damaris, you don't understand; perhaps you won't understand. I'd go with you—if I could—"

"You didn't really mean it, when you said that she—"

"Wanted to kill me? Yes, I did mean it."

"You can bribe her—pay her—"

"Money isn't all she wants."

"I know, I know. She hates you. That's natural—to hate where you have most deeply offended. But if you offered her enough—"

"Nothing less than the whole will satisfy her." He sat up, keeping his arms around me; I saw his eyes scanning the darkness. "The situation is made to order. You see, my brother, poor devil, is still alive. His will leaves all he has to me, and, should I predecease him, to Annabelle. If I inherit from him I can make a will leaving the money away from my daughter. I have done this; that was the packet I sent to Edinburgh with you. But my will accomplishes nothing if I die before my brother. In that case his whole, enormous estate goes directly to Annabelle—and thus to Andrew and Mary. With me out of the way they can reach her easily.

It was so simple, and so deadly, that it took my breath away.

"If you could communicate with Lord Dunnoch—explain—get him to change his will—"

"It's too late for that. I tried; but he is barely conscious I doubt if he could understand the problem, much less make a new will."

"But then—you've got to get away from here, now! You said you would help me back down the cliff. Let's hurry!"

His arms held me fast. Almost indifferently, he said, "I was being optimistic. Actually, I think you could get down alone. If I didn't think so I wouldn't have suggested it. But we can't both do it."

"Why not?"

"Because they're looking for me right now, all over the glen. The house is full of Mary's hired assassins, and there are men patrolling all the known paths and some that aren't so well known. You happened, by sheer luck, to miss the fellow who's on this ridge. But we can't count on luck going down. If we were spotted, two well-placed stones would solve Mary's problem."

"I see," I said slowly. "You intend to stay behind, so that I can escape. But, Gavin—why can't it work the other way? I'll lead the guard off, and you go down. They won't hurt me, even if they do catch me."

His arms tightened. He rocked me back and forth, his breath stirring my hair in gasps of voiceless laughter.

"I have to laugh, or I'll cry, or curse. Damaris, my poor, innocent love, don't you know that you've been Mary's strongest weapon against me? Have you forgotten the night you fell from this very cliff? Whose hand was it, do you think, that refused to hold yours?"

"Andrew's?" I whispered.

"I wish to God it had been; but he hasn't the courage. When my dear wife found that she had lost her old hold on me she found a new one. You had two adventures that might have proved fatal—the cliff, and the horse that bolted. A tack under the saddle is easy to fix."

"But—" I searched my memory. It was with actual relief that I said eagerly, "But she never left the room during that visit—when Flame threw me."

"Andrew was Mary's agent in that case. He has enough intestinal fortitude for long-distance murder. And perhaps then not much harm was intended. It was a warning, to me. The only way I could protect you adequately was to send you away—or to tell you the whole story. I should have done it, Damaris; but I was so afraid I'd lose you."

In the ensuing silence, a sound arose, like the moan of an evil spirit. My hair literally rose on end. It took me several seconds to identify the source, and when I did my hair stayed on end. The cat was growling.

Gavin pulled himself away from me. There was a faint clink of metal, and the light vanished as he slid the cover on to the brazier. Toby's growl stopped.

The blackness, which obliterated sight, sharpened hearing. The walls were stone, several feet thick, but I heard —a shuffle, a scrape, a clatter. Movement, within the hollow shell of the tower.

I could hear Toby again. Gavin had him muffled in his plaid; surely the sound wouldn't be audible outside, above the whisper of the wind in the trees.

Something brushed my bare shoulder, and I bit back a cry. It was Gavin, clutching a furious Toby in his arms. He put his face up against mine and whispered, "He's in the Tower. The man I mentioned. Don't move."

"What are you going to do?"

"Take him. If he gives me a chance. Hold Toby."

"No, wait. One shout and we're done."

I heard his teeth grit together. "Got to do something."

"The entrance," I breathed. "Into this room. Where does it go?"

"Outside."

"Then he'll hear you. Gavin—the other path?"

"Which?"

"To the pool—the pass—"

I felt, if I could not see, that his head shook in emphatic negation. "Too far. Cold. You couldn't."

A dull blow struck the walls just beside our heads. The guard was sounding the stones.

My breathing stopped. Gavin's cheek, against mine, was rigid as wood. The sound was not repeated. After a long agonizing wait I ventured another whisper.

"I can. I must. If we can get into the pines—"

"It's better than the cliff," Gavin admitted, in a whisper.

Then we heard another sound, which froze us again— the sound of a human voice.

It went on and on. I couldn't make out words, but there was an odd rhythm to the sound, not like the rise and fall of conversation. Gavin was listening as intently as I. Finally I felt his breath come out in what would have been a laugh if he had dared risk sound.

"Singing, by heaven! He has a bottle. Typical. . . . We've got a chance now."

CHAPTER 15

We waited. At last the singing stopped; but still Gavin made no move. Finally his head came close to mine once more.

"We'll have to risk it now," came the sibilant whisper near my ear. "It's late. Dawn soon. He's quiet."

"The cliff?"

"Too risky. There are men all over the place. We'll try the woods."

While we waited I had put on my dress and shoes and muffled myself again in my cloak.

"I'm ready," I said.

Stone grated on stone; then I saw, first a slit, then a widening square, of pale snow. The moon was sinking. Soon it would be down.

I followed Gavin through the opening, which was so low we had to crawl on hands and knees. Toby followed us and then stalked off, without a glance in our direction, around the base of the Tower towards the cliff.

"I like dogs," said Gavin, with a faint grin. "But at this moment I'm glad Toby isn't one. We'd make a pretty sort of flight with a faithful pup yapping at our heels."

"Gavin . . ."

He put his arm around me and drew me to his side.

"It's all right. We'll make it."

Ahead of us lay the long ragged backbone of the ridge, falling steeply away southward to the glen. The slope was a jumbled pattern of black and grey, of bare slanted stone and drifted snow. The moon sank below the hills even as I looked at it, but a bright scattering of stars blazed against the black velvet of the sky, and the snow patches seemed to give off a pale glow of their own. We would have to avoid the snow. Any object moving against it would be visible from a great distance.

I looked to the right, towards the glen, and my breath caught. The house was a blaze of light. The gold of candles and lamplight moved behind windows, in the court a column of red flame lit the night with a hellish glow. Even at that distance I fancied I could see black, insectlike forms passing to and fro in front of the flames.

"The hunters," said Gavin in a dry whisper. "Pray that they remain occupied there."

He reached for my hand, and we started walking. The bare, rock-strewn hill stretched for half a mile from the base of the Tower. Then the pines began. Once under those massive branches we would be hidden, comparatively safe. I racked my brain trying to remember how far the strip of woods extended. I couldn't remember whether they reached all the way to the pool or not. If they did, we had a chance.

We had covered three quarters of the rocky distance when Gavin stopped behind a high boulder and drew me to his side. The woods were very close, and to me they were as beautiful as a sanctuary. But before the first pines began, there was a wide open stretch, frosted with snow. The slope was gradual and it extended, smooth and white as a counterpane, for hundreds of feet.

Gavin's eyes followed the slope down to the lower end of the snowfield. Then he looked at me and smiled. There was no need to speak. We had known it wouldn't be easy, and this choice was plain. Time was our enemy as well as as space. Dawn would be breaking in a few hours, and surely the narrow bottleneck of the glen would be watched. If we couldn't get through the gap before daylight our chances of escape were small.

Since secrecy was impossible here, we ran. Gavin's long legs could have covered the space like a deer's, but my shorter strides and hampering skirts held us back. With every step we sank into snow that dragged at our feet and soaked our shoes. I fixed my eyes on the eaves of the wood and floundered on, trying to lift my heavy skirts with my free hand.

The nearest branches were only yards away. I was gasping for breath, but I nerved myself for the last dash. Surely we could rest when we reached the woods. . . . Then a man stepped out of the trees and stood before us, barring the way.

I didn't know him at first. It was dark, and the shock of discovery when freedom seemed so close, fogged my eyes. But Gavin recognised him. He let out a wordless hiss of anger and started forward again, dragging me with him. The gnarled dark form, barely visible against the black pines, lifted one hand, and Gavin halted.

My heart was pounding so hard it seemed to shake my ribs. Why didn't the man seize us? Why didn't he speak, or call out? In that still night, a shout would carry for miles and would alert the waiting hunters. Then the silent figure moved, dropping the folds of the plaid that had been wrapped around his head. My pent breath came out in a gasp.

"It's Angus," I said. "Angus, Gavin. Come . . ."

His arm went out like a bar across my breast. He didn't speak, or take his eyes from the wrinkled face of his servant. Angus had never looked more like an evil spirit than he did then, crouched and huddling his plaid against the cold, and glaring, speechlessly, at Gavin.

I never learned how the resolution took place. I could hardly make out Angus's features, and he never once spoke. But Gavin sensed, somehow, when the conflict of hatred and loyalty was resolved. He sprang, more like a giant bird than a man, his plaid billowing out in winglike folds over his extended arms. He was too slow, by a split second. As his body struck the old man, knocking him down into the snow, an eldritch yell burst from Angus's throat. It echoed from hill to hill through the star-still night and ended in a shaken silence as Gavin's hand slapped down across the parted lips.

I ran forward. Angus was down, with Gavin on top of him. One of the Master's black hands covered the wrinkled lips, cutting off sound; the other pinned the old man's right hand against the ground. In that hand was a long thin blade—a Highland dirk. The position left one of Angus's hands free, and he was using it to claw and pound at Gavin's face. When Gavin's head twisted, avoiding a thrust at his eyes, I saw another mark across his scarred cheek—the threefold mark of Angus's tearing nails.

Dancing up and down on the trampled snow in an agony of fear, I glanced quickly over my shoulder at the house and saw a sight that froze the blood in my veins. The lights were going out. They were giving up the search there. That meant only one thing.

Gavin couldn't see what I had seen, but he knew as well as I the need for haste. He lifted his hand from Angus's mouth and suddenly grabbed the dirk. The old man's breath sucked in, and Gavin struck him on the temple with the heavy hilt just in time to cut off another shout.

Then Gavin was on his feet, dragging at my hand.

"Run!" he ordered, and we were off, without a backward look.

The shelter of the pines closed over us like welcoming arms. We ran on for a while in silence. It was wonderful to be out of the open, to be running so effortlessly. There was little snow here to hinder the feet, but light was almost nonexistent. Gavin seemed to find his way by second sight, twisting and winding around the heavy boles, tugging me with him. After a time my first exhilaration wore off; my weary muscles protested and my skirts clung and dragged at my ankles. Each breath brought a small sharp pain; but even above my own panting breaths I heard Gavin's. We were making too much noise. The pine needles underfoot were wet, but the branches crackled as we fled through them.

I wasn't aware that Gavin was faltering; I was too occupied with the necessity for going on when every limb cried out for rest. But then he stopped with a jerk, and an exclamation, and I realised that he had run headlong into one of the tree trunks he had been avoiding so deftly. I caught at him to steady him; and he winced away from my touch with another muttered sound.

"You're hurt," I said. "Gavin, your arm—"

"It's only a cut. But I'm afraid—"

His head came up in a quick, startled movement, lifting towards the north. I heard it too : a muffled, muted sound, rising and falling, oddly inhuman.

"Dogs," Gavin said. "Make haste, Damaris. Curse it, I've been dripping blood for two miles."

I bound up the gash in his forearm, using one of my petticoats.

"You've lost too much blood," I muttered, working as fast as I could. "On top of your other wound—"

"That arm won't be of much use, no. A pity, and I may yet need two, before the night's done. . . . That's enough. We've got to go on now"

"The dogs—" I gave a start, as the hollow baying rose again, closer.

"My dogs won't bother us." Gavin shook down his sleeve. "But they may have a strange one. Even without a dog, they'll find Angus, and blood on the snow where we fought. With lanterns they can follow our trail easily."

He took my hand again, and we went on, at a walk now. I should have spared my breath, but there was one thing I had to say.

"Angus was on their side."

"Angus is a little mad, I think. Oh, with cause."

"Why does he hate you so?"

"It's not me he hates. It's the house and the family. They say that he's my grandfather's son."

I remembered the first day in the library, when the likeness between the two men had struck me.

"Is it true?" I gasped.

"From what I remember of my grandfather, it could be true. But the truth doesn't matter, Angus believes it.

"And so do you. You could have killed him, when you had his dirk."

"Well . . . one never knows," said Gavin dryly. "I've

217

enough on my conscience without taking a chance like that."

The woods were pitch black, save where small clearings gave a view of a patch of sky spangled with stars, and we avoided these places when we could. We stopped to rest twice more. The second time I collapsed, telling myself I mustn't sleep. I couldn't sleep ... And then I woke with a start of terror to feel Gavin's hand urgent on my shoulder.

"I'm sorry, darling, but we must go on. Listen."

I listened, and the hairs on my neck lifted. The dogs! No—it was so close now that I could tell there was only one throat making that unearthly sound. Momentarily I expected to see it appear between the aisles of pines. Between the howls I thought I made out another sound.

I was on my feet by then, shaking with fatigue and terror.

"How could I have slept? You shouldn't have let me. ... Do you hear the horses too?"

"I hear them." Gavin was moving, tugging me with him. "I didn't think they'd dare use them in the woods. We've not had the best of luck tonight. There's only one dog; but it's not one of mine."

We ran on, through the unending pines. I was almost at the end of my endurance; the baying of the dog had finished what fatigue and fright had begun. I hung on to Gavin's arm like a dead weight, and it seemed to me that I could see him more clearly. Surely the darkness was not quite so dark as before.

We came out, with the suddenness of a dream ending, on to the rock-strewn plateau I had seen once before. In front of us lay the pool. I could see it clearly, because dawn was breaking over the ragged backbone of the eastern ridge.

There was no sun as yet, not even real light; only a lessened darkness. I could see shapes, but no colours. Sky and earth and water were of the same dull grey; so was Gavin's face.

We reached the beginning of the pool and ran parallel

to it. In its centre the rocks stood up like talons, waiting to catch and tear. The water was dark, almost black, but a gleam of reflected light from the east caught in the slow deadly whirl of the current, which coiled like a pallid snake. I stumbled, almost falling, and wrenched my eyes away from the grim fascination of the water. And then I heard the thunder of the horses as they broke out of the wood.

There were two of them. Ahead of both, trailing the lead rope that one of the riders had just dropped, came the dog. It was a giant breed, as long as a man was tall, with massive jaws and a barrel chest. It covered the broken ground in great leaps, giving tongue with excitement as it came.

Gavin stopped. There was no need to run any longer. He pushed me behind him and snatched Angus's dirk from his belt. He had just enough time for that before the dog leaped.

Time froze. The great hound seemed to hang suspended in mid air, its gaping jaws wide and its heavy paws outstretched. The two riders stopped, and sat watching. One wore long skirts that trailed down over the horses's flank. Directly before me Gavin stood braced to receive the hound's weight. His left arm was lifted to shield his face and throat. In his right hand was the dagger. The light was better now. I could see the rent in his right sleeve, and the dark stains that covered it.

The paralysis of time broke. Gavin had gone down with the dog upon him. I fell to the ground, groping frantically in the snow. I found what I was seeking and rose up, swaying in my icebound skirts, with a slab of broken stone lifted on both hands.

Th dog's muzzle was buried in the space between Gavin's chin and breast; from its throat came a muffled worrying growl. Above its back Gavin's other arm rose and fell. The blade of his dirk was dark with the animal's blood, but it showed no signs of being weakened. I took two steps forward, pulled off balance by the weight of the stone suspended above my head. I let it fall. There was a hideous howl from the dog, and silence.

Gavin rolled out from under the dead weight. There was blood on his left sleeve now, to match the right. The thick wool of his plaid was ravelled where the dog had chewed it. Slowly he raised himself to one knee, but his strength would take him no farther. His empty hands dangled, touching the snow.

I looked for the knife and saw it buried hilt-deep in the dog's neck, just behind the shattered skull. Even to save both our lives it was more than I could bring myself to do, to drag it out of its place.

The riders had not moved. Dully, I wondered why. Perhaps they were prolonging the torment, hoping we would try to run again. Mary would enjoy that. . . .

I brushed my forehead with the back of my hand, and my eyes came into focus once more The two riders were talking. Yes, there were only two of them—Mary and Andrew. Of course, they would take on this part of the hunt themselves. But the hunters didn't seem to agree. Mary wasn't looking at us; she was turned towards Andrew and the gestures of her head and arms suggested that she was urging him on to something. He was unwilling; I saw his head shake in a sullen sign of negation.

The woman turned from him with a gesture of contempt. Her arm rose, brandishing her riding crop. I saw it go down against the horse's flank, and then the animal broke into a gallop. Straight at us they came, Mary's arm flailing up and down, the maddened horse snorting and rearing. I looked down at Gavin's bent head. He had seen the danger approaching and was struggling to rise, but his body would no longer obey his will. So this, I thought, is the end. It never occurred to me to plead with her—not because I was so brave, but because I knew it wouldn't do any good.

They were almost upon us when the horse baulked. It stopped not six feet away, bringing all four hooves down together with a decisive thud. I had been too absorbed by the riders to look at their mounts, but now I realised that this one was familiar.

"Flame!" A sudden outrageous upsurge of hope gave strength to my voice. "Flame, don't you know me?"

She knew the voice; perhaps she had already recognised me. She started forward at a walk, nose naively outstretched for the apple or bit of sugar I usually had for her. Mary, a snarl of fury contorting her face, raised her crop and struck again.

I had never touched Flame with a whip. This last blow was too much for her. She rose almost upright on her hind legs, and tossed the rider neatly over her tail.

I caught her reins as she came trotting up to me. I was laughing—or crying, I'm not sure which. It's strange how the loyalty of even a dumb beast can strengthen the heart. Indeed, Flame was not the only animal that had helped us that night.

Gavin was suddenly on his feet.

"Mount, Damaris. Mount and ride!"

I didn't answer. He knew perfectly well that I would do nothing of the sort. I couldn't look at him; I was afraid to take my eyes off Mary. She had scrambled to her feet, snow spotting her immaculate black habit, but without the horse she was relatively harmless. I blessed the chance that had given Flame to her instead of to Andrew.

Andrew had ridden up by that time, at a gentle walk, as if he were going calling.

"I told you that brute wouldn't obey," he remarked to Mary.

"Yours will," she said.

With the same affected leisureliness Andrew looked us over. He looked at Mary, who was glaring at him as if the strength of a stare could force him to do her will; at myself, a tattered, dripping scarecrow; and at Gavin, erect but barely conscious. An odd expression came over the boy's face as he gazed down at the man whom he had wronged so grievously, and I wondered just what it was that held Andrew back. Fear of the ultimate crime, perhaps, or even—stranger things have happened—some last expiring gleam of conscience or honour. He shook his head.

"No. By God, Mary, there are limits—even for me."

"Then why don't you give him your horse," she said in a strangled voice, "and let them go?"

"Oh, gad, we can't do that."

"Then what do you intend to do? Stand here until we take root in the ground? You fool, have you forgotten what's at stake?"

Sir Andrew's face altered. I think for a few moments he had forgotten. But fifty thousand pounds a year is a figure that sticks in the mind. Slowly the boy raised his arm. Then Gavin spoke.

"Good lad, Andrew. Do what the lady says. If anyone hangs for murder, it won't be she."

Andrew bit his lip and let his poised arm drop. He hesitated a moment longer, but the words had been too well chosen to be ignored. He started to swing himself off his horse.

"I won't ride down a defenceless man," he said sullenly. "I'll give him a fair chance—man to man."

Mary caught me as I lunged for him, beside myself with fury. Dear heaven, but she was strong! I tried to fight her, with teeth and nails, like the wild animal to which necessity had reduced me; but I was too weakened. I could only writhe helplessly in her grip, and watch the last act being played out.

Gavin retreated, stumbling back with more haste than dignity. His dragging steps and limp hands told all of us what we already knew; that he was too worn out to block the most casual attack. He had put about ten feet between himself and Andrew before the boy got off his horse. Andrew went after him, walking with a kind of contemptuous slowness. I couldn't see his face, but I fancied he was smiling. His chivalry was only skin-deep.

Still Gavin stumbled back. I watched with growing terror, and opened my lips to cry out a warning. He was moving directly towards the edge of the lake, where the burn ran into it and the banks fell sheer into the ice-rimmed water. A horrid thought, bred of fear and fatigue, slid into my mind. He must know where his steps were taking him. He was a strong swimmer. Without me to weigh him down, he might reach the other shore. At worst, the water would be kinder than the other way.

I fought down the suspicion. It was unworthy of him. Beaten and worn as he was, he wouldn't do that. But the same thought had occurred to Andrew, and he had no standards of decency by which to judge others. Nor did he know, I think, about the current. He threw himself forward, arms extended to catch his prey before it could elude him.

Then it happened. It had happened once before. I should have remembered the duel—the slow retreat, the deliberate opening of the guard to invite an opening on the opponent's part. Perhaps Andrew did remember, in the last split second. By then it was too late. He had over-balanced himself in his wild lunge, and Gavin, dropping down and to one side, lifted one leg and tipped the boy's body over the brink.

He screamed, once, as he went down. The sound ended in a splash and a crack of shattered ice. Then there was nothing except the angry gurgle of the burn, rushing on over rocks towards the falls.

Mary never spoke. She let me go, so suddenly that I fell to my knees. For a moment I saw her swaying on the brink, staring down into the dark waters. The first rim of the sun pushed its way up over the ridge; a ray of sunlight caught her hair and set it ablaze. One last glimpse of her hair, like a halo of gold around a haggard witch's face—and then she was gone, gone without a sound. The current took her with a chuckle of broken water, and flowed on.

On my hands and knees I crept to Gavin where he stood at the edge of the bank. I had to force myself to look, as he was looking, over the brink. But there was nothing there—nothing but the dark water and the shattered ice, and the foam of the burn beating against submerged rocks.

The horses were standing where we had left them. Gavin lifted me on to Flame's back, and she turned her head with a little whicker of pleasure. He mounted Andrew's chestnut. We turned our backs to the burn and rode south—towards the mouth of the glen, and the world. The sun rose over the eastern ridge, flooding the snow with radiance.